PUFFIN BOOKS

THE WONDERFUL ADVENTURES OF NILS

Selma Lagerlöf

Nils Holgersson has spent years bullying the birds and animals around him. Then, one day, he does the same to an elf and is punished for his wickedness. He finds himself transformed into the size of an elf and suddenly has to learn to survive in a world of giant birds and animals. Nils' extraordinary adventures begin when he takes up with a flock of wild geese on their journey to the North. He encounters enormous rats, sheep, storks, crows and butterflies and learns respect and humility along the way.

The Wonderful Adventures of Nils was first published in Sweden in 1906. Its sequel, *The Further Adventures of Nils*, was published in 1907. They are still considered to be Selma Lagerlöf's greatest work. In 1909, partly due to the immense success of *Nils*, the author was awarded the Nobel Prize for Literature. Selma Lagerlöf died in 1940.

Also by Selma Lagerlöf

THE FURTHER ADVENTURES OF NILS

The Wonderful Adventures of Nils

SELMA LAGERLÖF

Translated by Velma Swanston Howard

Illustrated by
HANS BAUMHAUER

PUFFIN BOOKS

PUFFIN BOOKS

Published by the Penguin Group
Penguin Books Ltd, 27 Wrights Lane, London w8 5tz, England
Viking Penguin, a division of Penguin Books USA Inc.
375 Hudson Street, New York, New York 10014, USA
Penguin Books Australia Ltd, Ringwood, Victoria, Australia
Penguin Books Canada Ltd, 2801 John Street, Markham, Ontario, Canada l3r 1b4
Penguin Books (NZ) Ltd, 182–190 Wairau Road, Auckland 10, New Zealand

Penguin Books Ltd, Registered Offices: Harmondsworth, Middlesex, England

First published in Sweden in 1906
First published in Great Britain in 1950
First published in one volume with *The Further Adventures of Nils*
by J. H. Dent & Sons Ltd 1984
Published in Puffin Books 1990
1 3 5 7 9 10 8 6 4 2

Printed in England by Clays Ltd, St Ives plc

CONTENTS

THE BOY   I

AKKA FROM KEBNEKAISE   25

THE WONDERFUL JOURNEY OF NILS   47

GLIMMINGE CASTLE   75

THE GREAT CRANE DANCE ON KULLABERG   93

IN RAINY WEATHER   107

THE STAIRWAY WITH THE THREE STEPS   115

BY RONNEBY RIVER   121

KARLSKRONA   134

THE TRIP TO ÖLAND   146

ÖLAND'S SOUTHERN POINT   152

THE BIG BUTTERFLY   163

LITTLE KARL'S ISLAND   169

TWO CITIES   186

THE LEGEND OF SMÅLAND   203

THE CROWS   210

THE OLD PEASANT WOMAN   238

FROM TABERG TO HUSKVARNA   254

THE BIG BIRD LAKE   259

ULVÅSA-LADY   281

THE HOMESPUN CLOTH   288

PART ONE

THE BOY

☆

Chapter One

THE ELF

ONCE there was a boy. He was—let us say—something like fourteen years old; long and loose jointed and tow-headed. He wasn't good for much, that boy. His chief delight was to eat and sleep, and after that he liked best to get into mischief.

It was a Sunday morning and the boy's parents were getting ready to go to church. Nils sat on the edge of the table, in his shirt-sleeves, and thought how lucky it was that both father and mother were going out, and the coast would be clear for a couple of hours. 'Good! Now I can take down father's gun and fire off a shot without anybody's meddling interference,' he said to himself.

But it was almost as if father had guessed the boy's thoughts, for just as he was on the threshold, ready to start, he stopped short, and turned to Nils.

'Since you won't come to church with mother and me,' he said, 'the least you can do is to read the service at home. Will you promise to do so?'

'Yes,' said Nils, 'that I can do easily enough.' And he thought, of course, that he wouldn't read any more than he felt like reading.

The boy thought that never had his mother been quicker to act. In a second she was over by the shelf near the fireplace, and had taken down Luther's Commentary and laid it on the table in front of the window —opened at the service for the day. She also opened the New Testament and placed it beside the Commentary. Finally she drew up the big arm-chair, which was bought at the parish auction the year before, and which, as a rule, no one but father was permitted to occupy.

Nils sat thinking that his mother was giving herself altogether too much trouble with this elaborate arrangement; for he had no intention of reading more than a page or so. But now, for the second time, it was almost as if his father were able to see right through him. He walked up to the boy and said in a severe tone: 'Now, remember, that you are to read carefully! For when we come back I shall question you thoroughly; and if you have skipped a single page it will not go well with you.'

'The service is fourteen and a half pages long,' said his mother, just as if she wanted to heap up the measure of his misfortune. 'You 'll have to sit down and begin the reading at once if you expect to get through with it.'

With that they departed. And as Nils stood in the doorway watching them he thought that he had been caught in a trap. 'There they go congratulating themselves, I suppose, in the belief that they 've hit upon something so good that I 'll be forced to sit and pore over the sermon the whole time they are away,' thought he.

But his father and mother were certainly not congratulating themselves upon anything of the sort; on the contrary, they were very much distressed. They were poor farmers, and their ground was not much bigger than a garden plot. When they first moved there the place couldn't feed more than one pig and a pair of chickens; but they were uncommonly industrious and capable folk —and now they had both cows and geese. Things had turned out very well for them; and they would have gone to church that beautiful morning satisfied and happy if they hadn't had their son to think of. Father complained that he was dull and lazy; he had not tried to learn anything at school, and he was such an all-round good-for-nothing that he could barely be made to tend geese. Mother did not deny that this was true; but she was most distressed because he was wild and bad, cruel to animals, and ill-tempered toward human beings. 'May God soften his hard heart and give him a better disposition!' said the mother, 'or else he will be a misfortune, both to himself and to us.'

Nils stood for a long time and pondered whether he should read the service or not. Finally he came to the conclusion that, this time, it was best to be obedient. He seated himself in the easy chair and began to read. But when he had been rattling away in an undertone for a little while, this mumbling seemed to have a soothing effect upon him and he began to nod.

It was the most beautiful weather outside. It was only the twentieth of March; but the boy lived in West Vemmenhög parish, down in Southern Skåne, where the spring was already in full swing. It was not as yet green, but it was fresh and budding. There was water in all the ditches, and the colt's-foot on the edge was in bloom. All the weeds that grew in among the stones were brown and shiny. The beech woods in the distance seemed to swell and grow thicker with every second. The skies were high and a clear blue. The cottage door stood ajar, and the lark's trill could be heard in the room. The hens and geese pattered about in the yard, and the cows, who felt the spring air away in their stalls, lowed their approval every now and then.

Nils read and nodded and fought against drowsiness. 'No! I don't want to fall asleep,' thought he, 'for then I 'll not finish this thing this morning.'

But, somehow, he fell asleep.

He did not know whether he had slept a short while, or a long while; but he was awakened by hearing a slight noise behind him.

On the window-sill, facing him, stood a small looking-glass; and almost the entire room could be seen in this. As Nils raised his head he happened to look in the glass; and then he saw that the lid to his mother's chest had been opened.

His mother owned a great, heavy, iron-bound oak chest, which she permitted no one but herself to open. Here she treasured all the things she had inherited from her mother, and of these she was especially careful. Here lay a couple of old-time peasant dresses of red homespun cloth, with short bodices and plaited skirts, and pearl-bedecked smocks. There were starched white linen head-dresses, and heavy silver ornaments and chains. People don't care to go about dressed like that in these days, and several times his mother had thought of getting rid of the old things; but somehow she hadn't had the heart to do it.

Now Nils saw distinctly, in the glass, that the chest lid was open. He could not understand how this had happened, for his mother had closed the chest before she went away. She never would have left that precious chest open when he was at home, alone.

He became low spirited and apprehensive. He was afraid that a thief had sneaked his way into the cottage. He didn't dare to move, but sat still and stared into the looking-glass.

While he sat there and waited for the thief to make his appearance, he began to wonder what that dark shadow was which fell across the edge of the chest. He looked and looked—and did not want to believe his eyes. But the thing, which at first seemed shadowy, became more and more clear to him; and soon he saw that it was something real. It was no less a thing than an elf who sat there astride the edge of the chest!

To be sure Nils had heard stories about elves, but he had never dreamed that they were such tiny creatures. He was no taller than a hand's breadth, this one, who sat on the edge of the chest. He had an old, wrinkled, and beardless face, and was dressed in a black frock-coat, knee-breeches, and a broad-brimmed black hat. He was very trim and smart, with his white laces about the throat and wristbands, his buckled shoes, and the bows on his garters. He had taken from the chest an embroidered smock, and sat and looked at the old-fashioned handiwork with such an air of veneration, that he did not observe the boy had awakened.

Nils was somewhat surprised to see the elf, but, on the other hand, he was not particularly frightened. It was impossible to be afraid of one who was so little. And since the elf was so absorbed in his own thoughts that he neither saw nor heard, the boy thought that it would be great fun to play a trick on him; to push him over into the chest and shut the lid on him, or something of that kind.

But Nils was not so courageous that he dared to touch the elf with his hands; instead he looked around the room for something to poke him with. He let his gaze wander from the sofa to the table, from the table to the fireplace. He looked at the kettles, then at the coffee-pot, which stood on a shelf near the fireplace; on the water bucket near the door; and on the spoons and knives and forks and saucers and plates, which could be seen through the half-open cupboard door. He looked at his father's gun which hung on the wall, beside the portrait of the Danish royal family, and on the geraniums and fuchsias which blossomed in the window. And last he caught sight of an old butterfly-net that hung on the window frame.

He had hardly set eyes on that butterfly-net, before he reached over and snatched it and jumped up and swung it alongside the edge of the chest. He was himself astonished at the luck he had. He hardly knew how he had managed it—but he had actually snared the elf. The poor little chap lay, head downward, in the bottom of the long net, and could not free himself.

For the first moment Nils hadn't the least idea what he should do with his prize. He was only careful to swing the net backwards and forwards, to prevent the elf from getting a foothold and clambering up.

The elf began to speak, and begged, oh! so pitifully, for his freedom. He had brought them good luck, these many years, he said, and deserved better treatment. Now if the boy would set him free he would give him an old coin, a silver spoon, and a gold penny, as big as the case of his father's silver watch.

The boy didn't think that this was much of an offer; but it so happened that after he had got the elf in his power he was afraid of him. He felt that he was in touch with something weird and uncanny; something which did not belong to his world, and he was only too glad to get rid of the horrid thing.

For this reason he agreed at once to the bargain, and held the net still so the elf could crawl out of it. But when the elf was almost out of the net, Nils happened to think that he ought to have bargained for large estates, and all sorts of good things. He should at least have made this stipulation: that the elf must conjure the sermon into his head. 'What a fool I was to let him go!' he thought, and began to shake the net violently, so that the elf would tumble down again.

But the instant Nils did this he received such a stinging box on the ear that he thought his head would fly in pieces. He was dashed first against one wall then against the other; he sank to the floor and lay there senseless.

When he awoke he was alone in the cottage. He saw no trace of the elf. The lid of the chest was down, and the butterfly-net hung in its usual place by the window.

If he had not felt how his right cheek burned from that box on the ear, he would have been tempted to believe the whole thing had been a dream. 'At any rate, father and mother will be sure to insist that it was nothing else,' he thought. 'They are not likely to make any allowances for that old sermon on account of the elf. It's best for me to get at that reading again.'

But as he walked toward the table he noticed something remarkable. It couldn't be possible that the cottage had grown. But why was he obliged to take so many more steps than usual to get to the table? And what was the matter with the chair? It looked no bigger than it did a while ago; but now he had to step on the rung first, and then clamber up in order to reach the seat. It was the same thing with the table. He could not look over the top without climbing to the arm of the chair.

'What in all the world is this?' said Nils. 'I believe the elf has bewitched both the arm-chair and the table— and the whole cottage.'

The Commentary lay on the table and, to all appearances, it was not changed; but there must have been something queer about that too, for he could not manage to read a single word of it without actually standing right on the book itself.

He read a couple of lines, and then he chanced to look up. With that, his glance fell on the looking-glass; and then he cried aloud: 'Look! There's another one!'

For in the glass he saw plainly a little, little creature who was dressed in a hood and leather breeches.

'Why, that one is dressed exactly like me!' said Nils, and clasped his hands in astonishment. But then he saw that the thing in the mirror did the same thing. Then he began to pull his hair and pinch his arms and swing round; and instantly he did the same thing after him; he, who could be seen in the mirror.

Nils ran round the glass several times, to see if there wasn't a little man hidden behind it, but he found no one there; and then he began to shake with terror. For now he understood that the elf had bewitched him, and that the creature whose image he saw in the glass was he, himself.

Chapter Two

THE WILD GEESE

NILS simply could not make himself believe that he had been transformed into an elf. 'It can't be anything but a dream—a queer fancy,' he thought. 'If I wait a few moments I 'll surely be turned back into a human being again.'

He placed himself before the glass and closed his eyes. He opened them again after a couple of minutes, and then expected to find that it had all passed over—but it hadn't. He was, and remained, just as little. In other respects, he was the same as before. The straw-coloured hair, the freckles across his nose, the patches on his leather breeches, and the darns on his stockings were all as they used to be, with this exception—that they had become smaller.

No, it would do him no good to stand still and wait—of this he was certain. He must try something else. And he thought the wisest thing that he could do was to try and find the elf and make his peace with him.

And while he sought, he cried and prayed and promised everything he could think of. Nevermore would he break his word to any one; never again would he be naughty; and never, never would he fall asleep again over the sermon. If he might only be a human being once more he would be such a good and helpful and obedient boy. But no matter how much he promised it did not help him the least little bit.

Suddenly he remembered that he had heard his mother say that all the tiny folk made their home in the cowsheds; and, at once, he decided to go there and see if he couldn't find the elf. It was a lucky thing that the cottage door stood partly open, for he never could have reached the bolt and opened it; but now he slipped through without any difficulty.

When he came out in the hall he looked round for his wooden shoes; for in the house, to be sure, he had gone about in his stocking-feet. He wondered how he should manage with these big, clumsy, wooden shoes; but just then he saw a pair of tiny shoes on the door-step. When he realized that the elf had been so thoughtful that he had also bewitched the wooden shoes, he was even more troubled. It was evidently planned that this affliction should last a long time.

On the wooden path in front of the cottage hopped a grey sparrow. He had hardly set eyes on the boy before he called out: 'Teetee! Teetee! Look at Nils goosey-boy! Look at Tummetott![1] Look at Nils Holgersson Tummetott!'

Instantly both the geese and the chickens turned and stared at the boy; and then they set up a fearful cackling. 'Cock-el-i-coo,' crowed the cock, 'good enough for him! Cock-el-i-coo, he has pulled my comb.' 'Ka, ka, kada, serves him right!' cried the hens; and with that they kept up a continuous cackle. The geese got together in a tight group, stuck their heads together, and asked: 'Who can have done this? Who can have done this?'

But the strangest thing of all was that Nils understood what they said. He was so astonished that he stood there, as if rooted to the door-step, and listened. 'It must be because I am changed into an elf,' he said. 'This is probably why I understand bird-talk.'

He thought it was unbearable that the hens would not

[1] Swedish word for Tom Thumb.

stop saying that it served him right. He threw a stone at them and shouted: 'Shut up, the pack of you!'

But it hadn't occurred to him before that he was no longer the sort of boy the hens need fear. The whole farmyard made a rush for him and formed a ring round

him; then they all cried at once: 'Ka, ka, kada, served you right! Ka, ka, kada, served you right!'

Nils tried to get away, but the chickens ran after him and screamed, until he thought he'd lose his hearing. It is more than likely that he never could have got away from them if the house cat hadn't come along just then. As soon as the chickens saw the cat they quieted down and pre-tended to be thinking of nothing else than just to scratch in the earth for worms.

Immediately the boy ran up to the cat. 'You dear pussy!' said he. 'You must know all the corners and hiding places about here. You'll be a good little kitty and tell me where I can find the elf.'

The cat did not reply at once. It seated itself, curled its tail into a graceful ring around its paws, and stared at Nils. It was a large black cat with one white spot on its chest. Its fur lay sleek and soft and shone in the sunlight. Its claws were drawn in, and its eyes were a dull grey, with just a little narrow dark streak down the centre. The cat looked thoroughly good-natured and harmless.

'I know well enough where the elf lives,' it said in a soft voice, 'but that doesn't say that I'm going to tell *you* about it.'

'Dear pussy, you must tell me where the elf lives!' said Nils. 'Can't you see how he has bewitched me?'

The cat opened its eyes a little so that green wickedness began to shine forth. It spun round and purred with satisfaction before it replied. 'Shall I perhaps help you because you have so often grabbed me by the tail?' it said at last.

Then Nils was furious and forgot entirely how little and helpless he was now. 'Oh! I can pull your tail again, I can,' said he, and ran toward the cat.

The next instant the cat was so changed that the boy could scarcely believe it was the same animal. Every separate hair on its body stood on end. Its back was arched; its legs grew longer; its claws scraped the ground; its tail had grown thick and short; its ears were laid back; its mouth was frothy; and its eyes were wide open and glistened like sparks of red fire.

Nils didn't want to let himself be scared by a cat and he took a step forward. Then the cat made one spring and landed right on the boy; knocked him down and stood over him—its forepaws on his chest, and its jaws wide apart over his throat.

The boy felt how the sharp claws sank through his vest and shirt and into his skin, and how the sharp teeth touched his throat. He shrieked for help, as loudly as he could, but no one came. He thought surely that his last hour had come. Then he felt that the cat drew in its claws and let go the hold on his throat.

'There!' it said, 'that will do now. I'll let you go this time, for my mistress's sake. I only wanted you to know which one of us two has the power now.'

With that the cat walked away—looking as smooth and pious as it did when it first appeared on the scene. Nils was so crestfallen that he didn't say a word, but only hurried to the cowhouse to look for the elf.

There were not more than three cows, all told. But when the boy came in, there was such a bellowing and such a kick-up that one might easily have believed that there were at least thirty.

'Moo, moo, moo!' bellowed Mayrose. 'It is well there is such a thing as justice in this world.'

'Moo, moo, moo!' The three of them took up the chorus. He couldn't hear what they said, for each one tried to out-bellow the others.

Nils wanted to ask after the elf, but he couldn't make himself heard because the cows were in full uproar. They carried on as they used to do when he let a strange dog in on them. They kicked with their hind legs, shook their necks, stretched their heads, and threatened him with their horns.

'Come here, you,' said Mayrose, 'and you'll get a kick that you won't forget in a hurry!'

'Come here,' said Gold Lily, 'and you shall dance on my horns!'

'Come here, and you shall taste how it felt when you threw your wooden shoes at me, as you did last summer!' bawled Star.

'Come here, and you shall be repaid for that wasp you let loose in my ear!' bellowed Gold Lily.

Mayrose was the oldest and the wisest of them, and she was the angriest. 'Come here,' said she, 'that I may pay you back for the many times that you have jerked the milk pail away from your mother; and for all the snares you laid for her when she came carrying the milk pails; and for all the tears she has stood here and wept over you!'

Nils wanted to tell them how sorry he was that he had been unkind to them; and that never, never—from now on—should he be anything but good, if they would only tell him where the elf was. But the cows didn't listen to him. They made such a racket that he began to fear one of them would succeed in breaking loose; and he thought that the best thing for him to do was to go quietly away from the cowhouse.

When he came out he was thoroughly disheartened. He could understand that no one on the place wanted to help him find the elf. And little good would it do him, probably, if the elf were found.

He crawled up on the broad stone wall which surrounded the farm, and which was overgrown with briars and brambles. There he sat down to think about how it would go with him, if he never became a human being again. When father and mother came home from church there would be a surprise for them. Yes, a surprise—it would be all over the land; and people would come flocking from East Vemmenhög and from Torp and from Skurup. The whole Vemmenhög parish would come to stare at him. Perhaps father and mother would take him with them and show him at the fair in Kivik.

No, that was too horrible to think about. He would rather that no human being should ever see him again.

His unhappiness was simply frightful! No one in all

the world was so unhappy as he. He was no longer a human being but a freak.

Little by little he began to understand what it meant to be no longer human. He was separated from everything now; he could no longer play with other boys, he could not take charge of the farm after his parents were gone, and certainly no girl would think of marrying *him*.

He sat and looked at his home. It was a little half-timbered cottage which lay as if it had been crushed down to earth, under the high, sloping roof. The out-houses were also small; and the patches of ground were so narrow that a horse could barely turn around on them. But little and poor though the place was it was much too good for him *now*. He couldn't ask for any better place than a hole under the stable floor.

It was wondrously beautiful weather. It budded, and it rippled, and it murmured, and it twittered all around him. But he sat there with such a heavy sorrow. He would never be happy any more about anything.

Never had he seen the skies as blue as they were to-day. Birds of passage came on their travels. They came from foreign lands, and had travelled over the East sea, by way of Smygehuk, and were now on their way north. They were of many different kinds; but he was only familiar with the wild geese, who came flying in two long rows, which met at an angle.

Several flocks of wild geese had already flown by. They flew very high, but still he could hear how they called: 'To the hills! Now we 're off to the hills!'

When the wild geese saw the tame geese who walked about the farm they sank nearer the earth and called: 'Come along! Come along! We 're off to the hills!'

The tame geese could not resist the temptation to raise

their heads and listen, but they answered very sensibly:
'We 're pretty well off where we are. We 're pretty well
off where we are.'

It was, as we have said, an uncommonly fine day, with
an atmosphere that it must have been a real delight to
fly in, so light and bracing. And with each new wild
geese flock that flew by, the tame geese became more and
more restless. A couple of times they flapped their wings
as if they had half a mind to fly along. But then an old
mother goose would always say to them: 'Now don't be
silly. Those creatures will have to suffer both hunger
and cold.'

There was a young gander whom the wild geese had
fired with a passion for adventure. 'If another flock
comes this way I 'll follow them,' said he.

Then there came a new flock, who called like the
others, and the young gander answered: 'Wait a minute!
Wait a minute! I 'm coming.'

He spread his wings and raised himself into the air;
but he was so unaccustomed to flying that he fell to the
ground again.

At any rate, the wild geese must have heard his call,
for they turned and flew back slowly to see if he was
coming.

'Wait, wait!' he cried, and made another attempt to
fly.

All this Nils heard where he lay on the stone wall.
'It would be a great pity,' he thought, 'if the big gander
should go away. It would be a big loss to father and
mother if he were gone when they came home from
church.'

When he thought of this, once again he entirely forgot
that he was little and helpless. He took one leap right

down into the flock of geese and threw his arms round the neck of the gander. 'Oh, no! You don't fly away this time, sir!' cried he.

But just about then the gander had found out what he should do to raise himself from the ground. He couldn't stop to shake the boy off so Nils had to go with him up in the air.

They flew on toward the heights so rapidly that Nils fairly gasped. Before he had time to think that he ought to let go his hold around the gander's neck, he was so high up that he would have been killed instantly if he had fallen to the ground.

The only thing that he could do to make himself a little more comfortable was to try and get upon the gander's back. And there he wriggled himself forthwith; but not without considerable trouble. And it was not an easy matter, either, to hold himself secure on the slippery back, between two swaying wings. He had to dig deep into feathers and down with both hands to keep from tumbling to the ground.

Chapter Three

THE BIG CHECKED CLOTH

Nils had grown so giddy that it was a long time before he came to himself. The winds howled and beat against him, and the rustle of feathers and swaying of wings sounded like a great storm. Thirteen geese flew around him, flapping their wings and honking. They danced before his eyes and they buzzed in his ears. He didn't know whether they were flying high or low or in what direction they were travelling.

After a bit he regained just enough sense to understand that he ought to find out where the geese were taking him. But this was not so easy, for he didn't know how he should ever muster up courage enough to look down. He was sure he'd faint if he attempted it.

The wild geese were not flying very high because the new travelling companion could not breathe in the very thinnest air. For his sake they also flew a little slower than usual.

At last Nils just made himself cast one glance down to earth. Then he thought that a great big rug lay spread beneath him, which was made up of an incredible number of large and small checks.

'Where in all the world am I now?' he wondered.

He saw nothing but check after check. Some ran crosswise, and some were long and narrow, but everywhere there were straight lines. Nothing was round, and nothing was twisting.

'What kind of a big checked cloth is this that I'm

looking down on?' said Nils to himself, without expecting any one to answer him.

But instantly the wild geese who flew about him called out: 'Fields and meadows. Fields and meadows.'

Then he realized that the big checked cloth that he was

travelling over was the flat land of southern Sweden; and he began to understand why it looked so checked and multi-coloured. The bright-green checks he recognized first; they were rye-fields that had been sown in the autumn and had kept themselves green under the winter snows. The yellowish-grey checks were stubble fields—the remains of the oat crop which had grown there the summer before. The brownish ones were old clover meadows, and the black ones deserted grazing lands or ploughed-up fallow pastures. The brown checks with the yellow edges were, undoubtedly, beech-tree forests; for in these you 'll find the big trees which grow in the heart of the forest are bare in winter; while the little beech-trees, which grow along the borders, keep their dry, yellowed leaves into the spring. There were also dark checks with grey centres: these were the large farms with their blackening thatched roofs built round paved court-yards. And then there were checks green in the middle with brown borders: these were the orchards, where the grass was already turning green, although the trees and bushes around them were still in their bare, brown bark.

Nils could not keep from laughing when he saw how checked everything looked.

But when the wild geese heard him laugh they called out reprovingly: 'Fertile and good land. Fertile and good land.'

The boy had already become serious. 'To think that you can laugh; you, who have met with the most terrible misfortune that can possibly happen to a human being!' he thought. And for a moment he was depressed; but it wasn't long before he was laughing again.

Now that he had grown somewhat accustomed to the ride and the speed, so that he could think of something besides holding himself on the gander's back, he began to notice how full the air was of birds flying northward. And there was a shouting and a calling from flock to flock. 'So you came over to-day?' cried some. 'Yes,' answered the geese. 'How do you think the spring's getting on?' 'Not a leaf on the trees and ice-cold water in the lakes,' came back the answer.

When the geese flew over a place where they saw some tame fowl they shouted: 'What 's the name of this place? What 's the name of this place?' Then the cock raised

his head and answered: 'Its name's Lillgärde this year
—the same as last year; the same as last year.'

Most of the cottages were probably named after their
owners—which is the custom in Skåne. But instead of
saying this is 'Per Matssons,' or 'Ola Bossons,' the
cockerels hit upon the kind of names which, to their way
of thinking, were more appropriate. Those who lived
on small farms, and belonged to poor cottagers, cried:
'This place is called Grainscarce.' And those who
belonged to the poorest hut-dwellers screamed: 'The
name of this place is Little-to-eat, Little-to-eat, Little-
to-eat.'

The big, well-cared-for farms got high-sounding names
from the cockerels—such as Luckymeadow, Eggberga,
and Moneyville.

But the cocks on the great landed estates were too high
and mighty to condescend to anything like jesting. One
of them crowed and called out with such gusto that it
sounded as if he wanted to be heard clear up to the sun:
'This is Dybeck's estate; the same this year as last year;
this year as last year.'

A little farther on strutted one cock who crowed:
'This is Swanholm, surely all the world knows that!'

The boy observed that the geese did not fly straight
forward; but zigzagged hither and thither over the whole
south country, just as though they were glad to be in
Skåne again and wanted to pay their respects to every
separate place.

They came to one place where there were a number of
big, clumsy-looking buildings with great, tall chimneys,
and all around these were a lot of smaller houses. 'This
is Jordberga Sugar Refinery,' cried the cocks. The boy
gave a start as he sat there on the goose's back. He

ought to have recognized this place, for it was not very far from his home.

Here he had worked the year before as a watch-boy; but, to be sure, nothing looked quite the same when one saw it like that—from up above.

And think! Just think! Osa the goose-girl and little Mats, who were his comrades last year! Indeed Nils would have been glad to know if they still were anywhere about here. Fancy what they would have said had they suspected that he was flying over their heads!

Soon Jordberga was lost to sight, and they travelled toward Svedala and Skaber Lake and back again over Börringe Cloister and Häckeberga. The boy saw more of Skåne in this one day than he had ever seen before—in all the years that he had lived.

Whenever the wild geese came across any tame geese, they had the best fun. They flew forward very slowly and called down: 'We 're off to the hills. Are you coming along? Are you coming along?'

But the tame geese answered: 'It 's still winter in this country. You 're out too soon. Fly back! Fly back!'

The wild geese flew lower that they might be heard a little better, and called: 'Come along! We 'll teach you how to fly and swim.'

Then the tame geese got angry and wouldn't answer them with a single honk.

The wild geese came down still lower until they almost touched the ground—then, quick as lightning, they raised themselves, just as if they 'd been terribly frightened. 'Oh, oh, oh!' they exclaimed. 'Those things are not geese. They are only sheep, they are only sheep.'

The geese on the ground were beside themselves with

rage and shrieked: 'May you be shot, the whole lot o'
you! The whole lot o' you!'

When the boy heard all this teasing he laughed. Then
he remembered how badly things had gone with him
and he cried. But the next second he was laughing
again.

Never before had he ridden so fast; and to ride fast
and recklessly—that he had always liked. And, of
course, he had never dreamed that it could be as fresh
and bracing as it was up in the air; or that there rose
from the earth such a fine scent of resin and soil. Nor
had he ever dreamed what it could be like to ride so
high above the earth. It was just like flying away from
sorrow and trouble and annoyances of every kind that
could be thought of.

PART TWO

AKKA FROM KEBNEKAISE

☆

Chapter One

EVENING

THE big tame gander that had followed them up in the air felt very proud of being permitted to travel back and forth over the southern plains with the wild geese, and crack jokes with the tame birds. But in spite of his happiness he began to tire as the afternoon wore on. He tried to take deeper breaths and quicker wing-strokes, but even so he remained several goose-lengths behind the others.

When the wild geese, who flew last, noticed that the tame one couldn't keep up with them, they began to call to the goose who flew in the centre of the angle and led the flock: 'Akka from Kebnekaise! Akka from Kebnekaise!'

'What do you want of me?' asked the leader.

'The white one will be left behind; the white one will be left behind.'

'Tell him it's easier to fly fast than slow!' called the leader, and raced on as before.

The gander certainly tried to follow the advice and increase his speed; but then he became so exhausted that he sank down to the pollarded willows that bordered the fields and meadows.

'Akka, Akka, Akka from Kebnekaise!' cried those

who flew last and saw what a hard time he was having.

'What do you want now?' asked the leader—and she sounded very angry.

'The white one sinks to the earth; the white one sinks to the earth.'

'Tell him it's easier to fly high than low!' shouted the leader, and she didn't slow up the least little bit but raced on as before.

The gander tried to follow this advice, too; but when he wanted to raise himself, he became so winded that he almost burst his breast.

'Akka, Akka!' again cried those who flew last.

'Can't you let me fly in peace?' asked the leader, and she sounded even more angry than before.

'The white one is ready to collapse.'

'Tell him that he who has not the strength to fly with the flock can go back home!' cried the leader. She certainly had no idea of decreasing her speed—but raced on as before.

'Oh! is that the way the wind blows,' thought the gander. He understood at once that the wild geese had never intended to take him along up to Lapland. They had only lured him away from home in sport.

He felt very annoyed to think that his strength should fail him now, so that he wouldn't be able to show these vagabonds that even a tame goose was good for something. But the most provoking thing of all was that he had fallen in with Akka from Kebnekaise. Tame gander that he was, he had heard about a leader-goose, named Akka, who was more than a hundred years old. She had such a big name that the best wild geese in the world followed her. But no one had such a contempt for tame geese as

Akka and her flock, and gladly would he have shown them that he was their equal.

He flew slowly behind the rest, while he deliberated whether he should turn back or continue. Finally the little creature that he carried on his back said: 'Dear Morten gander, you know well enough that it is simply impossible for you, who have never flown, to go with the wild geese all the way up to Lapland. Won't you turn back before you kill yourself?'

But the farmer's lad was about the worst thing the gander knew anything about, and as soon as it had dawned on him that this puny creature actually believed that he couldn't make the trip, he decided to stick it out. 'If you say another word about this, I'll drop you into the first ditch we ride over!' said he, and at the same time his fury gave him so much strength that he began to fly almost as well as any of the others.

It isn't likely that he could have kept this pace up very long, neither was it necessary; for just then the sun sank quickly; and at sunset the geese flew down, and before the boy and the gander knew what had happened they stood on the shores of Vomb Lake.

'They probably mean to spend the night here,' thought the boy, and jumped down from the gander's back.

He stood on a narrow beach by a fair-sized lake. It was ugly to look upon, because it was almost entirely covered with an ice-crust that was blackened and uneven and full of cracks and holes—as spring ice generally is.

The ice was already breaking up. It was loose and floating and had a broad belt of dark, shiny water all around it; but there was still enough of it left to spread chill and winter terror over the place.

On the other side of the lake there appeared to be open and light country, but where the geese had lighted was a belt of thick pines. It looked as if the forest of firs and pines had the power to bind the winter to itself. Everywhere else the ground was bare; but beneath the sharp pine branches lay snow that had been melting and freezing, melting and freezing, until it was as hard as ice.

The boy thought he had struck an arctic wilderness, and he was so miserable that he wanted to scream. He was hungry too. He hadn't eaten a bite the whole day. But where should he find any food? Nothing eatable grew on either ground or tree in the month of March.

Yes, where was he to find food, and who would give him shelter, and who would make his bed, and who would protect him from the wild beasts?

For now the sun was away and frost came from the lake, and darkness sank down from heaven and terror stole forward on the twilight's trail, and in the forest it began to patter and rustle.

Now the happiness which the boy had felt when he was up in the air was gone, and in his misery he looked around for his travelling companions. He had no one but them to cling to now.

Then he saw that the gander was having even a worse time of it than he. He was lying prostrate on the spot where he had alighted; and it looked as if he were ready to die. His neck lay flat against the ground, his eyes were closed, and his breathing sounded like a feeble hissing.

'Dear Morten gander,' said the boy, 'try to get a swallow of water! It isn't two steps to the lake.'

But the gander didn't stir.

Nils had certainly been cruel to all animals, and to the gander in times gone by; but now he felt that he was the only comfort he had left, and he was dreadfully afraid of losing him.

At once the boy began to push and drag him to get him into the water, but the gander was big and heavy, and it was very hard work for the boy; but at last he succeeded.

The gander got in head first. For an instant he lay motionless in the slime, but soon he poked up his head, shook the water from his eyes, and sniffed. Then he swam, proudly, between reeds and seaweed.

The wild geese were in the lake before him. They had not looked round for either the gander or for his rider, but had made straight for the water. They had bathed and primped, and now they lay and gulped half-rotten pondweed and water-clover.

The white gander had the good fortune to spy a perch. He grabbed it quickly, swam ashore with it, and laid it down in front of the boy. 'Here's a thank you for helping me into the water,' said he.

It was the first time the boy had heard a friendly word that day. He was so happy that he wanted to throw his arms around the gander's neck, but he refrained; and he was also thankful for the gift. At first he must have thought that it would be impossible to eat raw fish and then he thought he would try it.

He made sure that he still had his sheath-knife with him and, fortunately, there it hung on the back button of his trousers, although it was now so small that it was hardly as long as a match. Well, at any rate, it served to scale and clean fish with; and it wasn't long before the perch was eaten.

When the boy had satisfied his hunger, he felt a little ashamed because he had been able to eat a raw thing.

'It's evident that I'm not a human being any longer, but a real elf,' he thought.

While Nils ate, the gander stood silently beside him. But when he had swallowed the last bite, he said in a low voice: 'It's a fact that we have run across stuck-up goose folk who despise all tame birds.'

'Yes, I've noticed that,' said the boy.

'What a triumph it would be for me if I could follow them clear up to Lapland, and show them that even a tame goose can do things!'

'Y-e-e-s,' said the boy, hesitating because he didn't believe the gander could ever do it; yet he didn't wish to contradict him. 'But I don't think I can get along all alone on such a journey,' said the gander. 'I'd like to ask if you could come along and help me?' Nils, of course, had only expected to return to his home as soon as possible, and he was so surprised that he hardly knew what he should reply. 'I thought that we were enemies, you and I,' said he. But this the gander seemed to have forgotten entirely. He only remembered that the boy had just saved his life.

'I suppose I really ought to go home to father and mother,' said the boy.

'Oh! I'll get you back to them some time in the autumn,' said the gander. 'I shall not leave you until I put you down on your own door-step.'

The boy thought it might be just as well for him if he did not present himself before his parents for a time. He was not disinclined to favour the scheme, and was just on the point of saying that he agreed to it when they heard a loud rumbling behind them. It was the wild geese who had come up from the lake all together and stood shaking off the water. After that they arranged themselves in a long row—with the leader-goose at the head, and came toward them.

As the white gander regarded the wild geese he felt ill at ease. He had expected that they would be more like tame geese, and that he would feel a closer kinship with them. They were much smaller than he and none of them was white. They were all grey with a sprinkling of brown. He was almost afraid of their eyes. They were yellow, and shone as if a fire had been kindled behind them. The gander had always been taught that it was most fitting to move slowly and with a rolling motion, but these creatures did not walk—they half ran. He grew most alarmed, however, when he looked at their feet. These were large, and the soles were torn and ragged looking. It was evident that the wild geese never minded what they tramped upon. They took no by-paths. They were very neat and well cared for in other respects, but one could see by their feet that they were poor wilderness folk.

The gander only had time to whisper to the boy 'Speak up quickly for yourself, but don't tell them who you are!' before the geese were upon them.

When the wild geese had stopped in front of them, they curtsied with their necks many times, and the gander did likewise many more times. As soon as the ceremonies were over the leader-goose said: 'Now I presume we shall hear what kind of creatures you are.'

'There isn't much to tell about me,' said the gander. 'I was born in Skanor last spring. In the autumn I was sold to Holger Nilsson of West Vemmenhög, and there I have lived ever since.'

'You don't seem to have any pedigree to boast of,' said the leader-goose. 'What is it, then, that makes you so high-minded that you wish to associate with wild geese?'

'It may be because I want to show you wild geese that

we tame ones may also be good for something,' said the gander.

'Yes, it would be well if you could show us that,' said the leader-goose. 'We have already observed how much you know about flying; but you are more skilled, perhaps, in other sports. Possibly you would be strong in a swimming match?'

'No, I can't boast that I am,' said the gander. It seemed to him that the leader-goose had already made up her mind to send him home, so he didn't much care how he answered. 'I never swam any farther than across a marl-ditch,' he continued.

'Then I presume you 're a crack sprinter,' said the goose.

'I have never seen a tame goose run, nor have I ever done it myself,' said the gander; and he made things appear much worse than they really were.

The big white one was sure now that the leader-goose would say that under no circumstances could they take him along. He was very much astonished when she said: 'You answer questions courageously; and he who has courage can become a good travelling companion, even if he is ignorant in the beginning. What do you say to stopping with us for a couple of days until we can see what you are good for?'

'That suits me!' said the gander—and he was thoroughly happy.

Thereupon the leader-goose pointed with her bill and said: 'But who is that you have with you? I've never seen anything like him before.'

'That's my comrade,' said the gander. 'He's been a goose-tender all his life. He'll be useful all right to take with us on the trip.'

'Yes, he may be all right for a tame goose,' answered the wild one. 'What do you call him?'

'He has several names,' said the gander hesitatingly, not knowing what he should say in a hurry, for he didn't want to reveal the fact that the boy had a human name. 'Oh! his name is Tummetott,' he said at last.

'Does he belong to the elf family?' asked the leader-goose.

'At what time do you wild geese usually go to bed?' said the gander quickly—trying to evade that last question. 'My eyes close of their own accord about this time.'

One could easily see that the goose who talked with the gander was very old. The whole of her feathers were ice-grey without any dark streaks. The head was larger, the legs coarser, and the feet were more worn than any of the others. The feathers were stiff; the shoulders knotty; the neck thin. All this was due to age. It was only upon the eyes that time had had no effect. They shone brighter—as if they were younger—than any of the others.

She turned, very haughtily, toward the gander.

'Understand, Mr. Tame-goose, that I am Akka from Kebnekaise! And that the goose who flies nearest me to the right is Yksi from Vassijaure, and the one to the left is Kaksi from Nuolja. Understand, also, that the second right-hand goose is Kolmi from Sarjektjakko, and the second left is Neljä from Svappavaara; and behind them fly Viisi from Oviksfjällen and Kuusi from Sjangeli. And know that these, as well as the six goslings who fly last—three to the right and three to the left—are all high mountain geese of the finest breed. You must not take us for landlubbers who strike up a chance acquaintance with any and every one! And you must not think that we permit any one to share our quarters who will not tell us who his ancestors were.'

While Akka, the leader-goose, talked in this way, Nils stepped briskly forward. It had distressed him that the gander, who had spoken up so glibly for himself, should give such evasive answers when it concerned him. 'I don't care to make a secret of who I am,' said he. 'My name is Nils Holgersson. I 'm a farmer's son, and until to-day I have been a human being; but this morning——' He got no further. As soon as he had said that he was human the leader-goose staggered three steps backwards, and the rest of them even farther back. They all stretchéd their necks and hissed angrily at him.

'I have suspected this ever since I first saw you here on these shores,' said Akka; 'and now you can clear out of here at once. We tolerate no human beings among us.'

'It isn't possible,' said the gander, mediating, 'that you wild geese can be afraid of any one who is so tiny! By to-morrow, of course, he 'll turn back home. You can surely let him stay with us overnight. None of us

can afford to let such a poor little creature wander off by
himself in the night among weasels and foxes.'

The wild goose came nearer. But it was evident that
it was hard for her to master her fear. 'I have been
taught to fear everything in human shape be it big or
little,' said she. 'But if you will be responsible for this
one, and swear that he will not harm us, he can stay with
us to-night. But I don't believe our night quarters are
suitable either for him or you, for we intend to roost on
the broken ice out here.'

She thought, of course, that the gander would hesitate
when he heard this, but he never let on. 'You are very
wise to choose such a safe bed,' said he.

'You will be responsible for his return to his own
to-morrow.'

'Then I, too, will have to leave you,' said the gander.
'I have promised not to leave him.'

'You are free to fly whither you will,' said the leader-
goose.

With this she raised her wings and flew out over the
ice, and one after another the wild geese followed her.

Nils was very sad to think that his trip to Lapland
would not come off, and he was also afraid of the chilly
night quarters. 'It will be worse and worse,' said he.
'In the first place, we'll freeze to death on the ice.'

But the gander was quite cheerful. 'There's no
danger,' said he. 'Only make haste, please, and gather
together as much grass and litter as you can well carry.'

When Nils had his arms full of dried grass the gander
grabbed him by the shirt-band, lifted him, and flew out
on the ice, where the wild geese were already fast asleep
with their bills tucked under their wings.

'Now spread out the grass on the ice, so there'll be

something to stand on, to keep me from freezing fast. You help me and I 'll help you,' said the gander.

This the boy did. And when he had finished the gander picked him up, once again, by the shirt-band, and tucked him under his wing. 'I think you 'll lie snug and warm there,' said the gander as he covered him with his wing.

Nils was so embedded in down that he couldn't answer, and he was nice and comfy. Oh, but he was tired! And in less than two winks he was fast asleep.

Chapter Two

NIGHT

IT is a fact that ice is always treacherous and not to be trusted. In the middle of the night the loosened ice-cake on Vomb Lake moved about, until one corner of it touched the shore. Now it happened that Mr. Smirre Fox, who lived at this time in Öved Cloister Park—on the east side of the lake—caught a glimpse of that one corner, while he was out on his night hunt. Smirre had seen the wild geese early in the evening, and hadn't dared to hope that he might get at one of them, but now he walked right out on the ice.

When Smirre was very near to the geese, his claws scraped the ice, and the geese awoke, flapped their wings and prepared for flight. But Smirre was too quick for them. He darted forward as though he 'd been shot, grabbed a goose by the wing, and ran toward land again.

But this night the wild geese were not alone on the ice, for they had a human being among them—little as he was. The boy had awakened when the gander spread his wings. He had tumbled down on the ice and was sitting there, dazed. He hadn't grasped the whys and wherefores of all this confusion until he caught sight of a little, short-legged dog who ran over the ice with a goose in his mouth.

In a minute the boy was after that dog, to try and take the goose away from him. He must have heard the gander call to him : 'Have a care, Tummetott ! Have a care !' But the boy thought that such a little runt of a dog was nothing to be afraid of and he rushed ahead.

The wild goose that Smirre Fox tugged after him heard the clatter as the boy's wooden shoes beat against the ice, and she could hardly believe her ears. 'Does that tiny boy think he can take me away from the fox?' she wondered. And in spite of her misery she began to cackle right merrily, deep down in her windpipe. It was almost as if she had laughed.

'The first thing he knows, he'll fall through a crack in the ice,' she thought.

But dark as the night was the boy saw distinctly all the cracks and holes there were, and took daring leaps over them. This was because he had the elf's good eyesight now and could see in the dark. He saw both lake and shore just as clearly as if it had been daylight.

Smirre Fox left the ice where it touched the shore. And just as he was working his way up to the bank the boy shouted to him: 'Drop that goose, you sneak!' Smirre didn't know who was calling to him, and wasted no time in looking around, but increased his pace.

The fox made straight for a forest of big beech-trees and the boy followed him, with never a thought of the danger he was running. On the contrary, he thought all the while about the contemptuous way in which he had been received by the wild geese that evening; and he made up his mind to let them see that a human being was something higher than all else created.

He shouted again and again to that dog to make him drop his game. 'What kind of a dog are you, who can steal a whole goose and not feel ashamed of yourself? Drop her at once or you'll see what a beating you'll get. Drop her, I say, or I'll tell your master how you behave!'

When Smirre Fox saw that he had been mistaken for a

fierce dog he was so amused that he very nearly dropped the goose. Smirre was a great plunderer who wasn't satisfied with only hunting rats and pigeons in the fields, but he also ventured into the farmyards to steal chickens and geese. He knew that he was feared throughout the district; and anything as idiotic as this he had not heard since he was a cub.

The boy ran so fast that the thick beech-trees appeared to be running past him—backward, and he caught up with Smirre. Finally he was so close to him that he got hold of his tail. 'Now I'll take the goose from you anyway,' he cried, and held on as hard as ever he could, but he hadn't strength enough to stop Smirre. The fox dragged him along until the dry foliage whirled around him.

But now it began to dawn on Smirre how harmless the creature was that pursued him. He stopped short, put the goose on the ground, and stood on her with his forepaws so that she couldn't fly away. He was just about to bite off her head but couldn't resist the desire to tease the boy a little. 'Hurry off and complain to the master, for now I'm going to bite the goose to death!' he said.

Certainly it was the boy who was surprised when he saw what a pointed nose, and heard what a hoarse and angry voice that dog had, which he was pursuing. But now he was so enraged because the fox had made fun of him that he never thought of being frightened. He took a firmer hold on the tail, braced himself against a beech trunk, and just as the fox opened his jaws over the goose's throat he pulled as hard as he could. Smirre was so astonished that he let himself be pulled backward a couple of steps and the wild goose got away. She fluttered upward feebly and heavily. One wing was so badly wounded that she could barely use it. In addition to this she could not see in the night darkness of the forest but was as helpless as the blind. Therefore she could in no way help Nils; so she groped her way through the branches and flew down to the lake again.

Then Smirre made a dash for the boy. 'If I don't get the one I shall certainly have the other,' said he; and you could tell by his voice how angry he was. 'Oh, don't you believe it!' said the boy, who was in the best of spirits because he had saved the goose. He held himself fast by the fox-tail, and swung with it to one side when the fox tried to catch him.

There was such a dance in that forest that the dry beech leaves fairly flew! Smirre swung round and round, but the tail swung too, while Nils kept a tight grip on it, so that the fox couldn't grab him.

The boy was so gay after his success that, in the beginning, he only laughed and made fun of the fox. But Smirre was persevering—as old hunters generally are—and Nils began to fear that he would be captured in the end.

Then he caught sight of a little, young beech-tree that had shot up as slender as a rod that it might soon reach the free air above the canopy of branches which the old beeches spread over it.

Quick as a flash he let go of the fox-tail and climbed the beech-tree. Smirre Fox was so excited that he continued to dance around after his tail for a long time.

'Don't bother with the dance any longer!' said Nils.

But Smirre couldn't endure the humiliation of his

failure to get the better of such a little creature, so he lay down under the tree so that he might keep a close watch on him.

Nils didn't have any too good a time of it where he sat, astride a frail branch. The young beech did not, as yet, reach the high roof of branches, so the boy couldn't get over to another tree and he didn't dare to come down again. He was so cold and numb that he almost lost his hold round the branch; and he was dreadfully sleepy; but he didn't dare fall asleep for fear of tumbling down.

Goodness, it was dismal to sit in that way the whole night through, out in the forest! He never before understood the real meaning of 'night.' It was just as if the whole world had become petrified and never could come to life again.

Then the dawn came. The boy was glad that everything began to look more normal again, although the chill was even sharper than it had been during the night.

When the sun finally rose, it wasn't yellow but red. Nils thought it looked as though it were angry and he wondered what it was angry about. Perhaps it was because the

night had made it so cold and gloomy on earth while the sun was away.

The sunbeams came down in great clusters to see what the night had been up to. It could be seen how everything blushed as if they had guilty consciences. The clouds in the skies; the satiny beech limbs; the little intertwined branches of the forest canopy; the hoar-frost that covered the leaves on the ground—everything grew flushed and red. More and more sunbeams came bursting through space, and soon the night's terrors were driven away and a marvellous lot of living things appeared. The black woodpecker, with the red neck, began to hammer with its bill on the trunk of a tree. The squirrel ran out from its nest with a nut, and sat down on a branch and began to shell it. The starling came flying with a fibre of root and the chaffinch sang in the tree top.

Then the boy understood that the sun had said to all these tiny creatures: 'Wake up now, and come out of your nests! I'm here! Now you need be afraid of nothing.'

The wild-goose call was heard from the lake as they were preparing for flight; and soon all fourteen geese came flying above the forest. The boy tried to call to them, but they flew so high that his voice couldn't reach them. They probably believed the fox had eaten him up, and they didn't trouble themselves to look for him.

The boy came near crying with regret; but the sun stood up there—orange-coloured and happy—and put courage into the whole world. 'It isn't worth while, Nils Holgersson, for you to be troubled about anything as long as I'm here,' said the sun.

Chapter Three

GOOSE-PLAY

EVERYTHING remained unchanged in the forest about as long as it takes a goose to eat her breakfast. But just as the morning was verging on forenoon, a goose came flying, all by herself, under the thick tree-canopy. She groped her way, hesitatingly, between the stems and branches and flew very slowly. As soon as Smirre Fox saw her he left his place under the beech-tree and sneaked up towards her. The wild goose didn't avoid the fox, but flew very close to him. Smirre made a high jump for her but he missed her, and the goose went on her way down to the lake.

It was not long before another goose came flying. She took the same route as the first one, and flew still lower and slower. She, too, flew close to Smirre Fox, and he made such a high spring for her, that his ears brushed her feet. But she, too, got away from him unhurt, and went her way toward the lake, silent as a shadow.

A little while passed and then there came another wild goose. She flew still slower and lower; and it seemed even more difficult for her to find her way between the beech branches. Smirre made a powerful spring. He was within a hair's breadth of catching her, but that goose also managed to save herself.

Just after she had disappeared came a fourth. She flew so slowly, and so badly, that Smirre Fox thought he could catch her without much effort, but he was afraid of failure now and meant to let her fly past unmolested. She took the same direction the others had taken; and

43

just as she came right above Smirre she sank down so
far that he was tempted to jump for her. He jumped so
high that he touched her with his paw. But she flung
herself quickly to one side and saved her life.

Before Smirre had finished panting three more geese
come flying in a row. They flew just like the rest, and
Smirre made high springs for them all, but he did not
succeed in catching any one of them.

After that came five geese, but these flew better than
the others. And although it seemed as if they wanted to
lure Smirre to jump he withstood the temptation. After
quite a long time came one single goose. It was the
thirteenth. This one was so old that she was grey all
over, without a dark speck anywhere on her body. She
didn't appear to use one wing very well, but flew so
wretchedly and crookedly that she almost touched the
ground. Smirre not only made a high leap for her, but
he pursued her, running and jumping all the way down
to the lake. But not even this time did he get anything
for his trouble.

When the fourteenth goose came along it looked very
pretty because it was white. And as its great wings
swayed it glistened like a light in the dark forest. When
Smirre Fox saw this one he mustered all his resources
and jumped half-way to the tree tops. But the white one
flew by unhurt like the rest.

Now it was quiet for a moment under the beeches. It
looked as if the whole wild goose flock had travelled past.

Suddenly Smirre remembered his prisoner and raised
his eyes toward the young beech-tree. And just as he
might have expected—the boy had disappeared.

But Smirre didn't have much time to think about him;
for now the first goose came back again from the lake

and flew slowly under the trees. In spite of all his ill
luck, Smirre was glad that she came back, and darted
after her with a high leap. But he had been in too much
of a hurry and hadn't taken the time to aim properly,
and he landed at one side of the goose. Then there came
still another goose; then a third; a fourth; a fifth; and
so on, until the line was completed with the old ice-grey
one and the big white one. They all flew low and slow.
Just as they soared above Smirre Fox they sank down
as if inviting him to seize them. Smirre ran after them
and made leaps a couple of fathoms high but he couldn't
manage to get hold of a single one of them.

It was the most awful day that Smirre Fox had ever
experienced. The wild geese kept on travelling over his
head. They came and went—came and went. Great
splendid geese, who had eaten themselves fat on the
German heaths and grain fields, swayed all day through
the woods, and so close to him that he touched them
many times; yet he was not permitted to appease his
hunger with a single one of them.

The winter was hardly gone yet, and Smirre recalled
nights and days when he had been forced to drift about
in idleness with not so much as a hare to hunt; when the
birds of passage were away, when the rats hid themselves
under the frozen earth, and when the chickens were shut
up. But all the winter's hunger had not been as hard
to endure as this day's disappointment.

Smirre was no young fox. He had had the hounds
after him many a time, and had heard the bullets whizz
around his ears. He had lain in hiding, down in the lair,
while the dachshunds crept into the crevices and all but
found him. But all the anguish that Smirre Fox had
been forced to suffer from this hot chase was not to be

compared with what he suffered every time that he missed one of the wild geese.

In the morning, when the play began, Smirre Fox had looked so splendid that the geese were amazed when they saw him. Smirre loved display. His coat was a brilliant red; his breast white; his nose black; and his tail was as bushy as a plume. But when the evening of this day was come Smirre's coat was ragged. He was bathed in sweat; his eyes were lustreless, his tongue hung far out from his gaping jaws; and froth oozed from his mouth.

In the afternoon Smirre was so exhausted that he grew delirious. He saw nothing before his eyes but flying geese. He made leaps for sun-spots which he saw on the ground, and for a poor little butterfly that had come out of his chrysalis too soon.

The wild geese flew and flew, unceasingly. All day long they continued to torment Smirre. They were not moved to pity because Smirre was done up, fevered, and out of his mind. They continued without a let-up, although they understood that he hardly saw them, and that he jumped after their shadows.

Only when Smirre Fox sank down on a pile of dry leaves, weak and powerless and almost ready to give up the ghost, did they stop teasing him.

'Now you know, Mr. Fox, what happens to the one who dares to come near Akka of Kebnekaise!' they shouted in his ear, and with that they left him in peace.

PART THREE

THE WONDERFUL JOURNEY OF NILS

☆

Chapter One

ON THE FARM

JUST at that time a thing happened in Skåne which
created a good deal of discussion and even got into the
newspapers, but which many believed to be a myth
because they had not been able to explain it.

The story was this: a squirrel had been captured in the hazel brush that grew on the shores of Vomb Lake, and carried to a farmhouse close by. Every one on the farm —both young and old—were delighted with the pretty creature with the bushy tail, the wise, inquisitive eyes, and the neat little feet. They intended to amuse themselves all the summer by watching her nimble movements, her ingenious way of shelling nuts, and her droll play. They immediately put in order an old squirrel cage which consisted of a little green house and a round wire wheel. The little house, which had both doors and windows, the squirrel was to use as a dining-room and bedroom. For this reason they placed in it a bed of leaves, a bowl of milk, and some nuts. The wheel, on the other hand, she was to use as a play-house, where she could run and climb and swing round.

The people believed that they had arranged things very comfortably for the squirrel, and they were astonished because she didn't seem to be contented, but, instead, sat there, downcast and moody, in a corner of her room. Every now and again, she would let out a shrill, agonized cry. She did not touch the food, and not once did she swing round on the wheel. 'It's probably because she's frightened,' said the farmer folk. 'To-morrow, when she feels more at home, she will both eat and play.'

Meanwhile, the women on the farm were making preparations for a feast; and on the very day when the squirrel was captured they were busy with an elaborate bake. But they had bad luck with something: either the dough wouldn't rise, or else they were slow, for they were obliged to work long after dark.

Naturally there was a great deal of excitement and bustle in the kitchen, and probably no one there had time to think about the squirrel, or to wonder how she was getting on. But there was an old grandmother in the house who was too aged to take a hand in the baking; she understood this, but just the same she did not relish the idea of being left out of everything. She felt rather downhearted; and for this reason she did not go to bed but seated herself by the sitting-room window and looked out.

They had opened the kitchen door on account of the heat, and through it a clear ray of light streamed out on the yard; and it became so well lighted out there that the old woman could see all the cracks and holes in the plastering on the wall opposite. She also saw the squirrel cage which stood just where the light fell clearest. And she noticed how the squirrel ran from her room to the wheel, and from the wheel to her room, all night long, without stopping an instant. She thought it was a strange sort of unrest that had come over the animal; but she believed, of course, that the strong light kept her awake.

Between the cowhouse and the stable there was a broad, roofed-in carriage-gate; this too came within the ray of light. As the night wore on the old grandmother saw a tiny creature, no bigger than a hand's breadth, cautiously steal his way through the gate. He was dressed in leather breeches and wooden shoes like any other working man. The old grandmother knew at once that it was the elf, and she was not the least bit frightened. She had always heard that the elf kept himself somewhere about the place, although she had never seen him before; and an elf, to be sure, brought good luck wherever he appeared.

As soon as the elf came into the stone-paved yard, he

ran right up to the squirrel cage. And since it stood so high that he could not reach it, he went over to the storehouse for a stick; placed it against the cage, and swung himself up in the same way that a sailor climbs a rope. When he had reached the cage he shook the door of the little green house as if he wanted to open it; but the old grandmother didn't move, for she knew that the children had put a padlock on the door, as they feared that the boys on the neighbouring farms would try to steal the squirrel. The old woman saw that when the boy could not get the door open the squirrel came out to the wire wheel. There they held a long conference together. And when the boy had listened to all that the imprisoned animal had to say to him, he slid down the rod to the ground, and ran out through the carriage-gate.

The old woman didn't expect to see anything more of the elf that night, nevertheless, she remained at the window. After a few moments had gone by he returned. He was in such a hurry that it seemed to her as though his feet hardly touched the ground, and he rushed right up to the squirrel cage. The old woman, with her far-sighted eyes, saw him distinctly; and she also saw that he carried something in his hands, but what it was she couldn't imagine. The thing he carried in his left hand he laid down on the pavement, but that which he held in his right hand he took with him to the cage. He kicked so hard with his wooden shoes on the little window that the glass was broken. He poked in the thing which he held in his hand to the squirrel. Then he slid down again, and took up the thing he had laid upon the ground, and climbed up to the cage with that also. The next instant he ran off again with such haste that the old woman could hardly follow him with her eyes.

He poked in the thing which he held in his hand to the squirrel

But now the old grandmother could no longer sit still in the cottage, and she very slowly went out to the back yard and stationed herself in the shadow of the pump to await the elf's return. And there was one other who had also seen him and had become curious. This was the house cat. He crept along slyly and stopped close to the wall, just two steps away from the stream of light. They both stood and waited, long and patiently, on that chilly March night, and the old woman was just beginning to think about going in again when she heard a clatter on the pavement, and saw that the little mite of an elf came trotting along once more, carrying a burden in each hand as he had done before. That which he bore squealed and squirmed. And now a light dawned on the old grandmother. She understood that the elf had hurried down to the hazel grove and brought back the mother squirrel's babies; and that he was carrying them to her so they shouldn't starve to death.

The old grandmother stood very still so as not to disturb them; and it did not look as if the elf had noticed her. He was just going to lay one of the babies on the ground so that he could swing himself up to the cage with the other one—when he saw the cat's green eyes glisten close beside him. He stood there, bewildered, with a young one in each hand.

He turned around and looked in all directions; then he became aware of the old grandmother's presence. Then he did not hesitate long, but walked forward, stretched his arms as high as he could reach, for her to take one of the baby squirrels.

The old grandmother did not wish to prove herself unworthy of the trust, so she bent down and took the baby squirrel, and stood there and held it until the boy had swung himself up to the cage with the other one. Then he came back for the one he had entrusted to her care.

The next morning, when the farm folk had gathered together for breakfast, it was impossible for the old woman to refrain from telling them of what she had seen the night before. They all laughed at her, of course, and said that she had been only dreaming. There were no baby squirrels so early in the year.

But she was sure of her ground, and begged them to take a look into the squirrel cage and this they did. And there lay on the bed of leaves, four tiny half-naked, half-blind baby squirrels, who were at least a couple of days old.

When the farmer himself saw the young ones he said: 'Be this as it may, one thing is certain, we, on this farm, have behaved in such a manner that we are shamed before both animals and human beings.' And thereupon he took the mother squirrel and all her young ones from the cage, and laid them in the old grandmother's lap. 'Go thou out to the hazel grove with them,' said he, 'and let them have their freedom back again!'

It was this event that was so much talked about, and which even got into the newspapers, but which the majority would not credit because they were not able to explain how anything like that could have happened.

Chapter Two

VITTSKÖVLE

Two days later another strange thing happened. A flock of wild geese came flying one morning, and lit on a meadow down in Eastern Skåne not very far from Vittskövle manor. In the flock were thirteen wild geese of the usual grey variety, and one white gander, who carried on his back a tiny lad dressed in yellow leather breeches, green vest, and a white woollen toboggan hood.

They were now very near the Baltic Sea, and on the meadow where the geese had alighted the soil was sandy, as it usually is on the sea-coast. It looked as if, formerly, there had been flying sand in this vicinity which had to be held down, for in several directions large plantations of pine woods could be seen.

When the wild geese had been feeding for a time, two children came along, and walked along the edge of the meadow. The goose who was on guard at once raised herself into the air with noisy wing-strokes, so the whole flock should hear that there was danger on foot. All the wild geese flew upward; but the white one trotted along on the ground unconcerned. When he saw the others fly he raised his head and called after them: 'You needn't fly away from these! They are only a couple of children!'

The little creature who had been riding on his back, was sitting upon a knoll on the outskirts of the wood and had picked a pine-cone to pieces that he might get at the seeds. The children were so close to him that he did not dare to run across the meadow to the white one. He hid himself under a big, dry thistle leaf, and at the same time gave a warning cry. But the white one had evidently made up his mind not to let himself be scared. He walked along on the ground all the time and not once did he look to see in what direction they were going.

Meanwhile they turned from the path, walked across the field, getting nearer and nearer to the gander. When he finally did look up they were right upon him. He was dumbfounded, and become so confused that he forgot that he could fly, and tried to get out of their reach by running. But the children followed, chasing him into a ditch, and there they caught him. The larger of the two stuck him under his arm and carried him off.

When Nils, who was lying under the thistle leaf saw this, he sprang up as if he wanted to take the gander away from them; then he must have remembered how little and powerless he was, for he threw himself on the knoll and beat upon the ground with his clenched fists.

The gander cried with all his might for help: 'Tummetott, come and help me! Oh, Tummetott, come and help me!' The boy began to laugh in the midst of his distress. 'Oh, yes! I 'm just the right one to help anybody, I am!' he cried.

But he got up and followed the gander. 'I can't help him,' he said, 'but I shall at least find out where they are taking him.'

The children had a good start; but the boy had no difficulty in keeping them within sight until they came to a hollow where a brook gushed forth. But here he was obliged to run alongside it for some little time, before he could find a place narrow enough for him to jump over.

When he came up from the hollow the children had

disappeared. He could see their footprints on a narrow path which led to the woods, and these he continued to follow.

Soon he came to cross-roads. Here the children must have separated, for there were footprints in two directions. It seemed now to Nils as if all hope had fled. Then he saw a little white down on a heather knoll, and he understood that the gander had dropped this by the wayside to let him know in which direction he had been carried, and therefore he continued his search. He followed the children through the entire wood. The gander he did not see; but wherever he was likely to miss his way lay a little white down to put him right.

Nils continued faithfully to follow the bits of down. They led him out of the wood, across a couple of meadows, up along a road, and finally through the entrance of a broad avenue. At the end of the avenue there were red-tiled gables and towers, decorated with bright borders and other ornamentations that glittered and shone. When the boy saw that this was some great castle he thought he knew what had become of the gander. 'No doubt the children have carried him to the castle and sold him there. By this time he's probably butchered,' he said to himself. But he was not satisfied with anything less than proof positive, and with renewed courage ran forward. He met no one in the avenue and that was well, for such as he are generally afraid of being seen by human beings.

The castle which he came to was a splendid, old-time building with four great wings which enclosed a court-yard. On the east wing, there was a high archway leading into the courtyard. This far the boy ran without hesitation, but when he got there he stopped. He dared not venture farther, but stood still and pondered what he should do now.

There he stood, with his finger on his nose, thinking, when he heard footsteps behind him; and as he turned around he saw a whole crowd of people march up the avenue. In haste he stole behind a water-barrel which stood near the arch and hid himself.

Those who came up were some twenty young men from a folk-high-school, out on a walking tour. They were accompanied by one of the instructors. When they had come as far as the arch, the teacher requested them to wait there a moment, while he went in and asked if they might see the old castle of Vittskövle.

The newcomers were warm and tired, as if they had had a long tramp. One of them was so thirsty that he went over to the water-barrel and stooped down to drink. He had a tin box such as botanists use hanging about his neck. He evidently thought that this was in his way, for he threw it down on the ground. With this the lid flew open and one could see that there were a few spring flowers in it.

The botanist's box dropped just in front of Nils and he must have thought that here was his opportunity to get into the house and find out what had become of the gander. He smuggled himself quickly into the box and concealed himself as well as he could under the anemones and coltsfoot.

He was hardly hidden before the young man picked the box up, hung it round his neck, and shut down the lid.

Then the teacher came back and said that they had been given permission to enter the castle. At first he conducted them no farther than the courtyard. There he stopped and began to talk to them about this ancient building.

He called their attention to the first human beings who had inhabited this country, and who had been obliged to live in mountain clefts and earth caves, in tents made of animals' skins and in huts of twigs, and how a very long period had elapsed before they learned to build themselves huts from the trunks of trees. And afterwards how long had they not been forced to labour and struggle before they had advanced from the log cabin, with its single room, to the building of a castle with a hundred rooms—like Vittskövle!

It was about three hundred and fifty years ago that the rich and powerful built such castles for themselves, he said. It was evident that Vittskövle had been built at a time when wars and robbers made it unsafe in Skåne. All round the castle was a deep moat filled with water, and across this there had been a bridge in bygone days that could be hoisted up. Over the gateway there is, even to this day, a watch-tower, and all along the sides of the castle ran sentry galleries, and in the corners stood towers with walls three feet thick. Yet the castle had not been erected in the most savage war times; for Jens Brahe, who built it, had also tried to make it beautiful and decorative. If they could see the big, solid stone structure at Glimminge, which had been built only a generation earlier, they would readily see that Jens Holgersen Ulfstand, the builder, had only thought of building a big and strong and secure house, without bestowing a thought upon making it beautiful and comfortable. If they visited such castles as Marsvinsholm, Svenstorp, and Öved Cloister—which were erected a hundred years or so later—they would find that the times had become less warlike. The men who built these places had not furnished them with fortifications, but had only taken pains to provide themselves with great, splendid dwelling-houses.

The teacher talked at length and in detail, and Nils, who lay shut up in the box, was pretty impatient; but he must have lain very still, for the owner of the box hadn't the least suspicion that he was carrying him along.

Finally the party went into the castle. But if Nils had hoped for a chance to crawl out of that box he was disappointed; for the student carried it with him all the time and the boy was obliged to accompany him through all the rooms. It was a tedious tour. The teacher stopped every other minute to explain and instruct.

In one room he found an old fireplace, and before this he stopped to talk about the different kinds of fireplaces that had been used throughout the ages. The first indoor fireplace had been a big, flat stone in the centre of the room, with an opening in the roof which let in both wind and rain. The next had been a big stone hearth with no opening in the roof; this must have made the hut very warm, but it also filled it with soot and smoke. When Vittskövle was built the people had advanced as far as the open fireplace, which, at that time, had a wide chimney for the smoke; but it also took most of the warmth up in the air with it.

If Nils had ever in his life been cross and impatient, he was given a good lesson in patience that day. It must have been a whole hour now that he had lain perfectly still.

In the next room they came to the teacher stopped before an old-time bed with its high canopy and rich curtains. Immediately he began to talk about the beds and bed places of olden days.

The teacher didn't hurry himself; but then he did not know, of course, that a poor little creature lay shut up in a botanist's box, and only waited for him to end. When they came to a room with gilded leather hangings he talked to them about how the people had covered their walls and ceilings ever since the beginning of time. And when he came to an old family portrait he told them all about the different changes in dress. And in the banquet halls he described ancient customs of celebrating weddings and funerals.

Thereupon the teacher talked a little about the excellent men and women who had lived in the castle; about the old Brahes and the old Barnekows; of Christian Barnekow, who had given his horse to the king to help him escape; of Margareta Ascheberg, who had been married to Kjell Barnekow and who, when a widow, had managed the estates and the whole district for fifty-three years; of banker Hagerman, a crofter's son from Vittskövle, who had grown so rich that he had bought the entire estate; about the Stjernsvärds, who had given the people of Skåne better ploughs, which enabled them to discard the ridiculous old wooden ploughs that three oxen were hardly able to drag. During all this the boy lay still. If he had ever been mischievous and shut the cellar door on his father or mother, he understood now how they had felt; for it was hours and hours before that teacher finished.

At last the teacher went out into the courtyard again. And there he discoursed upon the tireless labour of mankind to procure for themselves tools and weapons, clothes and houses and ornaments. He said that such an old

castle like Vittskövle was a mile-post on time's highway.
Here one could see how far people had advanced three
hundred and fifty years ago; and one could judge for
oneself whether things had gone forward or backward
since their time.

But this dissertation the boy escaped hearing; for the
student who carried him was thirsty again, and stole into
the kitchen to ask for a drink of water. When the boy
was carried into the kitchen he must have tried to look
round for the gander. He had begun to move, and as
he did so he happened to press too hard against the lid
—and it flew open. As botanists' box lids are always
flying open the student thought no more about the
matter but pressed it down again. Then the cook asked
him if he had a snake in the box.

'No, I have only a few plants,' the student replied.
'It was certainly something that moved there,' insisted
the cook. The student threw back the lid to show her
that she was mistaken. 'See for yourself—if——'

But he got no farther, for now Nils dared not stay in
the box any longer, but with one bound he stood on the
floor and out he rushed. The maids hardly had time to
see what it was that ran, but they hurried after it,
nevertheless.

The teacher was still talking when he was interrupted
by shrill cries. 'Catch him, catch him!' shrieked those
who had come from the kitchen; and all the young men
raced after the boy, who slipped away faster than a rat.
They tried to intercept him at the gate, but it was not so
easy to catch such a little creature, so, luckily, he got
out into the open.

Nils did not dare to run down toward the open avenue,
but turned in another direction. He rushed through the

garden into the back yard. All the while the people raced after him, shrieking and laughing. The poor little thing ran as hard as ever he could to get out of their way; but still it looked as though the people would catch up with him.

As he rushed past a labourer's cottage he heard a goose cackle, and saw some white down lying on the door-step. There, at last, was the gander! He had been on the wrong track before. He thought no more of the house-maids and men who were hounding him but climbed up the steps—and into the hallway. Farther he couldn't go for the door was locked. He heard how the gander cried and moaned inside, but he couldn't get the door open. The hunters that were pursuing him came nearer and nearer, and, in the room, the gander cried more and more pitifully. In this direst of needs the boy finally plucked up courage and pounded on the door as hard as he could.

A child opened it, and Nils looked into the room. In the middle of the floor sat a woman who held the gander tight—to clip his quill-feathers. It was her children who had found him and she didn't want to do him any harm. She meant to let him in among her own geese, if she could succeed in clipping his wings so that he couldn't fly away. But a worse fate could hardly have happened to the gander, and he shrieked and moaned with all his might.

And a lucky thing it was that the woman hadn't started the clipping sooner. Now only two quills had fallen under the shears when the door was opened and the boy stood in the doorway. But a creature like that the woman had never seen before. She could only believe that it was Goa-Nisse himself; and in her terror she dropped the shears, clasped her hands, and forgot to hold on to the gander.

As soon as he felt himself freed he ran toward the door. He didn't give himself time to stop; but, as he ran past him, he grabbed Nils by the shirt-band and carried him along with him. In the porch he spread his wings and flew up in the air, and at the same time he made a graceful sweep with his neck and seated the boy on his smooth, downy back.

And off they flew—while all Vittskövle stood and stared after them.

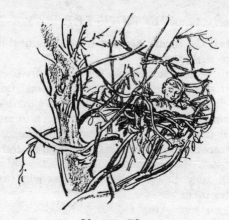

Chapter Three

IN ÖVED CLOISTER PARK

ALL that day, when the wild geese played with the fox, the boy lay and slept in a deserted squirrel nest. When he awoke, towards evening, he felt very uneasy. 'Well, now I shall soon be sent home again! Then I 'll have to show myself to father and mother, 'he thought. But when he looked up and saw the wild geese, who lay and bathed in Vomb Lake, not one of them said a word about his going. 'They probably think the white one is too tired to travel home with me to-night,' thought Nils.

The next morning the geese were awake at daybreak, long before sunrise. Now the boy felt sure that he 'd have to go home; but, curiously enough, both he and the white gander were permitted to follow the wild ones on their morning flight. The boy couldn't understand the reason for the delay, but he thought that the wild geese did not want to send the gander on such a long journey until he had eaten his fill. Come what might, Nils was only thankful for every moment that should pass before he must face his parents.

The wild geese travelled over Öved Cloister estate which was situated in a beautiful park east of the lake, and looked very imposing with its great castle, its well-planned court surrounded by low walls and pavilions; its fine old-time garden with covered arbours, streams, and fountains; its wonderful trees, trimmed bushes, and its evenly mown lawns with their beds of beautiful spring flowers.

When the wild geese flew over the estate in the early morning hour there was no human being about. When they had made quite sure of this they flew down towards the dog kennel, and shouted: 'What kind of a little hut is this? What kind of a little hut is this?'

Instantly the dog came out of his kennel—furiously angry—and barked at the air.

'Do you call this a hut, you tramps! Can't you see that this is a great stone castle? Can't you see what fine terraces, and what a lot of lovely walls and windows and great doors it has, bow, wow, wow, wow? Don't you see the grounds? Can't you see the garden? Can't you see the greenhouses? Can't you see the marble statues? You call this a hut, do you? Do huts have parks with beech woods and hazel bushes and groves and oak-trees and firs and hunting grounds filled with game, wow, wow, wow? Do you call this a hut? Have you seen huts with so many outhouses around them that they look like a whole village? You must know of a lot of huts that have their own church and their own parsonage, and that rule over manors and farms and villages and cottages, wow, wow, wow? Do you call this a hut? To this hut belong the richest possessions in Skåne, you beggars! You can't see a bit of land from where you hang in the clouds that does not belong to this hut, wow, wow, wow!'

All this the dog managed to cry out in one breath; and the wild geese flew back and forth over the estate, and listened to him until he was winded. But then they cried: 'What are you so angry about? We didn't ask about the castle; we only wanted to know about your kennel, stupid!'

When Nils heard this joke, he laughed; then a thought stole in on him which at once made him serious. 'Think how many of these amusing things you would hear, if you could go with the wild geese through the whole country, all the way up to Lapland!' he said to himself. 'And just now, when you are in such a bad fix, a trip like that would be the best thing you could possibly do.'

The wild geese travelled to one of the wide fields, east of the estate, to eat grass-roots, and they kept this up for hours. In the meantime, the boy wandered in the great park which bordered the field. He hunted up a hazel wood and began to look up at the bushes, to see if a nut from last autumn still hung there. But again and again the thought of the trip came over him, as he walked in the park. He pictured to himself what a fine time he would have if he went with the wild geese. To freeze and starve: that he believed he should have to do often enough; but as a reward he would escape both work and study.

As he walked there, the old grey leader-goose came up to him, and asked if he had found anything eatable. No, that he hadn't, he replied, and then she tried to help him.

She couldn't find any nuts either, but she discovered a couple of hips that hung on a brier bush. These the

boy ate with a good relish. But he wondered what
mother would say if she knew that he now lived on raw
fish and old winter-dried hips.

When the wild geese had finally eaten themselves full
they bore off toward the lake again, where they amused
themselves with games until almost dinner time.

The wild geese challenged the white gander to take
part in all kinds of sports. They had swimming races,
running races, and flying races with him. The big tame
one did his level best to hold his own, but the clever wild
geese beat him every time. All the while, Nils sat on
the gander's back and encouraged him, and had as much
fun as the rest. They laughed and screamed and cackled,
and it was remarkable that the people on the estate
didn't hear them.

When the wild geese were tired of play, they flew out
on the ice and rested for a couple of hours. The afternoon they spent in pretty much the same way as the
forenoon. First a couple of hours feeding, then bathing
and play in the water near the ice edge until sunset, when
they immediately arranged themselves for sleep.

'This is just the life that suits me,' thought the boy
when he crept in under the gander's wing. 'But to-
morrow, I suppose, I 'll be sent home.'

Before he fell asleep, he lay and thought that if he
might go with the wild geese, he would escape all the
scoldings because he was lazy. Then he could cut loose
every day, and his only worry would be to get something
to eat. But he needed so little nowadays, and there
would always be a way to get that.

So he pictured the whole scene to himself; what he
should see, and all the adventures that he would have.
Yes, it would be something different from the wear and

tear at home. 'If I could only go with the wild geese on their travels, I shouldn't feel so unhappy because I 've been bewitched,' thought Nils.

He wasn't afraid of anything except being sent home; but not even on Wednesday did the geese say anything to him about going. That day passed in the same way as Tuesday; and the boy grew more and more contented with the outdoor life. He thought that he had the lovely Öved Cloister Park—which was as large as a forest—all to himself; and he wasn't anxious to go back to the stuffy cabin and the little patch of ground there at home.

On Wednesday he believed that the wild geese thought of keeping him with them; but on Thursday he lost hope again.

Thursday began just like the other days; the geese fed on the broad meadows, and the boy hunted for food in the park. After a while Akka came to him and asked if he had found anything to eat. No, he had not; and then she discovered a dry caraway herb that had kept all its tiny seeds intact.

When Nils had eaten Akka said that she thought he ran around in the park altogether too recklessly. She wondered if he knew how many enemies he had to guard against, he who was so little. No, he didn't know anything at all about that. Then Akka began to list them for him.

Whenever he walked in the park, she said, he must look out for the fox and the marten; when he came to the shores of the lake, he must think of the otters; as he sat on the stone wall, he must not forget the weasels, who could creep through the smallest holes; and if he wished to lie down and sleep on a pile of leaves, he must first find out if the adders were not sleeping their winter sleep in the same pile. As soon as he came out in the open fields, he should keep an eye out for hawks and buzzards, for eagles and falcons, that soared in the air. In the bramble bush he could be captured by the sparrow-hawk; magpies and crows were found everywhere and in these he mustn't place any too much confidence. As soon as it was dusk he must keep his ears open and listen for the big owls, who flew along with such soundless wing-strokes that they could come right up to him before he was aware of their presence.

When Nils heard that there were so many who were after his life, he thought that it would be simply impossible for him to escape. He was not particularly afraid to die, but he didn't like the idea of being eaten up, so he asked Akka what he should do to protect himself from the wild beasts.

Akka answered at once that Nils should try to get on good terms with all the small animals in the woods and fields: with the squirrel-folk and the hare family; with bullfinches and titmice and woodpeckers and larks. If he made friends with them they could warn him against dangers, find hiding places for him, and protect him.

But later in the day when the boy tried to profit by this counsel, and turned to Sirle Squirrel to ask for his protection, it was evident that he did not care to help him. 'You surely can't expect anything from me, or the rest of the small animals!' said Sirle. 'Don't you think we know that you are Nils the goose-boy, who tore down the swallow's nest last year, crushed the starling's eggs, threw baby crows in the marl-ditch, caught thrushes in snares, and put squirrels in cages? You just help yourself as well as you can; and you may be thankful that we do not form a league against you, and drive you back to your own kind!'

This was just the sort of answer the boy would not have let go unpunished, in the days when he was Nils the goose-boy. But now he was only fearful lest the wild geese, too, had found out how wicked he could be. He had been so afraid he wouldn't be permitted to stay with the wild geese, that he hadn't dared to get into the least little mischief since he joined their company. It was true that he didn't have the power to do much harm now, but, little as he was, he could have destroyed many birds' nests, and crushed many eggs, if he'd had a mind to. But he had been good. He hadn't pulled a feather from a goose wing, or given any one a rude answer; and every morning when he called upon Akka he had always removed his cap and bowed.

All day Thursday he thought it was surely on account of his wickedness that the wild geese did not care to take him with them up to Lapland. And in the evening, when he heard that Sirle Squirrel's wife had been stolen, and her children were starving to death, he made up his mind to help them. And we have already been told how well he succeeded.

When the boy came into the park on Friday, he heard the bullfinches sing in every bush, of how Sirle Squirrel's wife had been carried away from her children by cruel robbers, and how Nils, the goose-boy, had risked his life among human beings, and taken the little squirrel children to her.

'And who is so honoured in Öved Cloister Park now, as Tummetott!' sang the bullfinch; 'he whom all feared when he was Nils the goose-boy? Sirle Squirrel will give him nuts; the poor hares are going to play with him;

the deer will carry him on their backs and fly away with him when Smirre Fox approaches. The titmice are going to warn him against the hawk, and the finches and larks will sing of his valour.'

Nils was absolutely certain that both Akka and the wild geese had heard all this. But still Friday passed and not one word did they say about his remaining with them.

Until Saturday the wild geese fed in the fields around Öved, undisturbed by Smirre Fox.

But on Saturday morning when they came out in the meadows, he lay in wait for them and chased them from one field to another, and they were not allowed to eat in peace. When Akka understood that he didn't intend to leave them in peace she came to a decision quickly, raised herself into the air, and flew with her flock several miles away, over Färs' plains and Linderödsosen's hills. They did not stop before they had arrived in the district of Vittskövle.

But at Vittskövle the gander was stolen, and how it happened has already been related. If the boy hadn't used all his powers to help him he would never again have been found.

On Saturday evening, as Nils came back to Vomb Lake with the gander, he thought that he had done a good day's work; and he speculated a good deal on what Akka and the wild geese would say to him. The wild geese were not at all sparing in their praises, but they did not say the word he was longing to hear.

Then Sunday came again. A whole week had gone by since the boy had been bewitched, and he was still just as little.

But he didn't appear to be giving himself any extra

worry on account of that. On Sunday afternoon he sat huddled up in a big, fluffy, osier bush, down by the lake, and blew on a reed-pipe. All around him there sat as many finches and bullfinches and starlings as the bush could well hold—who sang songs which he tried to teach himself to play. But Nils was not at home in this art. He blew so out of tune that the feathers stood on end on the little music-masters and they shrieked and fluttered in despair. The boy laughed so heartily at their excitement that he dropped his pipe.

He began once again, and that went just as badly. Then all the little birds wailed: 'To-day you play worse than usual, Tummetott!' You don't make one true note! Where are your thoughts, Tummetott?'

'They are elsewhere,' said the boy—and this was true. He sat there and pondered how long he would be allowed to remain with the wild geese, or if he should be sent home perhaps to-day.

Finally Nils threw down his pipe and jumped from the bush. He had seen Akka and all the wild geese coming toward him in a long row. They walked in such a slow and dignified way that the boy immediately understood that now he should learn what they intended to do with him.

When they stopped at last, Akka said: 'You may well have reason to wonder at me, Tummetott, who have not said thanks to you for saving me from Smirre Fox. But I am one of those who would rather give thanks by deeds than words. And now, Tummetott, I think I have managed to help you. I have sent word to the elf that bewitched you. At first he didn't want to hear anything about curing you; but I have sent message upon message to him, and told him how well you have conducted yourself among us. He now sends word to you that as soon as you turn back home you shall be human again.'

But think of it! Just as happy as the boy had been when the wild geese began to speak, just as miserable was he when they had finished. He didn't say a word, but turned away and wept.

'What in all the world is this?' said Akka.

'It looks as though you had expected more of me than I have offered you.'

But Nils was thinking of the carefree days and the fun, and of adventure and freedom and travel, high above the earth, that he should miss, and he actually sobbed with grief. 'I don't want to be human,' he said. 'I want to go with you to Lapland.'

'I'll tell you something,' said Akka. 'That elf is very touchy, and I'm afraid that if you do not accept his offer now it will be difficult for you to coax him another time.'

It was a strange thing about that boy—as long as he had lived he had never cared for any one. He had not cared for his father or mother; nor for the school teacher; nor for his schoolmates; nor for the boys in the neighbourhood. All that they had wanted him to do—whether it had been work or play—he had only thought tiresome. Therefore there was no one whom he missed or longed for.

The only ones that he had got on fairly well with were Osa the goose-girl and little Mats—a couple of children who had tended geese in the fields, like himself. But he didn't care particularly for them either. No, far from it!

'I don't want to be human,' sobbed Nils. 'I want to go with you to Lapland. That's why I've been good for a whole week!'

'I don't want to forbid you to come along with us as far as you like,' said Akka, 'but think first if you wouldn't rather go home again. A day may come when you will regret this.'

'No,' said the boy, 'that's nothing to regret. I have never been as well off as here with you.'

'Well then, let it be as you wish,' said Akka.

'Oh, thank you!' said Nils, and he felt so happy that he had to cry for very joy—just as he had cried before from sorrow.

PART FOUR

GLIMMINGE CASTLE

☆

Chapter One

BLACK RATS AND GREY RATS

In south-eastern Skåne, not far from the sea, there is an old castle called Glimminge. It is a large and solid stone house which can be seen over the plain for miles around. It is not more than four storeys high; but it is so enormous that an ordinary farmhouse, which stands on the same estate, looks like a little children's doll's house in comparison.

The big stone house has such thick ceilings and walls that there is scarcely room inside for anything but the thick walls. The stairs are narrow, the entrances small, and the rooms few. That the walls might retain their strength, there are only the fewest number of windows in the upper storeys, and none at all are found in the lower ones, only narrow openings to let in the light. In the old war times, the people were just as glad that they could shut themselves up in a strong and massive house like this, as one is nowadays to be able to creep into furs in a bitter cold winter. But when the time of peace came they did not care to live in the dark and cold stone halls of the old castle any longer. They have long since deserted the big Glimminge castle, and moved into dwelling places where the light and air can penetrate.

At the time when Nils Holgersson wandered round with the wild geese there were no human beings in Glimminge castle; but for all that, it was not without inhabitants. Every summer there lived a pair of storks in a large nest on the roof. In a nest in the attic lived a pair of grey owls; in the secret passages hung bats; in the kitchen oven lived an old cat; and down in the cellar there were hundreds of old black rats.

Rats are not held in very high esteem by other animals; but the black rats at Glimminge castle were an exception. They were always mentioned with respect, because they had shown great valour in battle with their enemies, and much endurance under the great misfortunes which had befallen their kind. For they belonged to a rat tribe who, at one time, had been very numerous and powerful, but who were now dying out. During a long period of time, the black rats owned Skåne and the whole country. They were found in every cellar, in every attic, in larders and cowhouses and barns, in breweries and flour-mills, in churches and castles, in every man-constructed building. But now they were banished from all this and were almost exterminated. Only in some old and secluded places could one run across a few of them, and nowhere were they to be found in such large numbers as in Glimminge castle.

When an animal people dies out, it is generally the

human kind who are the cause of it; but not in this case. The people had certainly fought with the black rats, but they had not been able to do them any harm worth mentioning. Those who had conquered them were an animal people of their own kind: the grey rats.

These grey rats had not lived in the land since time immemorial like the black rats, but were descended from a couple of poor immigrants who landed in Malmö from a Libyan sloop about a hundred years ago. They were homeless, starved wretches who stuck close to the harbour, swam among the piles under the bridges, and ate refuse that was thrown into the water. They never ventured into the city, which was owned by the black rats.

But gradually, as the grey rats increased in number, they grew bolder. At first they moved over to some deserted and condemned old houses which the black rats had abandoned. They hunted for their food in gutters and dirt heaps, and made the most of all the rubbish that the black rats did not deign to worry about. They were hardy, contented, and fearless, and within a few years they had become so powerful that they started to drive the black rats out of Malmö. They took from them attics, cellars, and store-rooms, and starved them out or bit them to death, for they were not at all afraid of fighting.

When Malmö was captured they marched forward in small and large companies to conquer the whole country. It is almost impossible to understand why the black rats did not organize themselves into a great, united army to exterminate the grey rats while these were still few in numbers. But the black rats were so certain of their power that they could not believe it possible for them to lose it. They sat still on their estates, and in the meantime the grey rats took from them farm after farm, city after city. They were starved out, forced out, rooted out. In Skåne they had not been able to remain in a single place except Glimminge castle.

The old castle had such secure walls and such few rat passages led through them, that the black rats had managed to protect themselves, and to prevent the grey rats from crowding in. Night after night, year after year, the struggle had continued between the aggressors and the defenders; but the black rats had kept faithful watch, and had fought with the utmost contempt for death, and, thanks to the fine old house, they had always conquered.

It must be acknowledged that as long as the black rats were in power they were as much shunned by all other living creatures as the grey rats are in our day—and for just cause; they had thrown themselves upon poor, fettered prisoners and tortured them; they had ravished the dead; they had stolen the last turnip from the cellars of the poor; bitten off the feet of sleeping geese; robbed eggs and chicks from the hens; and committed a thousand depredations. But since they had come to grief, all this seemed to have been forgotten, and no one could help marvelling at the last of a race that had held out so long against its enemies.

The grey rats that lived in the courtyard at Glimminge and in the vicinity kept up a continuous warfare, and tried to watch for every possible chance to capture the castle. You might have imagined that they would have allowed the little company of black rats to occupy Glimminge castle in peace, since they themselves had acquired all the rest of the country; but you may be sure

this thought never occurred to them.   They were wont
to say that it was a point of honour with them to conquer
the black rats at some time or other.   But those who
knew the grey rats must have known that it was because
people used Glimminge castle as a grain storehouse that
the grey ones could not rest before they had taken
possession of the place.

Chapter Two

THE STORK

EARLY one morning the wild geese who stood and slept on the ice in Vomb Lake were awakened by long calls from the air. 'Trirop, trirop!' it sounded. 'Trianut, the crane, sends greetings to Akka, the wild goose, and her flock. To-morrow will be the day of the great crane dance on Kullaberg.'

Akka raised her head and answered at once: 'Greetings and thanks! Greetings and thanks!'

With that the cranes flew farther and the wild geese heard them for a long while where they travelled and called out over every field and every wooded hill: 'Trianut sends greetings. To-morrow will be the day of the great crane dance on Kullaberg.'

The wild geese were very happy over this invitation. 'You 're in luck,' they said to the white gander, 'to be permitted to attend the great crane dance on Kullaberg!'

'Is it then so remarkable to see cranes dance?' asked the gander.

'It is something that you have never even dreamed about!' replied the wild geese.

'Now we must think out what we shall do with Tummetott to-morrow, so that no harm can come to him while we run over to Kullaberg,' said Akka.

'Tummetott shall not be left alone!' said the gander. 'If the cranes won't let him see their dance then I 'll stay with him.'

'No human being has ever been permitted to attend the Animals' Congress at Kullaberg,' said Akka, 'and I shouldn't dare to take Tummetott with us. But we'll discuss this more at length later in the day. Now we must first and foremost think about getting something to eat.'

With that Akka gave the signal to move. On this day she also sought her feeding place a good distance away, on Smirre Fox's account, and she didn't alight until she came to the swampy meadows a little south of Glimminge castle.

All that day Nils sat on the edge of a little pond and blew on reed-pipes. He was unhappy because he wouldn't see the crane dance, and he just couldn't say a word, either to the gander or to any of the others.

It was pretty hard that Akka should still distrust him. When a boy had given up being human, just to travel about with a few wild geese, they surely ought to understand that he had no desire to betray them. Then, too, they ought to understand that when he had given up so much to follow them, it was their duty to let him see all the wonders they could show him.

'I'll have to speak my mind to them,' he thought. But hour after hour passed; still he couldn't make himself do it. It may sound remarkable—but the boy had actually come to have a kind of respect for the old leader-goose. He felt that it was not easy to pit his will against hers.

On one side of the swampy meadow, where the wild geese fed, there was a broad stone wall. Toward evening when the boy finally raised his head to speak to Akka his glance happened to rest on this wall. He uttered a little cry of surprise, and all the wild geese instantly looked up and stared in the same direction. At first both the geese and the boy thought that all the round,

grey stones in the wall had acquired legs, and were starting to run; but soon they saw that it was a company of
rats who ran over it. They moved very rapidly, and ran
forward, tightly packed, line upon line, and were so
numerous that, for some time, they covered the entire
stone wall.

The boy had been afraid of rats, even when he was a
big, strong human being. So what must his feelings be
now, when he was so tiny that two or three of them could
overpower him? One shudder after another travelled
down his spine as he stood and stared at them.

And strangely enough, the wild geese seemed to feel
the same aversion toward the rats that he did. They
did not speak to them; and when they were gone they
shook themselves as if their feathers had been mud-
bespattered.

'What a lot of grey rats abroad!' said Yksi from
Vassijaure. 'That's not a good omen.'

The boy intended to take advantage of this opportunity
to say to Akka that he thought she ought to let him go
with them to Kullaberg, but he was prevented anew, for
all of a sudden a big bird came down in the midst of the
geese.

One could believe, when one looked at this bird, that
he had borrowed body, neck, and head from a little white
goose. But in addition to this he had procured for himself large black wings, long red legs, and a heavy bill
which was too large for the little head, and weighed it
down until it gave him a sad and worried look.

Akka at once straightened out the feathers of her wings
and curtsied many times as she approached the stork.
She wasn't specially surprised to see him in Skåne so
early in the spring, because she knew that the male storks

are in the habit of coming over in good time to take a look at their nests, and see that they haven't been damaged during the winter, before the female storks go to the trouble of flying over the Baltic. But she wondered very much what it might signify that he sought her out, since storks prefer to associate with members of their own family.

'I can hardly believe that there is anything wrong with your house, Herr Ermenrich,' said Akka.

It was apparent now that it was true what people said: a stork can seldom open his bill without complaining. But what made the thing he said sound even more doleful was that it was difficult for him to speak out. He stood for a long time and only clattered with his bill; afterward he spoke in a hoarse and feeble voice. He complained about everything: the nest, which was situated at the very top of the roof-tree at Glimminge castle, had been totally destroyed by winter storms, and no food could he get any more in Skåne. The people of Skåne were appropriating all his possessions. They dug out his marshes and laid waste his swamps. He intended to move away from this country and never return to it again.

While the stork grumbled, Akka, the wild goose who had neither home nor protection, could not help thinking to herself: 'If I had things as comfortable as you have, Herr Ermenrich, I should be above complaining. You have remained a free and wild bird; and still you stand so well with human beings that no one will fire a shot at you, or steal an egg from your nest.' But all this she kept to herself. To the stork she only remarked that she couldn't believe he would be willing to move from a house where storks had lived ever since it was built.

Then the stork suddenly asked the geese if they had

seen the grey rats who were marching toward Glimminge castle. When Akka replied that she had seen the horrid creatures he began to tell her about the brave black rats who, for years, had defended the castle. 'But this night Glimminge castle will fall into the grey rats' power,' sighed the stork.

'And why just this night, Herr Ermenrich?' asked Akka.

'Well, because nearly all the black rats went over to Kullaberg last night,' said the stork, 'since they had counted on all the rest of the animals also hurrying there. But you see that the grey rats have stayed at home, and now they are mustering to storm the castle to-night, when it will be defended by only a few old creatures who are too feeble to go over to Kullaberg. They 'll probably accomplish their purpose. But I have lived here in harmony with the black rats for so many years that it does not please me to live in a place inhabited by their enemies.'

Akka understood now that the stork had become so enraged over the grey rats' plan of action, that he had sought her out as an excuse to complain about them. But after the manner of storks he had done nothing to avert the disaster.

'Have you sent word to the black rats, Herr Ermenrich?' she asked.

'No,' replied the stork, 'that wouldn't be of any use. Before they can get back the castle will be taken.'

'You mustn't be so sure of that, Herr Ermenrich,' said Akka. 'I know an old wild goose who will gladly prevent outrages of this kind.'

When Akka said this the stork raised his head and stared at her. And it was not surprising, for Akka had

neither claws nor bill that were fit for fighting; and she
was a day bird into the bargain,
and as soon as it grew dark she
fell helplessly asleep, while the
rats did their fighting at night.

But Akka had evidently made
up her mind to help the black
rats. She called Yksi from Vassijaure and ordered him to take
the wild geese over to Vomb
Lake, and when the geese made
excuses, she said authoritatively:
'I believe it will be best for us all
that you obey me. I must fly
over to the big stone house, and
if you follow me, the people on
the place will be sure to see us
and shoot us down. The only
one that I want to take with me
on this trip is Tummetott. He
can be of great service to me
because he has good eyes and
can keep awake at night.'

Nils was in his most contrary
mood that day. And when he
heard what Akka said, he raised
himself to his full height and
stepped forward, his hands behind him and his nose in the air,
and he intended to say that he,
most assuredly, did not wish to
take a hand in the fight with grey rats. She might look
around for assistance elsewhere.

But the instant the boy was seen, the stork began to move. He had stood before, as storks generally stand, with head bent downward and the bill pressed against the neck. But now a gurgle was heard deep down in his windpipe, as though he would have laughed. Quick as a flash, he lowered the bill, grabbed the boy, and tossed him a couple of yards in the air. This feat he performed seven times, while the boy shrieked and the geese shouted: 'What are you trying to do, Herr Ermenrich? That's not a frog. That's a human being, Herr Ermenrich.'

Finally the stork put the boy down entirely unhurt. Thereupon he said to Akka: 'I'll fly back to Glimminge castle now, mother Akka. All who live there were very much worried when I left. You may be sure they'll be very glad when I tell them that Akka, the wild goose, and Tummetott, the human elf, are on their way to rescue them.'

With that the stork stretched out his neck, spread his wings, and darted off like an arrow when it leaves a well-drawn bow. Akka understood that he was making fun of her but she didn't let it bother her. She waited until the boy had found his wooden shoes, which the stork had shaken off, then she put him on her back and followed the stork, and the boy made no objection, and said not a word about not wanting to go with her. Nils was so furious with the stork that he actually sat and puffed. That long, red-legged thing believed he was of no account just because he was little; but he would show him what kind of a man Nils Holgersson from West Vemmenhög was.

A couple of moments later Akka stood in the storks' nest at Glimminge castle. It was a fine, large nest. It had a wheel for foundation, and over this lay several grass mats and some twigs. The nest was so old that many shrubs and plants had taken root up there; and when the mother stork sat on her eggs in the round hole in the middle of the nest, she not only had the beautiful outlook over a goodly portion of Skåne to enjoy, but she had also the wild brier blossoms and house leeks to look upon.

Both Akka and the boy saw immediately that something was going on here which seemed to reverse the natural order of things. For on the edge of the storks' nest sat two grey owls, an old grey-streaked cat, and a dozen old decrepit rats with protruding teeth and watery eyes. They were not exactly the sort of animals one usually finds living peaceably together.

Not one of them turned round to look at Akka or to bid her welcome. They could only sit and stare at some long, grey lines, which were in sight here and there on the bare winter meadows.

All the black rats were silent. One could see that they were in deep despair, and probably knew that they could neither defend themselves nor the castle. The two owls sat and rolled their big eyes, and twisted their great, encircling eyebrows, and talked in hollow, ghost-like voices about the awful cruelty of the grey rats, and that they would have to move away from their nest, because they had heard it said of them that they spared neither eggs nor baby birds. The old grey-streaked cat was positive that the grey rats would bite him to death, since they were coming into the castle in such great numbers, and he scolded the black rats incessantly. 'How could you be so idiotic as to let your best fighters go away?' said he. 'How could you trust the grey rats? It is absolutely unpardonable!'

The twelve black rats did not say a word. But the stork, despite his misery, could not refrain from teasing the cat. 'Don't worry so, Monsie house-cat!' said he. 'Can't you see that mother Akka and Tummetott have come to save the castle? You can be certain that they'll succeed. Now I must stand up to sleep—and I do so with the utmost calm. To-morrow, when I awaken, there won't be a single grey rat in Glimminge castle.'

Nils winked at Akka, and made a sign—as the stork stood upon the very edge of the nest, with one leg drawn up, to sleep—that he wanted to push him down to the ground; but Akka stopped him. She did not seem to be the least bit angry. Instead, she said in a confident tone of voice: 'It would be pretty poor business if one who is as old as I am could not manage to get out of worse difficulties than this. If only Mr. and Mrs. Owl, who can stay awake all night, will fly off with a couple of messages for me, I think that all will go well.'

Both owls were willing. Then Akka bade Mr. Owl go and seek the black rats who had gone off, and counsel them to hurry home immediately. Mrs. Owl she sent to Flammea, the barn owl, who lived in Lund cathedral, with a commission which was so secret that Akka only dared to confide it to her in a whisper.

Chapter Three

THE RAT CHARMER

IT was getting on toward midnight when the grey rats. after a diligent search, succeeded in finding an open air-hole in the cellar. This was pretty high up on the wall; but the rats got up on one another's shoulders, and it wasn't long before the most daring among them sat in the air-hole, ready to force her way into Glimminge castle, outside whose walls so many of her forebears had fallen.

The grey rat sat still for a moment in the hole, and waited for an attack from within. The main army of the defenders was certainly away, but she assumed that the black rats who were still in the castle wouldn't surrender without a struggle. With thumping heart she listened for the slightest sound, but everything remained quiet. Then the leader of the grey rats plucked up courage and jumped down in the coal-black cellar.

One after another of the grey rats followed the leader. They all kept very quiet; and all expected to be ambushed by the black rats. Not until so many of them had crowded into the cellar that the floor couldn't hold any more, did they venture farther.

Although they had never before been inside the building, they had no difficulty in finding their way. They soon found the passages in the walls which the black rats had used to get to the upper floors. Before they began to clamber up these narrow and steep steps, they listened again with great attention. They felt more frightened because the black rats held themselves aloof in this way, than if they had met them in open battle. They could hardly believe their luck when they reached the first storey without any mishaps.

Immediately upon their entrance the grey rats caught the scent of the grain, which was stored in great bins on the floor. But it was not as yet time for them to begin to enjoy their conquest. They searched first, with the utmost caution, through the sombre, empty rooms. They ran up in the fireplace, which stood on the floor in the old castle kitchen, and they almost tumbled into the well in the inner room. Not one of the narrow peep-holes did they leave uninspected, but they found no black rats. When this floor was wholly in their possession they began, with the same caution, to acquire the next. Then they had to venture on a bold and dangerous climb through the walls, while, with breathless anxiety, they awaited an assault from the enemy. And although they were tempted by the most delicious smell from the grain bins, they forced themselves most systematically to inspect the old-time warriors' pillar-propped kitchen, their stone table and fireplace, the deep window-niches, and the hole in the floor—which in olden time had been opened to pour down boiling pitch on the intruding enemy.

All this time the black rats were invisible. The grey ones groped their way to the third storey, and into the lord of the castle's great banqueting hall—which stood there cold and empty, like all the other rooms in the old house. They even groped their way to the upper storey, which had but one big, barren room. The only place they did not think of exploring was the big storks' nest on the roof—where, just at this time, Mrs. Owl awakened Akka and informed her that Flammea, the barn owl, had granted her request, and had sent her the thing she wished for.

Since the grey rats had so conscientiously inspected the entire castle they felt at ease. They took it for granted that the black rats had flown and didn't intend to offer any resistance; and, with light hearts, they ran up into the grain bins.

But the grey rats had hardly swallowed the first wheat grains, before the sound of a little shrill pipe was heard from the yard. They raised their heads, listened anxiously, ran a few steps as if they intended to leave the bin, then they turned back and began to eat once more.

Again the pipe sounded a sharp and piercing note—and now something wonderful happened. One rat, two rats—yes, a whole lot of rats left the grain, jumped from the bins, and hurried down to the cellar by the shortest cut to get out of the house. Still there were many grey rats left. These thought of all the toil and trouble it had cost them to win Glimminge castle, and they did not want to leave it. But again they caught the tones from the pipe and had to follow them. With wild excitement they rushed up from the bins, slid down through the narrow holes in the walls, and tumbled over each other in their eagerness to get out.

In the middle of the courtyard stood a tiny creature who blew upon a pipe. All round him he had a whole circle of rats who listened to him, astonished and fascinated; and every moment brought more. Once he took the pipe from his lips—only for a second—put his thumb to his nose, and wiggled his fingers at the grey rats; and then it looked as if they would throw themselves on him and bite him to death, but as soon as he blew on his pipe they were in his power.

When the tiny creature had played all the grey rats out

of Glimminge castle, he began to wander slowly from the courtyard out on the highway, and all the grey rats followed him, because the tones from that pipe sounded so sweet to their ears that they could not resist them.

The tiny creature walked before them and charmed them along with him, on the road to Vallby. He led them into all sorts of crooks and turns and bends—on through hedges and down into ditches—and wherever he went they had to follow. He blew continuously on his pipe, which appeared to be made from an animal's horn, although the horn was so small that, in our days, there were no animals from whose foreheads it could have been taken. No one knew, either, who had made it. Flammea, the barn owl, had found it in a niche in Lund cathedral. She had shown it to Bataki, the raven; and they had both decided that this was the kind of horn that was used in former times by those who wished to gain power over rats and mice. But the raven was Akka's friend, and it was from him she had learned that Flammea owned a treasure like this.

And it was true that the rats could not resist the pipe. Nils walked before them and played as long as the starlight lasted, and all the while they followed him. He played at daybreak, he played at sunrise, and the whole time the entire procession of grey rats followed him, and were enticed farther and farther away from the big grain loft at Glimminge castle.

PART FIVE

THE GREAT CRANE DANCE ON KULLABERG

ALTHOUGH there are many magnificent buildings in Skåne, it must be acknowledged that there's not one among them that has such fine walls as old Kullaberg.

Kullaberg is low and rather long. It is not by any means a big or imposing mountain. On its broad summit you'll find woods and grain fields, and an occasional stretch of heather. Here and there round heather knolls and barren cliffs rise up. It is not especially beautiful up there. It looks a good deal like all the other upland places in Skåne.

He who walks along the path which runs across the middle of the mountain can't help feeling a little disappointed. Then he happens, perhaps, to turn away from the path, and wanders off toward the mountain's sides and looks down over the cliffs; and then, all at once, he will find there is so much that is worth seeing he hardly knows how he'll find time to take in the whole of it. For it happens that Kullaberg does not stand on the land, with plains and valleys round it, like other mountains; but it has plunged into the sea, as far out as it could get. Not even the tiniest strip of land lies below the mountain to protect it against the breakers, but these reach all the way up to the mountain walls, and can polish and mould them to suit themselves. This is why the walls stand there as richly ornamented as the sea and its helpmeet, the wind, have been able to effect. You'll find steep ravines that are deeply chiselled in the mountain's sides, and black crags that have become smooth and shiny under the constant lashing of the winds. There are solitary rock columns that spring right up out of the water, and dark grottoes with narrow entrances. There are barren, perpendicular precipices, and soft, leaf-clad slopes. There are small points and small inlets and small rolling stones that are rattlingly washed up and down with every rolling wave. There are majestic cliff arches that stand out over the water. There are sharp stones that are constantly dashed by a white foam; and others that mirror themselves in unchangeable dark-green still water. There are giant troll caverns shaped in the rock, and great crevices that lure the wanderer to venture into the mountain's depths —all the way to Kullman's Hollow.

And over and around all these cliffs and rocks crawl entangled tendrils and weeds. Trees grow there also, but the wind's power is so great that trees have to transform themselves into clinging vines, that they may get a firm hold on the steep precipices. The oaks creep along on the ground, while their foliage hangs over them like a low ceiling; and long-limbed beeches stand in the ravines like great leaf tents.

These remarkable mountain walls, with the blue sea beneath them and the clear penetrating air above them, are what make Kullaberg so dear to the people that great crowds of them haunt the place every day as long as the summer lasts. But it is more difficult to tell what it is that makes it so attractive to animals, that every year they gather there for a big play meeting. This is a custom that has been observed since time immemorial; and one should have been there when the first sea wave was dashed into foam against the shore, to be able to explain just why Kullaberg was chosen as a rendezvous in preference to all other places.

When the meeting is to take place, the stags and roebucks and hares and foxes and all the other four-footed animals make the journey to Kullaberg the night before, so as not to be seen by the human beings. Just before sunrise they all march up to the playground, which is a heath on the left side of the road, and not very far from the mountain's most extreme point. The playground is enclosed on all sides by rounded knolls, which conceal it from any and all who do not happen to come right upon it. And in the month of March it is not at all likely that any walkers will stray off up there. All the strangers who usually stroll round on the rocks and clamber up the mountain's sides have been driven away by the autumn storms these many months past. And the light-house keeper out there on the point, the old woman on the mountain farm, and the mountain peasant and his family go their accustomed ways, and do not run about on the desolate heather moors.

When the animals have arrived on the playground they take their places on the round knolls. Each animal family keeps to itself, although it is understood that, on a day like this, universal peace reigns, and no one need fear attack. On this day a little hare might wander over to the foxes' hill, without losing as much as one of his long ears. But still the animals arrange themselves into separate groups. This is an old custom.

After they have all taken their places they begin to look round for the birds. It is always beautiful weather on this day. The cranes are good weather prophets, and would not call the animals together if they expected rain. Although the air is clear, and nothing obstructs the

vision, the animals see no birds. This is strange. The
sun stands high in the heavens and the birds should
already be on their way.

But what the animals, on the other hand, do observe,
are several little dark clouds that come slowly forward
over the plain. And look! one of these clouds comes
gradually along the coast of Öresund and up toward
Kullaberg. When the cloud has come right over the
playground it stops, and, simultaneously, the entire
cloud begins to sing and chirp, as if it were made of
nothing but sound. It rises and sinks, rises and sinks, but
all the while it sings and chirps. At last the whole cloud
falls down over a knoll—all at once—and the next
instant the knoll is entirely covered with grey larks,
pretty red-white-grey bullfinches, speckled starlings, and
greenish-yellow titmice.

Soon after that another cloud comes over the plain.
This stops over every bit of land : over peasant cottage
and palace, over towns and cities, over farms and
railway stations, over fishing hamlets and sugar refineries.
Every time it stops it draws to itself a little whirling
column of grey dust-grains from the ground. In this
way it grows and grows. And at last, when it is all
gathered up and heads for Kullaberg, it is no longer a
cloud but a real mist, which is so big that it throws a
shadow on the ground all the way from Höganäs to
Mölle. When it stops over the playground it hides the
sun, and for a long time it has to rain grey sparrows on
one of the knolls, before those who had been flying in the
innermost part of the mist could again catch a glimpse
of the daylight.

But still the biggest of these bird clouds is the one
which now appears. This has been formed of birds who

have travelled from every direction to join it. It is dark bluish-grey, and no sun-ray can penetrate it. It is full of the ghastliest noises, the most frightful shrieks, the grimmest laughter, and most gloomy croaking! All on the playground are glad when it finally resolves itself into a storm of fluttering and croaking: of crows and jackdaws and rooks and ravens.

Thereupon not only clouds are seen in the heavens, but a variety of stripes and figures. Then straight, dotted lines appear in the east and north-east. These are forest birds from Göinge districts: black grouse and wood grouse who come flying in long lines a couple of yards apart. Swimming birds that live around Måk-läppen, just out of Falsterbo, now come floating over Öresund in many extraordinary figures: in triangular and long curves; in sharp hooks and semicircles.

To the great reunion held the year that Nils Holgersson travelled round with the wild geese, came Akka and her flock, later than all the others. And that was not to be wondered at, for Akka had to fly over the whole of Skåne to get to Kullaberg. Besides, as soon as she awoke she had been obliged to go out and hunt for Tummetott, who, for many hours, had gone and played to the grey rats, and lured them far away from Glimminge castle. Mr. Owl had returned with the news that the black rats would be at home immediately after sunrise; and there was no longer any danger in letting the barn owl's pipe be hushed, and to give the grey rats the liberty to go where they pleased.

But it was not Akka who discovered the boy where he walked with his long following, and quickly sank down over him and caught him with his bill and swung into the air with him, but it was Herr Ermenrich, the stork!

For Herr Ermenrich had also gone out to look for him; and, after he had borne him up to the storks' nest, he begged his forgiveness for having treated him with disrespect the evening before.

This pleased Nils immensely, and the stork and he became good friends. Akka, too, showed him that she felt very kindly toward him; she rubbed her old head several times against his arms, and commended him because he had helped those who were in trouble.

But this one must say to the boy's credit: he did not want to accept praise which he had not earned. 'No, mother Akka,' he said, 'you mustn't think that I lured the grey rats away to help the black ones. I only wanted to show Herr Ermenrich that I was of some consequence.'

He had hardly said this before Akka turned to the stork and asked if he thought it was advisable to take Tummetott along to Kullaberg. 'I mean, that we can rely on him as upon ourselves,' said she.

The stork at once advised, most enthusiastically, that Tummetott be allowed to go. 'Certainly you shall take Tummetott along to Kullaberg, mother Akka,' he said. 'It is fortunate for us that we can repay him for all that he has endured this night for our sakes. And since it still grieves me to think that I did not conduct myself in a becoming manner toward him the other evening, it is I who will carry him on my back—all the way to the meeting place.'

There isn't much that pleases us more than to receive praise from those who are themselves wise and capable; and the boy had certainly never felt so happy as he did when the wild goose and the stork talked about him in this way.

Thus Nils made the trip to Kullaberg, riding stork-back. Although he knew that this was a great honour, it caused him much anxiety, for Herr Ermenrich was a master flyer, and started off at a very different pace from the wild geese. While Akka flew her straight way with even wing-strokes, the stork amused himself by performing a lot of flying tricks. Now he lay still at an immeasurable height, and floated in the air without moving his wings, now he flung himself downward with such sudden haste that it seemed as though he would fall to the ground, helpless as a stone; now he had lots of fun flying all around Akka, in great and small circles, like a whirlwind. The boy had never been on a ride of this sort before; and although he sat there all the while in terror, he had to acknowledge to himself that he had never before known what a good flight meant.

Only a single pause was made during the journey, and that was at Vomb Lake when Akka joined her travelling companions, and called to them that the grey rats had been vanquished. After that the travellers flew straight to Kullaberg.

There they descended to the knoll reserved for the wild geese; and as the boy let his glance wander from knoll to knoll, he saw on one of them the many pointed antlers of the stags, and on another the grey herons' neck crests. One knoll was red with foxes, one was grey with rats; one was covered with black ravens who shrieked continually, one with larks who simply couldn't keep still, but kept on throwing themselves in the air and singing for very joy.

Just as it has ever been the custom on Kullaberg, it was the crows who began the day's games and frolics with their flying-dance. They divided themselves into two flocks, that flew toward each other, met, turned, and began all over again. This dance had many repetitions, and appeared to the spectators who were not familiar with the dance as altogether too monotonous. The crows were very proud of their dance, but all the others were glad when it was over. It appeared to the animals about as gloomy and meaningless as the winter storms' play with the snowflakes. It depressed them to watch it, and they waited eagerly for something that should give them a little pleasure.

They did not have to wait in vain, either; for as soon as the crows had finished, the hares came running. They dashed forward in a long row, without any apparent order. In some of the figures, one single hare came; in others, they ran three and four abreast. They had all raised themselves on two legs, and they rushed forward with such rapidity that their long ears swayed in all directions. As they ran they spun round, made high leaps, and beat their forepaws against their sides so that they rattled. Some performed a long succession of somersaults, others doubled themselves up and rolled over like wheels; one stood on one leg and swung round; one walked upon his forepaws. There was no plan whatever, but there was much that was droll in the hares' play, and the many animals who stood and watched them began to breathe faster. Now it was spring; joy and rapture were coming. Winter was over, summer was coming. Soon it was only play to live.

When the hares had romped themselves out, it was the great forest birds' turn to perform. Hundreds of wood grouse in shining dark brown array, and with bright red eyebrows, flung themselves up into a great oak that stood in the centre of the playground. The one who sat upon the topmost branch fluffed up his feathers, lowered his wings, and lifted his tail so that the white covert feathers were seen. Thereupon he stretched his neck and sent forth a couple of deep notes from his thick throat: 'Chack, chack, chack,' it sounded. More than this he could not utter. He only gurgled a few times way down in the throat. Then he closed his eyes and whispered: 'Sis, sis, sis. Hear how pretty! Sis, sis, sis.' At the same time he fell into such an ecstasy that he no longer knew what was going on around him.

While the first wood grouse was sissing, the three nearest—under him—began to sing; and before they had finished their song, the ten who sat lower down joined in; and thus it continued from branch to branch, until the entire hundred grouse sang and gurgled and sissed. They all fell into the same ecstasy during their song, and this affected the other animals like a contagious transport. Lately the blood had flowed lightly and agreeably; now it began to grow heavy and hot. 'Yes, this is surely spring,' thought all the animals. 'Winter chill has vanished. The fires of spring burn over the earth.'

When the black grouse saw that the brown grouse were having such a success, they could no longer keep quiet. As there was no tree for them to alight on, they rushed down on to the playground, where the heather stood so high that only their beautifully turned tail-feathers and their thick bills were visible—and they began to sing: 'Orr, orr, orr.'

Just as the black grouse began to compete with the brown grouse something unprecedented happened. While all the animals thought of nothing but the grouse game, a fox stole slowly over to the wild geese's knoll. He glided very cautiously, and came right up on the knoll before any one noticed him. Suddenly a goose

caught sight of him; and as she could not believe that a
fox had sneaked in among the geese for any good purpose,
she began to cry: 'Have a care, wild geese! Have a
care!' The fox struck her across the throat—mostly,
perhaps, because he wanted to make her keep quiet—
but the wild geese had already heard the cry and they

all flew up in the air.   And when they had flown up, the
animals saw Smirre Fox standing on the wild geese's
knoll, with a dead goose in his mouth.

But because he had in this way broken the play-day's
peace, such a punishment was meted out to Smirre Fox
that, for the rest of his days, he must regret he had not
been able to control his thirst for revenge, but had
attempted to approach Akka and her flock in this
manner.

He was immediately surrounded by a crowd of foxes,
and doomed in accordance with an old custom, which
demands that whosoever disturbs the peace on the great

play-day must go into exile.   Not a fox wished to lighten
the sentence, since they all knew that the instant they
attempted anything of the sort, they would be driven
from the playground, and would never more be permitted
to enter it.   Banishment was pronounced upon Smirre
without opposition.   He was forbidden to remain in
Skåne.   He was banished from wife and kindred, from
hunting grounds, home, resting places, and retreats, which
he had hitherto owned; and he must tempt fortune in
foreign lands.   So that all foxes in Skåne should know
that Smirre was outlawed in the district the oldest of the
foxes bit off his right earlap.   As soon as this was done,
all the young foxes began to yowl from blood-thirst, and
threw themselves on Smirre.   For him there was no
alternative except to take flight, and with all the young
foxes in hot pursuit he rushed away from Kullaberg.

All this happened while black grouse and brown grouse
were going on with their games.   But these birds lose
themselves so completely in their song, that they neither
hear nor see.   Nor had they permitted themselves to be
disturbed.

The forest birds' contest was barely over before the
stags from Häckeberga came forward to show their
wrestling game.   There were several pairs of stags who
fought at the same time.   They rushed at each other
with tremendous force, struck their antlers clashingly
together, so that their points were entangled, and tried
to force each other backwards.   The heather was torn
up beneath their hoofs, the breath came like smoke from
their nostrils, out of their throats came deep bellowings,
and the foam streaked their shoulders.

On the knolls round about there was breathless silence
while the skilled stag wrestlers clinched.   In all the

animals new emotions were awakened. Each and all felt courageous and strong, enlivened by returning powers, born again with the spring, gay, and ready for all kinds of adventures. They felt no enmity toward each other, although, everywhere, wings were lifted, neck feathers raised, and claws sharpened. If the stags from Häckeberga had continued another instant a wild struggle would have arisen on the knolls, for all had been gripped with a burning desire to show that they too were full of life because the winter's impotence was over and strength surged through their bodies.

But the stags stopped wrestling just at the right moment, and instantly a whisper went from knoll to knoll: 'The cranes are coming!'

And then came the grey, dusk-clad birds with plumes in their wings and red feather ornaments on their necks. The big birds with their tall legs, their slender throats, their small heads, came gliding down the knoll with an abandon that was full of mystery. As they glided forward they swung round—half flying, half dancing. With wings gracefully lifted they moved with an inconceivable rapidity. There was something marvellous and strange about their dance. It was as though grey shadows played a game which the eye could scarcely follow. It was as if they had learned it from the mists that hover over desolate swamps. There was witchcraft in it. All those who had never before been on Kullaberg understood why the whole meeting took its name from the cranes' dance. There was wildness in it, yet the feeling which it awakened was a delicious longing. No one thought any more about struggling. Instead, both the winged and those who had no wings all wanted to raise themselves eternally, lift themselves above the clouds,

*The Big Birds with . . . their slender throats . . . came gliding
down the knoll*

seek that which was hidden beyond them, leave the oppressive body that dragged them down to earth, and soar away toward the infinite.

Such longing after the unattainable, after the hidden mysteries beyond this life, the animals felt only once a year; and this was on the day when they beheld the great crane dance.

PART SIX

IN RAINY WEATHER

IT was the first rainy day of the trip. As long as the wild geese had remained in the vicinity of L. Vombsjön, they had had beautiful weather; but on the day when they set out to travel farther north it began to rain, and for several hours the boy had to sit on goose-back, soaking wet, and shivering with the cold.

In the morning when they started it had been clear and mild. The wild geese had flown high up in the air— evenly, and without haste—with Akka at the head maintaining strict discipline, and the rest in two oblique lines behind her. They had not wasted time in shouting any witty sarcasms to the animals on the ground, but, as it was simply impossible for them to keep perfectly silent, they sang out continually—in rhythm with the wingstrokes—their usual coaxing call: 'Where are you? Here am I. Where are you? Here am I.'

They all took part in this persistent calling, and only stopped, now and then, to show the gander the landmarks they were travelling over. The places on this route included Linderödsåsen's dry hills, Ovesholm's manor, Kristianstad's church steeple, Bäckaskog's royal castle on the narrow isthmus between Oppmannasjön and Lake Ivösjön, and Mt. Ryssberget's steep precipice.

It had been a monotonous trip, and when the rain clouds made their appearance Nils thought it was a real diversion. In the old days, when he had only seen a rain cloud from below, he had imagined that they were grey and disagreeable; but it was a very different thing to be up amongst them. Now he saw distinctly that the clouds were enormous carts, which drove through the heavens with sky-high loads. Some of them were piled up with huge, grey sacks, some with barrels; some were so large that they could hold a whole lake, and a few were filled with big jugs and bottles which were piled up to an immense height. And when so many of them had driven forward that they filled the whole sky it appeared as though someone had given a signal, for all at once water began to pour down over the earth, from jugs, barrels, bottles, and sacks.

Just as the first spring showers pattered against the ground, there arose such shouts of joy from all the small birds in groves and pastures, that the whole air rang with them and the boy leaped high where he sat. 'Now we'll have rain. Rain gives us spring; spring gives us flowers and green leaves; green leaves and flowers give us worms and insects; worms and insects give us food, and plentiful and good food is the best thing there is,' sang the birds.

The wild geese, too, were glad of the rain which came to awaken the plants from their long sleep, and to drive holes in the ice roofs on the lakes. They were not able to be serious any longer, but began to send merry calls over the neighbourhood.

When they flew over the big potato patches, which are so plentiful in the country around Christianstad—and which still lay bare and black—they screamed: 'Wake up and be useful! Here comes something that will awaken you. You have idled long enough now.'

When they saw people who hurried to get out of the rain, they reproved them saying: 'What are you in such a hurry about? Can't you see that it's raining rye loaves and cakes?'

It was a big, thick mist that moved northward briskly and followed close upon the geese. They seemed to think that they dragged the mist along with them; and now, when they saw great orchards beneath them, they called out proudly: 'Here we come with anemones; here we come with roses; here we come with apple blossoms and cherry buds; here we come with peas and beans and turnips and cabbages. He who wills can take them. He who wills can take them.'

Thus it had sounded while the first showers fell, and when all were still glad of the rain. But when it continued to fall the whole afternoon the wild geese grew impatient, and cried to the thirsty forests around Ivös lake: 'Haven't you got enough yet? Haven't you got enough yet?'

The heavens were growing greyer and greyer and the sun hid itself so well that one couldn't imagine where it was. The rain fell faster and faster, and beat harder and harder against the wings, as it tried to find its way between the oily outside feathers, into their skins. The earth was hidden by fogs; lakes, mountains, and woods floated together in an indistinct maze, and the landmarks could not be distinguished. The flight became slower and slower; the joyful cries were hushed; and Nils felt the cold more and more keenly.

But still he had kept up his courage as long as he had ridden through the air. And in the afternoon, when they had alighted under a little stunted pine, in the middle of a large swamp, where all was wet and all was cold; where some hillocks were covered with snow, and others stood up bare in a puddle of half-melted ice-water, even then he did not feel discouraged, but ran about in fine spirits, and hunted for cranberries and frozen

whortleberries. But then came evening, and darkness
sank down on them so closely that not even such eyes as
the boy's could see through it; and all the wilderness
became strangely grim and awful. Nils lay tucked in
under the gander's wing, but could not sleep because he
was cold and wet. He heard such a lot of rustling and
rattling and stealthy steps and menacing voices, that he
was terror-stricken and didn't know where he should go.
He must go somewhere, where there was light and heat, if
he wasn't going to be entirely scared to death.

'If I should venture where there are human beings,
just for this night?' Nils thought. 'Only so that I could
sit by a fire for a moment and get a little food. I could
get back to the wild geese before sunrise.'

He crept from under the wing and slid down to the
ground. He didn't awaken either the gander or any of
the other geese, but stole, silently and unobserved,
through the swamp.

He didn't know where on earth he was: if he was in
Skåne, in Småland, or in Blekinge. But just before he
had come down in the swamp he had caught a glimpse
of a large village, and thither he directed his steps. It
wasn't long, either, before he discovered a road; and
soon he was in the village street, which was long, and
had trees planted on both sides, and was bordered with
house after house.

Nils had come to one of the big church villages, which
are so common on the uplands, but can hardly be seen
at all down in the plain.

The houses were of wood and very prettily built.
Most of them had gables and fronts edged with carved
mouldings, and glass doors, with here and there a
coloured pane, opening on verandas. The walls were

painted in light oil-colours; the doors and window-frames shone in blues and greens, and even in reds. While the boy walked about and looked at the houses, he could hear, out in the road, how the people who sat in the warm cottages chattered and laughed. The words he could not distinguish, but he thought it was lovely to hear human voices. 'I wonder what they would say if I knocked and begged to be let in,' he thought.

This was, of course, what he had intended to do all along, but now that he saw the lighted windows his fear of the darkness was gone. Instead, he felt again that shyness which always came over him now when he was near human beings. 'I 'll take a look at the village for a while longer,' he thought, 'before I ask any one to take me in.'

On one house there was a balcony. And just as Nils walked by the doors were thrown open, and a yellow light streamed through the fine, sheer curtains. Then a pretty young woman came out on the balcony and leaned over the railing. 'It 's raining; now we shall soon have spring,' she said. When the boy saw her he had a strange feeling. It was as though he wanted to weep. For the first time he felt uneasy because he had shut himself away from the human beings.

Soon after that he walked by a shop. Outside the shop stood a red corn-drill. He stopped and looked at it, and finally crawled up to the driver's place and seated himself. When he had got there he clicked with his tongue and pretended that he sat and drove. He thought what fun it would be to be allowed to drive such a fine machine over a grain-field. For a moment he forgot what he was like now; then he remembered it, and jumped down quickly from the machine. Then a greater unrest came over him. After all, human beings were very wonderful and clever.

He walked by the post office, and then he thought of all the newspapers which came every day, with news from all the four corners of the earth. He saw the apothecary's shop and the doctor's home, and he thought about the power of human beings, which was so great that they were able to battle with sickness and death. He came to the church. Then he thought how human beings had built it that they might hear about another world than the one in which they lived, of God and the Resurrection and eternal life. And the longer he walked there the better he liked human beings.

Children never think any farther ahead than the length of their noses. That which lies nearest them, they want promptly, without caring what it may cost them. Nils Holgersson had not understood what he was losing when he chose to remain an elf; but now he began to be dreadfully afraid that, perhaps, he would never again get back his right form.

How on earth should he go to work to become human? This he wanted, oh! so much, to know.

He crawled up on a door-step, and seated himself in the pouring rain and meditated. He sat there one whole hour, two whole hours, and he thought so hard that his forehead lay in furrows; but he was none the wiser. It seemed as though the thoughts only rolled round and round in his head. The longer he sat there the more impossible it seemed to him to find any solution.

'This thing is certainly much too difficult for one who has learned as little as I have,' he thought at last. 'It will probably end by my having to go back among human beings after all. I must ask the minister and the doctor and the schoolmaster and others who are learned, and may know a cure for such things.'

This he concluded that he would do at once, and shook himself—for he was as wet as a dog that has been in a water-pool.

Just then he saw a big owl come flying along and alight on one of the trees that bordered the village street. The next instant a lady owl, who sat under the cornice of the house, began to call out: 'Kivitt, Kivitt! Are you at home again, Mr. Grey Owl? What kind of a time did you have abroad?'

'Thank you, Lady Brown Owl. I had a very comfortable time,' said the grey owl. 'Has anything out of the ordinary happened here at home during my absence?'

'Not here in Blekinge, Mr. Grey Owl, but in Skåne a marvellous thing has happened! A boy has been transformed by an elf into a goblin no bigger than a squirrel; and since then he has gone to Lapland with a tame goose.'

'That 's a remarkable bit of news, a remarkable bit of news. Can he never be human again, Lady Brown Owl? Can he never be human again?'

'That 's a secret, Mr. Grey Owl; but you shall hear it just the same. The elf has said that if the boy watches over the gander, so that he comes home safe and sound, and——'

'What more, Lady Brown Owl? What more? What more?'

'Fly with me up to the church tower, Mr. Grey Owl, and you shall hear the whole story! I fear there may be someone listening down here in the street.' With that the owls flew their way; but the boy flung his cap in the air, and shouted: 'If I only watch over the gander, so that he gets back safe and sound, then I shall become a human being again. Hurrah! Hurrah! Then I shall become a human being again!'

He shouted 'Hurrah!' until it was strange that they did not hear him in the houses—but they didn't, and he hurried back to the wild geese, out in the wet swamp, as fast as his legs could carry him.

PART SEVEN

THE STAIRWAY WITH THE
THREE STEPS

THE following day the wild geese intended to travel
northward through Allbo district, in Småland. They
sent Yksi and Kaksi to spy out the land. But when they
returned they said that all the water was frozen and all
the land was snow-covered. 'We may as well remain
where we are,' said the wild geese. 'We cannot travel
over a country where there is neither water nor food.'

'If we remain where we are we may have to wait here
until the next moon,' said Akka. 'It is better to go
eastward, through Blekinge, and see if we can't get to
Småland by way of Möre, which lies near the coast and
has an early spring.'

Thus Nils came to ride over Blekinge the next day.
Now that it was light again he was in a merry mood once
more, and could not understand what had come over
him the night before. He certainly didn't want to give
up the journey and the outdoor life now.

There lay a thick fog over Blekinge. Nils couldn't see
how it looked out there. 'I wonder if it is a good or a
poor country that I'm riding over,' he thought, and
tried to search his memory for the things which he had
heard about the country at school. But at the same time
he knew well enough that this was useless, as he had
never been in the habit of studying his lessons.

At once Nils saw the whole school before him. The
children sat by the little desks and raised their hands,

the teacher sat at his desk and looked displeased, and he himself stood before the map and ought to answer some question about Blekinge, but he hadn't a word to say. The schoolmaster's face grew darker and darker for every second that passed, and the boy thought he was more particular that they should know their geography than anything else. Now he came down from the desk, took the pointer from the boy, and sent him back to his seat.

'This won't end well,' Nils thought then.

But the schoolmaster had gone over to a window, and had stood there for a moment and looked out, and then he had whistled to himself once. Then he had gone on to the platform and said that he would tell them something about Blekinge. And what he then talked about had been so amusing that Nils had listened. If he only stopped and thought for a moment he remembered every word.

'Småland is a tall house with spruce-trees on the roof,' said the teacher, 'and leading up to it is a broad stairway with three big steps, and this stairway is called Blekinge. It is a stairway that is well constructed. It stretches forty-two miles along the frontage of Småland house, and any one who wishes to go all the way down to the Baltic, by way of the stairs, has twenty-four miles to wander.

'A good long time must have elapsed since the stairway was built. Both days and years have gone by since the steps were hewn from grey stones and laid down—evenly and smoothly—for a convenient track between Småland and the Baltic Sea.

'Since the stairway is so old, one can, of course, understand that it doesn't look just the same now, as it did when it was new. I don't know how much they troubled themselves about such matters at that time; but big as

it was no broom could have kept it clean. After a couple
of years moss and lichen began to grow on it. In the
autumn dry leaves and dry grass blew down over it; and
in the spring it was piled up with falling stones and
gravel. And as all these things were left there to mould,
they finally gathered so much soil on the steps that not
only herbs and grass, but even bushes and trees could
take root there.

'But at the same time a great difference has arisen
between the three steps. The topmost step, which lies
nearest Småland, is mostly covered with poor soil and
small stones, and no trees except birches and bird-cherry
and spruce—which can stand the cold on the heights,
and are satisfied with little—can thrive up there. One
understands best how poor and dry it is there, when one
sees how small the field-plots are, that are ploughed up
from the forest lands; and how small the cabins are that
the people build for themselves; and how far it is between
the churches. But on the middle step there is better soil,
and it does not lie bound down under such severe cold,
either. This one can see at a glance, since the trees are
both higher and of finer quality. There you'll find
maple and oak and linden and weeping-birch and hazel-
trees growing, but no cone-trees to speak of. And it is
still more noticeable because of the amount of cultivated
land that you will find there, and also because the people
have built themselves great and beautiful houses. On
the middle step there are many churches with large
towns around them; and in every way it has a better and
finer appearance than the top step.

'But the very lowest step is the best of all. It is covered
with good rich soil; and, where it lies and bathes in the
sea, it hasn't the slightest feeling of the Småland chill.

Beeches and chestnut and walnut-trees thrive down here; and they grow so big that they tower above the church roofs. Here lie also the largest grain-fields; but the people have not only timber and farming to live upon, but they are also occupied with fishing and trading and seafaring. For this reason you will find the most sumptuous houses and the prettiest churches here; and the parishes have developed into villages and cities.

'But this is not all that can be said of the three steps. For one must realize that when it rains on the roof of the big Småland house, or when the snow melts up there, the water has to go somewhere; and then, naturally, a lot of it is spilled over the big stairway. In the beginning it probably oozed over the whole stairway, big as it was: then cracks appeared in it, and, gradually, the water has accustomed itself to flow along it in well dug-out grooves. And water is water whatever one does with it. It never has any rest. In one place it cuts and files away, and in another it adds to. Those grooves it has dug into vales, and the walls of the vales it has covered with soil; and bushes and trees and creepers have clung to them ever since—so thick, and in such profusion, that they almost hide the stream of water that winds its way down there in the deep. But when the streams come to the landings between the steps, they throw themselves headlong over them; this is why the water comes with such a seething rush that it gathers strength with which to move mill-wheels and machinery—these, too, have sprung up by every waterfall.

'But this does not tell all that is said of the land with the three steps. It must also be told that up in the big house in Småland there lived once upon a time a giant, who had grown very old. And it fatigued him, in his extreme age, to be forced to walk down that long stairway in order to catch salmon from the sea. To him it seemed much more suitable that the salmon should come up to him where he lived.

'Therefore he went up on the roof of his great house, and there he stood and threw stones down into the Baltic. He threw them with such force that they flew over the whole of Blekinge and dropped into the sea. And when the stones came down, the salmon got so scared that they came up from the sea and fled toward the Blekinge streams, ran through the rapids, flung themselves with high leaps over the waterfalls, and stopped only when they were far inside Småland with the old giant.

'How true this is one can see by the number of islands and points that lie along the coast of Blekinge, and which are nothing but the big stones that the giant threw.

'One can also tell because the salmon always go up the Blekinge streams and work their way up through rapids and still water all the way to Småland.

'That giant is worthy of great thanks and much honour from the Blekinge people; for salmon in the streams, and stone-cutting on the island—that means work which gives food to many of them even to this day.'

PART EIGHT

BY RONNEBY RIVER

NEITHER the wild geese nor Smirre Fox had believed that they would ever run across each other after they had left Skåne. But now it happened that the wild geese took the route over Blekinge and thither Smirre Fox had also gone.

So far he had kept himself in the northern parts of the province, and since he had not as yet seen any manor parks, or hunting grounds filled with game and dainty young deer, he was more disgruntled than he could say.

One afternoon, when Smirre tramped around in the desolate forest district in the middle of Blekinge, not far from Ronneby River, he saw a flock of wild geese fly through the air. Instantly he observed that one of the geese was white, and then he knew, of course, with whom he had to deal.

Smirre began immediately to hunt the geese—just as much for the pleasure of getting a good square meal, as for the desire to be avenged for all the humiliation that they had heaped upon him. He saw that they flew eastward until they came to Ronneby River. Then they changed their course and followed the river toward the south. He understood that they intended to seek a sleeping place along the river bank, and he thought that he should be able to get hold of a pair of them without much trouble. But when Smirre finally discovered the place where the wild geese had taken refuge, he observed they had chosen such a well-protected spot, that he couldn't get near them.

Ronneby River is not a big or important stream; nevertheless, it is just as much talked of, for the sake of its attractive shores. At several points it forces its way between steep mountain walls that stand upright out of the water, and are entirely overgrown with honeysuckle and bird-cherry, mountain-ash and osier; and there isn't much that can be more delightful than to row out on the little dark river on a pleasant summer day, and look up at the soft green that fastens itself to the rugged mountain sides.

But now, when the wild geese and Smirre came to the river, it was cold and blustery spring weather; all the trees were bare, and there was probably no one who thought the least little bit about whether the shore was ugly or pretty. The wild geese thanked their good fortune that they had found a sand strip large enough for them to stand upon, by a steep mountain wall. In front of them rushed the river, which was strong and violent in the snow-melting time; behind them they had an impassable mountain rock wall, and overhanging branches screened them. They couldn't have it better.

The geese were asleep instantly; but Nils couldn't get a wink of sleep. As soon as the sun had disappeared he was seized with a fear of the darkness and a wilderness terror, and he longed for human beings. Where he lay —tucked in under the goose wing—he could see nothing, and only hear a little; and he thought if any harm came to the gander he couldn't save him.

Noises and rustlings were heard from all directions, and he grew so uneasy that he had to creep from under the wing and seat himself on the ground beside the goose.

Disappointed Smirre stood on the mountain's summit and looked down upon the wild geese and his jaw fell. 'You may as well give this pursuit up first as last,' he said to himself. 'You can't climb such a steep mountain; you can't swim in such a wild torrent; and there isn't the tiniest strip of land below the mountain which leads to the sleeping place. Those geese are too wise for you. Don't ever bother again to hunt them!'

But Smirre, like all foxes, found it hard to give up an undertaking already begun, and so he lay down on the extreme point of the mountain edge, and did not take his eyes off the wild geese. While he lay and watched them he thought of all the harm they had done him. Yes, it was their fault that he had been driven from Skåne, and had been obliged to move to poverty-stricken Blekinge. He worked himself up to such a pitch as he lay there that he wished the wild geese were dead, even if he himself should not have the satisfaction of eating them.

When Smirre's resentment had reached this height he heard a grating sound in a large pine that grew close to him, and saw a squirrel come down from the tree, hotly pursued by a marten. Neither of them noticed Smirre, and he sat quietly and watched the chase, which went from tree to tree. He looked at the squirrel, who moved among the branches as lightly as though he 'd been able to fly. He looked at the marten, who was not so skilled at climbing as the squirrel, but who still ran up and along the branches just as securely as if they had been even paths in the forest. 'If I could only climb half as well as either of them,' thought the fox, 'those things down there wouldn't sleep in peace very long!'

As soon as the squirrel had been captured and the chase was at an end Smirre walked over to the marten, but stopped two steps away from him, to signify that he did not wish to cheat him of his prey. He greeted the marten in a very friendly manner and wished him good luck with his catch. Smirre chose his words well—as foxes always do. The marten, on the contrary, who, with his long and slender body, his fine head, his soft skin, and his light-brown neck-piece, looked like a little marvel of beauty—but in reality was nothing but a cruel forest dweller—hardly answered him. 'It surprises me,' said Smirre, 'that such a fine hunter as you are should be satisfied with chasing squirrels when there is much better game within reach.' Here he paused; but when the marten only grinned impudently at him, he continued: 'Can it be possible that you haven't seen the wild geese that stand under the mountain wall, or are you not a good enough climber to get down to them?'

This time he had no need to wait for an answer. The marten rushed up to him with back bent and every

separate hair on end. 'Have you seen wild geese?' he
hissed. 'Where are they? Tell me instantly, or I'll
bite your neck off!'

'No! You must remember
that I'm twice your size—so be
a little polite. I ask nothing
better than to show you the wild
geese.'

The next instant the marten
was on his way down the steep;
and while Smirre sat and watched
how he swung his snake-like
body from branch to branch, he
thought: 'That pretty tree-
hunter has the wickedest heart in
all the forest. I believe that the
wild geese will have me to thank
for a bloody awakening.'

But just as Smirre was waiting
to hear the geese's death-rattle,
he saw the marten tumble from
branch to branch, and plump
into the river so that the water
splashed high. Soon after wings
beat loudly and strongly and all
the geese went up in a hurried
flight.

Smirre intended to hurry after
the geese, but he was so curious
to know how they had been
saved, that he sat there until the marten came clambering
up. That poor thing was soaked in mud and stopped
every now and then to rub his head with his forepaws.

'Now wasn't that just what I thought—that you were a booby, and would go and tumble into the river?' said Smirre contemptuously.

'I haven't acted boobyishly. You don't need to scold me,' said the marten. 'I sat, all ready, on one of the lowest branches and thought how I should manage to tear a whole lot of geese to pieces, when a little creature, no bigger than a squirrel, jumped up and threw a stone at my head with such force that I fell into the water; and before I had time to pick myself up——'

The marten didn't have to say any more. He had no audience. Smirre was already a long way off in pursuit of the wild geese.

In the meantime Akka had flown southward in search of a new sleeping place. There was still a little daylight; and, besides, the half-moon stood high in the heavens, so that she could see a little. Luckily she was well acquainted in these parts, because it had happened more than once that she had been wind-driven to Blekinge when she travelled over the Baltic Sea in the spring.

She followed the river as long as she saw it winding through the moon-lit landscape like a black, shining snake. In this way she came way down to Djupafors—where the river first hides itself in an underground channel—and then clear and transparent, as though it were made of glass, rushes down in a narrow cleft, and breaks into bits against its bottom in glittering drops and flying foam. Below the white falls lay a few stones, between which the water rushed away in a wild torrent cataract. Here mother Akka alighted. This was another good sleeping place—especially so late in the evening, when no human beings moved about. At sunset the geese would hardly have been able to camp there, for Djupafors does not lie in any wilderness. On one side of the falls is a pulp-mill; on the other, which is steep and tree-grown, is Djupadal's Park, where people are always strolling about on the steep and slippery paths to enjoy the wild stream's rushing movement down in the ravine.

It was about the same here as at the former place; none of the travellers thought the least little bit that they had come to a pretty and well-known place. They thought rather that it was ghastly and dangerous to stand and sleep on slippery, wet stones, in the middle of a rumbling waterfall. But they had to be content, if only they were protected from wild beasts.

The geese fell asleep instantly, while Nils could find no rest in sleep, but sat beside them that he might watch over the gander.

After a while Smirre came running along the river bank. He spied the geese immediately where they stood out in the foaming whirlpools, and understood that he couldn't get at them here, either. Still he couldn't make up his mind to abandon them, but seated himself on the shore and looked at them. He felt very much humbled, and thought that his entire reputation as a hunter was at stake.

All of a sudden he saw an otter come creeping up from the falls with a fish in his mouth. Smirre approached him but stopped within two steps of him, to show him that he didn't wish to take his game from him.

'You 're a remarkable one, who can content yourself with catching a fish, while the stones are covered with geese!' said Smirre. He was so eager that he hadn't taken the time to arrange his words as carefully as he

was wont to do. The otter didn't turn his head once in
the direction of the river. He was a vagabond—like all
otters—and had fished many times by Vomb Lake, and
probably knew Smirre Fox.

'I know very well how you act when you want to coax
away a salmon trout, Smirre,' said he.

'Oh, is it you, Gripe?' said Smirre, and was delighted;
for he knew that this particular otter was a quick and
accomplished swimmer. 'I don't wonder that you do
not care to look at the wild geese since you can't manage
to get out to them.' But the otter, who had swimming-
webs between his toes and a stiff tail—which was as good
as an oar—and a skin that was waterproof, didn't wish
to have it said of him that there was a waterfall that he
wasn't able to manage. He turned toward the stream,
and, as soon as he caught sight of the wild geese, he threw
the fish away and rushed down the steep shore and into
the river.

If it had been a little later in the spring, so that the
nightingales in Djupafors had been at home, they would
have sung for many a day of Gripe's struggle with the
rapid. For the otter was thrust back by the waves many
times and carried down river, but he fought his way
steadily up again. He swam forward in still water; he
crawled over stones, and gradually came nearer the wild
geese. It was a perilous trip, which might well have
earned the right to be sung by the nightingales.

Smirre followed the otter's course with his eyes as well
as he could. At last he saw that the otter was in the act
of climbing up to the wild geese. But just then it
shrieked shrill and wild. The otter tumbled backwards
into the water, and dashed away as if he had been a blind
kitten. An instant later there was a great crackling of

geese's wings. They raised themselves and flew away to
find another sleeping place.

The otter soon came on land. He said nothing, but
commenced to lick one of his forepaws. When Smirre
sneered at him because he hadn't succeeded, he broke
out: 'It was not the fault of my swimming, Smirre. I
had raced all the way over to the geese, and was about to
climb up to them when a tiny creature came running
and jabbed me in the foot with some sharp iron. It hurt
so, I lost my footing, and then the current took me.'

He didn't have to say any more. Smirre was already
far away after the wild geese.

Once again Akka and her flock had to take a night
flight. Fortunately the moon had not gone down, and
with the aid of its light she succeeded in finding another
of those sleeping places which she knew in that neighbourhood. Again she followed the shining river toward
the south. Over Djupadal's manor, and over Ronneby's
dark roofs and white waterfalls, she swayed forward
without alighting. But a little south of the city and not
far from the sea, lies Ronneby watering-place, with its
bath-house and spring-house; with its big hotel and
summer cottages for the spring's guests. All these stand
empty and desolate in winter—which the birds know
perfectly well; and many are the bird companies who
seek shelter on the deserted buildings' balustrades and
balconies during hard storm-times.

Here the wild geese lit on a balcony, and, as usual,
they fell asleep at once. The boy, on the contrary, could
not sleep because he didn't want to creep in under the
gander's wing.

The balcony faced south, so the boy had an outlook
over the sea. And since he could not sleep, he sat there

and saw how pretty it looked when sea and land meet, here in Blekinge.

You see, sea and land can meet in many different ways. In many places the land comes down toward the sea with flat, tufted meadows, and the sea meets the land with flying sand, which piles up in mounds and drifts. It looks as though they both disliked each other so much that they only wished to show the poorest they possessed. But it can also happen that, when the land comes toward the sea, it raises a wall of hills in front of it—as though the sea were something dangerous. When the land does this the sea comes up to it with fiery wrath, and beats and roars and lashes against the rocks, and looks as if it would tear the land-hill to pieces.

But in Blekinge it is altogether different when sea and land meet. There the land breaks itself up into points and islands and islets; and the sea divides itself into fiords and bays and sounds; and it is perhaps this which makes it look as if they must meet in happiness and harmony.

Think now first and foremost of the sea! Far out it lies desolate and empty and big, and has nothing else to do but to roll its grey billows. When it comes toward the land it comes across the first skerry. This it immediately overpowers, tears away everything green, and makes it as grey as itself. Then it meets still another skerry. With this it does the same thing. And still another. Yes, the same thing happens to this also. It is stripped and plundered, as if it had fallen into robbers' hands. Then the skerries come nearer and nearer together, and then the sea has to understand that the land sends toward it her smallest children in order to move it to pity. It also becomes more friendly the farther in it comes; rolls its waves less high, moderates its storms, lets the green plants stay in cracks and crevices, separates itself into small sounds and inlets, and becomes at last so harmless near the land that little boats dare venture out on it. It certainly cannot recognize itself— so mild and friendly has it grown.

And then think of the hillside! It looks monotonous and the same almost everywhere. It consists of flat grain-fields, with some birch groves between them; or else long stretches of forest ranges. It looks as if it had thought about nothing but grain and turnips and potatoes and spruce and pine. Then comes a sea fiord that cuts far into it. It doesn't mind that, but borders it with birch and alder, just as if it were an ordinary freshwater lake. Then still another wave comes driving in. Nor does the hillside bother itself about giving in to this, but it, too, gets the same covering as the first one. Then the fiords begin to broaden and separate; they break up fields and woods and then the hillside cannot help noticing them. 'I believe it is the sea itself that is coming,' says the hillside, and then it begins to adorn itself. It wreathes itself with blossoms, travels up and down in hills, and throws islands into the sea. It no longer cares about pines and spruces, but casts them off like old everyday clothes, and parades later with big oaks and lindens and chestnuts, and with blossoming leafy bowers, and becomes as gorgeous as a manor park. And when it meets the sea it is so changed that it doesn't know itself. All this one cannot see very well until summer-time; but, at any rate, Nils observed how mild and friendly nature was; and he began to feel calmer than he had been before, that night. Then suddenly he heard a sharp and ugly bark from the bath-house park, and when he stood up he saw, in the white moonlight, a fox standing on the pavement under the balcony. For Smirre had followed the wild geese once more. But when he had found the place where they were quartered, he had understood that it was impossible to get at them in any way, and he had not been able to keep from barking with disappointment.

When the fox barked in this manner, old Akka, the leader-goose, was awakened. Although she could see nothing she thought she recognized the voice. 'Is it you who are out to-night, Smirre?' she said.

'Yes,' said Smirre, 'it is I; and I want to ask what you geese think of the night that I have given you?'

'Do you mean to say that it is you who have sent the marten and otter against us?' asked Akka.

'A good turn shouldn't be denied,' said Smirre. 'You once played the goose game with me, now I have begun to play the fox game with you; and I 'm not inclined to let up on it so long as a single one of you still lives, even if I have to follow you the world over!'

'You, Smirre, ought at least to think whether it is right for you, who are weaponed with both teeth and claws, to hound us in this way; we who are without defence,' said Akka.

Smirre thought that Akka sounded scared, and he said quickly: 'If you, Akka, will take that Tummetott—who has so often opposed me—and throw him down to me, I 'll promise to make peace with you. Then I 'll never more pursue you or any of yours.'

'I 'm not going to give you Tummetott,' said Akka. 'From the youngest of us to the oldest, we would willingly give our lives for his sake!'

'Since you 're so fond of him,' said Smirre, 'I 'll

promise you that he shall be the first among you that I will wreak vengeance upon.'

Akka said no more, and after Smirre had sent up a few more barks, all was still. Nils lay all the while awake. Now it was Akka's words to the fox that prevented him from sleeping. Never had he dreamed that he should hear anything so great as that any one was willing to risk life for his sake. From that moment, it could no longer be said of Nils Holgersson that he did not care for any one.

PART NINE

KARLSKRONA

I⊤ was a moonlight evening in Karlskrona—calm and
beautiful. But earlier in the day there had been rain
and wind; and the people must have thought that the
bad weather still continued, for hardly one of them had
ventured out in the streets.

While the city lay there so desolate, Akka, the wild
goose, and her flock came flying toward it over Vemmön
and Pantarholmen. They were out in the late evening
to seek a sleeping place on the islands. They couldn't
remain inland because they were disturbed by Smirre
Fox wherever they lighted.

When the boy rode along high up in the air, and looked
at the sea and the islands which spread themselves before

him, he thought that everything appeared so strange and ghost-like. The heavens were no longer blue, but encased him like a globe of green glass. The sea was milk-white, and as far as he could see rolled small white waves tipped with silver ripples. In the midst of all this white lay numerous little islets, absolutely jet black. Whether they were big or little, whether they were as even as meadows or full of cliffs, they looked just as black. Even dwelling-houses and churches and windmills, which at other times are white or red, were outlined in black against the green sky. Nils thought it was as if the earth had been transformed and he had come to another world.

He thought that this night he wanted to be brave and not afraid—when he saw something that really frightened him. It was a rocky island, which was covered with big, rugged blocks; and between the blocks shone specks of bright, shining gold. He couldn't help thinking of Maglestone, by Trolle-Ljungby, which the trolls sometimes raised upon high gold pillars; and he wondered if this was something like that.

But the stones and the gold would not have mattered so much if it had not been for a lot of horrid things that were lying all round the island. They looked like whales and sharks and other big sea-monsters. But Nils took them to be sea trolls, who had gathered around the island and intended to crawl up on it, to fight with the land trolls who lived there. And those on the land were probably afraid, for he saw how a big giant stood on the highest point of the island and raised his arms—as if in despair over all the misfortune that should come to him and his island.

Nils was not a little terrified when he noticed that

Akka began to descend right over that particular
island! 'No, for pity's sake! We must not alight
there,' said he.

But the geese continued to descend, and soon the boy
was astonished that he could have mistaken things so
badly. In the first place, the big stone blocks were
nothing but houses. The whole island was a city; and
the shining gold specks were street lamps and lighted
window-panes. The giant who stood on the top of the
island and raised his arms was a church with two square
towers; all the sea trolls and monsters which he thought
he had seen were boats and ships of every description,
that lay anchored all around the island. On the side
which lay toward the land were mostly rowing boats
and sailing boats and small coastal steamers; but on the
side that faced the sea lay armour-clad battleships; some
were broad, with very thick, slanting funnels; others were
long and narrow, and so constructed that they could
glide through the water like fishes.

Now what city might this be? That Nils thought he
knew because he saw all the battleships. All his life he
had loved ships, although he had had nothing to do
with any, except the galleys which he had sailed in the
road ditches. He knew very well that this city—where
so many battleships lay—couldn't be any place but
Karlskrona.

Nils's grandfather had been an old sailor; and as long
as he had lived he had talked of Karlskrona every day;
of the great warship dock, and of all the other things to
be seen in that city. The boy felt perfectly at home, and
he was glad that he should see all this of which he had
heard so much.

But he only had a glimpse of the towers and fortifications which barred the entrance to the harbour, and the many buildings, and the shipyard—before Akka came down on one of the flat church towers.

This was a pretty safe place for those who wanted to get away from a fox, and the boy began to wonder if he couldn't venture to crawl in under the gander's wing for this one night. Yes, that he might safely do. It would do him good to get a little sleep. He would try to see a little more of the dock and the ships after it had grown light.

Nils himself thought it was strange that he could not keep still and wait until the next morning to see the ships. He certainly had not slept five minutes before he slipped out from under the wing and slid down the lightning-conductor and the water-pipe all the way down to the ground.

Soon he stood in a big square which opened in front of the church. It was covered with round stones, and was just as difficult for him to walk on, as it is for big people to walk on a tufted meadow. Those who are accustomed to live in the wilderness—or far out in the country—always feel uneasy when they come into a city, where the houses stand straight and forbidding, and the streets are open, so that every one can see who goes there. And it happened in the same way with Nils. When he stood in the big Karlskrona square, and looked at the German church, and the town hall, and the cathedral from which he had just descended, he couldn't do anything but wish that he was back on the tower again with the geese.

It was a lucky thing that the square was entirely deserted. There wasn't a human being about—unless he counted a statue that stood on a high pedestal. The boy gazed long at the statue, which represented a big, brawny man in a three-cornered hat, long coat, knee-breeches and coarse shoes, and wondered what kind of a person he was. He held a long stick in his hand, and he looked as if he would know how to make use of it, too—for he had a very severe countenance, with a big, hooked nose and an ugly mouth.

'What is that long-lipped thing doing here?' said Nils at last. He had never felt so small and insignificant as he did that night. He tried to cheer himself up a bit by saying something audacious. Then he thought no more about the statue, but betook himself to a wide street which led down to the sea.

But he hadn't gone far before he heard that someone was following him. Someone was walking behind him who stamped on the stone pavement with heavy foot-steps, and pounded on the ground with an iron-shod stick. It sounded as if the bronze man up in the square had gone out for a walk.

Nils listened to the steps while he ran down the street, and he became more and more convinced that it was the bronze man. The ground trembled and the houses shook. It couldn't be any one but he, who walked so heavily, and the boy grew panic-stricken when he thought of what he had just said to him. He did not dare to turn his head to find out if it really was he.

'Perhaps he is only out for a walk?' thought Nils. 'Surely he can't be offended with me for the words I spoke. They were not at all badly meant.'

Instead of going straight on and trying to get down to the dock Nils turned into a side street which led east. First and foremost he wanted to get away from the one who tramped after him.

But the next instant he heard that the bronze man had turned into the same street; and then the boy was so scared that he didn't know what to do with himself. And how hard it was to find any hiding places in a city where all the gates were closed! Then he saw on his right an old wooden church, which lay a short distance away from the street in the centre of a group of trees. Without a moment's hesitation he rushed on toward the church. 'If I can only get there, then I'll surely be shielded from all harm,' thought he.

As he ran forward he suddenly caught sight of a man who stood on a gravel path and beckoned to him. 'There is certainly someone who will help me!' thought the boy; he became intensely happy, and hurried off in that direction. He was actually so frightened that his heart fairly thumped in his breast.

But when he came up to the man who stood on the edge of the gravel path, upon a low pedestal, he was absolutely thunderstruck. 'Surely it can't have been that one who beckoned to me!' thought he; for he saw that the entire man was made of wood.

He stood there and stared at him. He was a thick-set man on short legs, with a broad, ruddy countenance, shiny black hair, and full black beard. On his head he wore a black wooden hat; on his body a brown wooden coat; around his waist a black wooden belt; on his legs he had wide, grey, wooden knee-breeches and wooden stockings; and on his feet black wooden shoes. He was newly painted and newly varnished so that he glistened and shone in the moonlight. This undoubtedly had a good deal to do with giving him such a good-natured appearance that the boy at once placed confidence in him.

In his left hand he held a wooden slate, and there Nils
read:

> Most humbly I beg you,
>   Though voice I may lack:
> Come drop a penny, do;
>   But lift my hat!

Oh ho! the man was only a poor-box. The boy felt
disappointed. He had expected this to be something
really remarkable. And now he remembered that
grandpapa had also spoken of the wooden man, and said
that all the children in Karlskrona were so fond of him.
And that must have been true, for he, too, found it hard
to part with the wooden man. He had something so
old-timey about him that one could well imagine him to
be many hundred years old; and at the same time he
looked strong and bold and lively—just as one might
imagine that folks looked in olden times.

Nils had so much fun looking at the wooden man that
he entirely forgot the one from whom he was fleeing.
But now he heard him. He turned from the street and
came into the churchyard. He followed him here too!
Where should Nils go?

Just then he saw the wooden man bend down to him
and stretch forth his big, broad hand. It was impossible
to believe anything but good of him; and with one jump
the boy stood in his hand. The wooden man lifted him
to his hat—and stuck him under it.

Nils was just hidden, and the wooden man had just
got his arm in its right place again, when the bronze
man stopped in front of him and banged the stick on the
ground so that the wooden man shook on his pedestal.
Thereupon the bronze man said in a strong and resonant
voice: 'Who might this be?'

The wooden man's arm went up so that it creaked in the old woodwork, and he touched his hat brim as he replied: 'Rosenbom, by Your Majesty's leave. Once upon a time boatswain of the man-of-war, *Dristigheten*; after completed service, sexton at the Admiral's church, and lately carved in wood and exhibited in the church-yard as a poor-box.'

Nils gave a start when he heard that the wooden man said 'Your Majesty.' For now, when he thought about it, he knew that the statue on the square represented the man who had founded the city. It was probably no less a person than Charles the Eleventh himself whom he had encountered.

'You give a good account of yourself,' said the bronze man. 'Can you also tell me if you have seen a little brat who runs around in the city to-night? He 's an impudent rascal; if I get hold of him I 'll teach him manners!' With that he again pounded on the ground with his stick and looked fearfully angry.

'By Your Majesty's leave, I have seen him,' said the wooden man; and the boy was so scared that he began to shake where he sat under the hat and looked at the bronze man through a crack in the wood. But he calmed down when the wooden man continued:

'Your Majesty is on the wrong track. That youngster certainly intended to run into the shipyard and conceal himself there.'

'Do you say so, Rosenbom? Well then, don't stand still on the pedestal any longer but come with me and help me find him. Four eyes are better than two, Rosenbom.'

But the wooden man answered in a doleful voice: 'I would most humbly beg to be permitted to stay where I am. I look well and sleek because of the paint, but I'm old and mouldy and cannot stand moving about.'

The bronze man was not one of those who liked to be contradicted. 'What sort of notions are these? Come along, Rosenbom!' Then he raised his stick and gave the other one a resounding whack on the shoulder. 'Do you not see that you hold together?'

With that they broke off and walked forward along the streets of Karlskrona—large and mighty—until they came to a high gate which led to the shipyard. Just outside and on guard walked one of the navy's jack tars, but the bronze man strutted past him and kicked the gate open without the jack tar pretending to notice it.

As soon as they had got into the shipyard they saw before them a wide, expansive harbour separated by pile bridges. In the different harbour basins lay the warships, which looked bigger, and more awe-inspiring close to, like this, than lately, when the boy had seen them from up above. 'Then it wasn't so crazy, after all, to imagine that they were sea trolls,' thought he.

'Where do you think it most advisable for us to begin the search?' said the bronze man.

'A fellow like him could most easily conceal himself in the hall of models,' replied the wooden man.

On a narrow land strip which stretched to the right from the gate, all along the harbour, lay ancient buildings. The bronze man walked over to a building with low walls, small windows, and a large roof. He pounded on the door with his stick until it burst open and tramped up a pair of worn-out steps. Soon they came into a large hall, which was filled with tackle and full-rigged little ships. The boy understood without being told that these were models for the ships which had been built for the Swedish navy.

There were ships of many different varieties. There were old men-of-war, whose sides bristled with cannon, and which had high structures fore and aft, and their masts weighed down with a network of sails and ropes. There were small island boats with rowing benches along the sides; there were undecked cannon sloops and richly gilded frigates, which were models of the ones the kings had used on their travels. Finally there were also the heavy, broad, armour-plated ships with towers and cannon on deck—such as are in use nowadays; and narrow, shining torpedo-boats which resembled long, slender fishes.

When the boy was carried around among all this he was awed. 'Fancy that such big, splendid ships have been built here in Sweden!' he thought to himself.

He had plenty of time to see all that was to be seen in there; for when the bronze man saw the models he forgot everything else. He examined them all, from the first to the last, and asked about them. And Rosenbom, the boatswain of the *Dristigheten*, told as much as he knew of the ships' builders, and of those who had manned them; and of the fates they had met. He told them about Chapman and Puke and Trolle; of Hogland and Svensksund—all the way along until 1809—after that he had not been there.

Both he and the bronze man had the most to say about the fine old wooden ships. The new battleships they didn't exactly appear to understand.

'I can hear that you don't know anything about these new-fangled things,' said the bronze man. 'Therefore, let us go and look at something else; for this amuses me, Rosenbom.'

By this time he had entirely given up his search for Nils, who felt calm and secure where he sat in the wooden hat.

Thereupon the two men wandered through the big establishment: sail-making shops, anchor smithy, machine and carpenter shops. They saw the mast sheers and the docks; the large magazines, the arsenal, the rope-walk, and the big discarded dock, which had been blasted out of the rock. They went out upon the pile bridges where the naval vessels lay moored, stepped on board and examined them like two old sea-dogs; wondered, disapproved, approved, and became indignant.

Nils sat in safety under the wooden hat and heard all about how they had laboured and struggled in this place to equip the navies which had gone out from here. He heard how life and blood had been risked; how the last penny had been sacrificed to build the warships; how skilled men had strained all their powers, in order to perfect these ships which had been their fatherland's safeguard. A couple of times the tears came to the boy's eyes as he heard all this.

Finally they went into an open court where the figureheads of old men-of-war were grouped; and a more remarkable sight the boy had never beheld; for these had inconceivably powerful and terror-striking faces. They were big, fearless, and savage, filled with the same proud spirit that had fitted out the great ships. They were from another time than his. He thought that he shrivelled up before them.

But when they came in here, the bronze man said to the wooden man: 'Take off thy hat, Rosenbom, to those that stand here! They have all fought for the fatherland.'

And Rosenbom—like the bronze man—had forgotten

why they had begun this walk. Without thinking he
lifted the wooden hat from his head and shouted:

'I take off my hat to him who chose the harbour and
founded the shipyard and re-created the navy, to the
monarch who has awakened all this into life!'

'Thanks, Rosenbom! That was well spoken. You
are a fine man. But what is this, Rosenbom?'

For there stood Nils Holgersson, right on the top of
Rosenbom's bald pate. He wasn't afraid any longer;
but raised his white toboggan hood and shouted:
'Hurrah for you, Longlip!'

The bronze man struck the ground hard with his stick,
but the boy never learned what he had intended to do,
for now the sun came up, and, at the same time, both the
bronze man and the wooden man vanished—as if they
had been made of mists. While he still stood and stared
after them the wild geese flew up from the church tower
and swayed back and forth over the city. Instantly they
caught sight of Nils Holgersson, and then the big white
one darted down from the sky and fetched him.

PART TEN

THE TRIP TO ÖLAND

THE wild geese went out to an island off the coast to feed. There they happened to run across a few grey geese, who were surprised to see them—since they knew very well that their kinsmen, the wild geese, usually travel over the interior of the country.

They were curious and inquisitive, and wouldn't be satisfied with less than that the wild geese should tell them all about the persecution which they had to endure from Smirre Fox. When they had finished, a grey goose, who appeared to be as old and as wise as Akka herself, said : 'It was a great misfortune for you that Smirre Fox was declared an outlaw in his own land. He 'll be sure to keep his word, and follow you all the way up to Lapland. If I were in your place I shouldn't travel north over Småland but would take the outside route over Öland instead, so that he 'll be thrown off the track entirely. To really mislead him you must remain for a couple of days on Öland's southern point. There you 'll find lots of food and lots of company. I don't believe you 'll regret it, if you go over there.'

It was certainly very sensible advice, and the wild geese decided to follow it. As soon as they had eaten all they could hold they started on the trip to Öland. None of them had ever been there before, but the grey goose had given them excellent directions. They only had to travel due south until they came to a large bird track, which extended all along the Blekinge coast. All the birds who spent the winter by the west sea, and who now intended to travel to Finland and Russia, flew forward there—and, in passing, they were always in the habit of stopping at Öland to rest. The wild geese would have no trouble in finding guides.

That day it was perfectly still and warm—like a summer's day—the best weather in the world for a sea trip. The only grave thing about it was that it was not quite clear, for the sky was grey and veiled. Here and there were enormous mist clouds which hung way down to the sea's outer edge and obstructed the view.

When the travellers had got away from the skerries, the sea spread itself so smooth and mirror-like that Nils as he looked down thought the water had disappeared. There was no longer any earth under him. He had nothing but mist and sky around him. He grew very dizzy, and held himself tight on the goose-back, more frightened than when he sat there for the

first time. It seemed as though he couldn't possibly
hold on; he must fall in some direction.

It was even worse when they reached the big bird
track of which the grey goose had spoken. Actually
there came flock after flock flying in exactly the same
direction. They seemed to follow a fixed route. There
were ducks and grey geese, surf-scoters and guillemots,
loons and pin-tail ducks, and mergansers and grebes and
oyster-catchers and sea grouse. But now, when the boy
leaned forward, and looked in the direction where the
sea ought to lie, he saw the whole bird procession
reflected in the water. But he was so dizzy that he didn't
understand how this had come about: he thought that
the whole bird procession flew with their bellies upside
down. Still he didn't wonder at this so much, for he did
not himself know which was up and which was down.

The birds were tired out and impatient to get on.
None of them called out or said a funny thing, and this
made everything seem peculiarly unreal.

'Think, if we have travelled away from the earth!'
Nils said to himself. 'Think, if we are on our way
up to heaven!'

He saw nothing but mists and birds around him, and
began to look upon it as reasonable that they were
travelling heavenward. He was glad, and wondered
what he should see up there. The dizziness passed all at
once. He was so exceedingly happy at the thought that
he was on his way to heaven and was leaving this earth.

Just then he heard a couple of loud shots and saw two
white smoke columns ascend.

There was a sudden awakening and an unrest among
the birds. 'Hunters! Hunters!' they cried. 'Fly high!
Fly away!'

Then the boy saw, finally, that they were travelling all the while over the sea, and that they certainly were not in heaven. In a long row lay small boats filled with hunters who fired shot upon shot. The first bird flocks hadn't noticed them in time. They had flown too low. Several dark bodies sank down toward the sea; and for every one that fell there arose cries of anguish from the living.

It was strange for one who had but lately believed himself in heaven to wake up suddenly to such fear and lamentation. Akka shot toward the heights as fast as she could, and the flock followed with the greatest possible speed. The wild geese got safely out of the way, but the boy couldn't get over his amazement. 'To think that any one could wish to shoot upon such as Akka and Yksi and Kaksi and the gander and the others! Human beings had no idea of what they were doing.'

So they went on again in the still air, and everything was as quiet as heretofore—except that some of the tired birds called out every now and then: 'Are we not there soon? Are you sure we 're on the right track?' Hereupon those who flew in the centre answered: 'We are flying straight to Öland; straight to Öland.'

The wild ducks were tired out, and the loons passed them. 'Don't be in such a rush!' cried the ducks. 'You 'll eat up all the food before we get there.'

'Oh, there 'll be enough for all of us,' answered the loons.

Before they had got so far that they saw Öland, there came a light wind against them. It brought with it something that resembled immense clouds of white smoke —just as if there was a big fire somewhere.

When the birds saw the first white spiral haze they

became uneasy and increased their speed. But that which resembled smoke blew thicker and thicker, and at last it enveloped them altogether. They smelled no smoke, and the smoke was not dark and dry, but white and damp. Suddenly Nils understood that it was nothing but a mist.

When the mist became so thick that one couldn't see a goose-length ahead, the birds began to carry on like real lunatics. All these, who before had travelled forward in such perfect order, began to play in the mist. They flew hither and thither, to entice one another astray. 'Be careful!' they cried. 'You're only travelling round and round. Turn back, for pity's sake! You'll never get to Öland in this way.'

They all knew perfectly well where the island was, but they did their best to lead each other astray. 'Look at those long-tailed ducks!' rang out in the mist. 'They are going back toward the North Sea!'

'Have a care, wild geese!' called someone from another direction. 'If you continue like this, you'll get clear up to Rügen.'

There was, of course, no danger that the birds who were accustomed to travel here would be lured in a wrong direction. But the ones who had a hard time of it were the wild geese. The jesters observed that they were uncertain as to the way, and did all they could to confuse them.

'Where do you intend to go, good people?' called a swan. He came right up to Akka and looked sympathetic and serious.

'We are going to Öland, but we have never been there before,' said Akka. She thought that this was a bird to be trusted.

'It 's too bad,' said the swan. 'They have lured you in the wrong direction. You're on the road to Blekinge. Now come with me and I 'll put you right!'

And so he flew off with them; and when he had taken them so far away from the track that they heard no calls, he disappeared in the mist.

They flew around for a while at random. They had barely succeeded in finding the birds again when a duck approached them. 'You had better lie down on the water until the mist clears,' said the duck. 'It is evident that you are not accustomed to look out for yourselves on journeys.'

Those rogues succeeded in making Akka's head swim. As far as the boy could make out the wild geese flew round and round for a long time.

'Be careful! Can't you see that you are flying upside down?' shouted a loon as he rushed by. The boy positively clutched the gander around the neck. This was something which he had feared for a long time.

No one can tell when they would have arrived if they hadn't heard a rolling and muffled shot in the distance.

Then Akka craned her neck, snapped hard with her wings, and rushed on at full speed. Now she had something to go by. The grey goose had told her not to light on Öland's southern point, because there was a cannon there which the people used to shoot the mist with. Now she knew the way, and now no one in the world should lead her astray again.

PART ELEVEN

ÖLAND'S SOUTHERN POINT

On the most southerly part of Öland lies a royal demesne, which is called Ottenby. It is a rather large estate which extends from shore to shore, straight across the island; and it is remarkable because it has always been a haunt for animals. In the seventeenth century, when the kings used to go over to Öland to hunt, the entire estate was nothing but a deer park. In the eighteenth century there was a stud there where thoroughbred race-horses were bred, and a sheep farm where several hundred sheep were maintained. In our days you'll find neither thoroughbreds nor sheep at Ottenby. In place of them are great herds of young horses which are to be used by the cavalry.

In all the land there is certainly no place that could be a better abode for animals. Along the extreme eastern shore lies the old sheep meadow, which is a mile and a half long, and the largest meadow in all Öland, where animals can graze and play and run about, as free as if they were in a wilderness. And there you will find the celebrated Ottenby grove with the hundred-year-old oaks, which give shade from the sun and shelter from the severe Öland winds. And we must not forget the long Ottenby wall which stretches from shore to shore, and separates Ottenby from the rest of the island, so that the animals may know how far the old royal demesne extends, and be careful about getting in on other ground where they are not so well protected.

You 'll find plenty of domestic animals at Ottenby, but that isn't all. One could almost believe that the wild ones also felt that on an old Crown property both the wild and the tame animals can count upon shelter and protection—since they venture there in such great numbers.

There are still a few stags of the old descent left, and hares and sheldrakes and partridges love to live there. But, moreover, it offers a resting place, in the spring and late summer, for thousands of migratory birds. Above all it is the swampy eastern shore below the sheep meadow where the migratory birds alight to rest and feed.

When the wild geese and Nils Holgersson had finally found their way to Öland they came down, like all the rest, on the shore near the sheep meadow. The mist lay thick over the island just as it had over the sea. But still the boy was amazed at all the birds which he discerned, only on the little narrow stretch of shore which he could see.

It was a low sand-shore with stones and pools, and a lot of cast-up seaweed. If Nils had been permitted to choose it isn't likely that he would have thought of alighting there; but the birds probably looked upon this as a veritable paradise. Ducks and geese walked about and fed on the meadow; nearer the water ran snipe and other coast birds. The loons lay in the sea and fished, but the life and movement was upon the long seaweed banks along the coast. There the birds stood side by side close together and picked grub-worms—which must have been found there in limitless quantities, for it was evident that there was never any complaint over a lack of food.

The great majority were going to travel farther and had only alighted to take a short rest; and as soon as the leader of a flock thought that his comrades had refreshed themselves sufficiently he said: 'If you are ready now we may as well move on.'

'No, wait, wait! We haven't had anything like enough,' said the followers.

'You surely don't believe that I intend to let you eat so much that you will not be able to move?' said the leader, and flapped his wings and started off. But more than once he had to turn back because he could not make the others follow him.

Along the outermost seaweed banks were a flock of swans. They didn't bother about going ashore, but rested themselves by lying and rocking on the water. Now and then they stretched down their long necks and brought up food from the sea-bottom. When they had got hold of anything very good they gave loud shouts that sounded like trumpet calls.

When Nils heard that there were swans on the shoals

he hurried out to the seaweed banks. He had never before seen wild swans at close range. He had luck on his side so that he got close up to them.

Nils was not the only one who had heard the swans. Wild geese and grey geese and loons swam out between the banks, laid themselves in a circle around the swans, and stared at them. The swans ruffled their feathers, raised their wings like sails, and lifted their necks high in the air. Occasionally one of them swam up to a goose, or a great loon, or a diving-duck, and said a few words. And then it appeared as though the one addressed hardly dared raise his bill to reply.

But then there was a little loon—a tiny mischievous creature—who couldn't stand all this ceremony. He dived suddenly and disappeared under the water's edge. Soon after that one of the swans let out a scream and swam off so quickly that the water foamed. Then he stopped and began to look majestic once more. But soon another one shrieked in the same way as the first one, and then a third.

The little loon wasn't able to stay under water any longer, but appeared on the water's edge, little and black and venomous. The swans rushed toward him; but when they saw what a poor little thing it was they turned abruptly—as if they considered themselves too good to quarrel with him. Then the little loon dived again and pinched their feet. It certainly must have hurt; and the worst of it was that they could not maintain their dignity. At once they took a decided stand. They began to beat the air with their wings so that it thundered, came forward a bit—as though they were running on the water, and finally got the wind under their wings and raised themselves.

When the swans were gone they were greatly missed; and those who had lately been amused by the little loon's antics scolded him for his thoughtlessness.

Nils walked toward land again. There he stopped to see how the pool snipe played. They resembled small cranes; like these, they had little bodies, long legs and necks, and light, swaying movements; only they were not grey, but brown. They stood in a long row on the shore where it was washed by waves. As soon as a wave rolled in the whole row ran backward; as soon as it receded they followed it. And they kept this up for hours.

The showiest of all the birds were the sheldrakes. They were undoubtedly related to the ordinary ducks, for, like these, they too had a thick-set body, broad bill, and webbed feet; but they were much more elaborately got up. The feather dress itself was white; around their necks they wore a broad gold band; the speculum shone in green, red, and black; and the wing edges were black, and the head was dark green and shimmered like satin.

As soon as any of these appeared on the shore the others said: 'Now, just look at those! They know how to tog themselves out.'

'If they were not so conspicuous they wouldn't have to dig their nests in the earth, but could lay above ground, like any one else,' said a brown mallard-duck.

'They may try as much as they please, still they'll never get anywhere with such noses,' said a grey goose. And this was actually true. The sheldrakes had a big knob on the base of the bill which spoiled their appearance.

Close to the shore seagulls and sea-swallows moved forward above the water and fished.

'What kind of fish are you catching?' asked a wild goose.

'It's stickleback. It's Öland stickleback. It's the best stickleback in the world,' said a gull. 'Won't you taste it?' And he flew up to the goose, with his mouth full of the little fishes, and wanted to give her some.

'Ugh! Do you think that I eat such filth?' said the wild goose.

The next morning it was just as cloudy. The wild geese were feeding on the meadow but Nils had gone to the seashore to gather mussels. There were plenty of them, and when he thought that the next day, perhaps, they would be in some place where they couldn't get any food at all, he decided that he would try to make himself a little bag which he could fill with mussels. He found old sedge on the meadow, which was strong and tough, and out of this he began to weave a knapsack. He worked at this for several hours, but he was well satisfied with it when it was finished.

At dinner time all the wild geese came running and asked him if he had seen the white gander.

'No, he has not been with me,' said the boy.

'We had him with us all along until just lately,' said Akka, 'but now we no longer know where he's to be found.'

Nils jumped up and was terribly frightened. He asked if any fox or eagle had appeared, or if any human being had been seen in the neighbourhood. But no one had noticed anything dangerous. The gander had probably lost his way in the mist.

But it was just as great a misfortune for Nils in whatever way the white one had been lost, and he started off immediately to hunt for him. The mist shielded him so that he could run wherever he wished without being seen, but it also prevented him from seeing. He ran southward along the shore—all the way down to the lighthouse and the mist cannon on the island's extreme point. There were crowds of birds everywhere, but no gander. He ventured over to Ottenby estate, and he searched every one of the old, hollow oaks in Ottenby grove, but he saw no trace of the gander.

He searched until it began to grow dark. Then he had to turn back again to the eastern shore. He walked with heavy steps and was thoroughly miserable. He didn't know what would become of him if he couldn't find the gander. There was no one whom he could spare less.

But when he wandered over the sheep meadow, what was that big, white thing that came toward him in the mist if it wasn't the gander? He was all right, and very glad that, at last, he had been able to find his way back to the others. The mist had made him so dizzy, he said, that he had wandered around on the big meadow all day long. The boy threw his arms around his neck for very joy, and begged him to take care of himself and not wander away from the others. And he promised, positively, that he never would do this again. No, never again.

But the next morning, when Nils went down to the beach and hunted for mussels, the geese came running and asked if he had seen the gander. No, of course he hadn't. Well, then the gander was lost again. He had gone astray in the mist, just as he had done the day before.

The boy ran off in great terror and began to search. He found one place where the Ottenby wall was so tumbledown that he could climb over it. Then he went about, first on the shore—which gradually widened and became so large that there was room for fields and meadows and farms—then up on the flat highland, which lay in the middle of the island, and where there were no buildings except windmills, and where the turf was so thin that the white limestone shone under it.

But he could not find the gander, and as it drew on toward evening, and Nils must return to the beach, he could believe only that his travelling companion was lost. He was so depressed he did not know what to do with himself.

He had just climbed over the wall again when he heard a stone crash down close beside him. As he turned to see what it was, he thought that he could distinguish something that moved on a stone pile which lay close to the wall. He stole nearer, and saw the gander come trudging wearily over the stone pile with several long roots in his mouth. The gander didn't see the boy, and the boy did not call to him, but thought it advisable to find out first why the gander, time and again, disappeared in this manner.

And he soon learned the reason for it. Up in the stone pile lay a young grey goose, who cried with joy when the gander came. The boy crept near, so that he heard what they said; then he found out that the grey goose had been wounded in one wing so that she could not fly, and that her flock had travelled away from her and left her alone. She had been near death's door with hunger when the white gander had heard her call, the other day, and had sought her out. Ever since he had been carrying food to her. They had both hoped that she would be well before they left the island, but as yet she could neither fly nor walk. She was very much worried over this, but he comforted her with the thought that he shouldn't leave for a long time. At last he bade her good night and promised to come the next day.

Nils let the gander go; and as soon as he was gone he stole, in turn, up to the stone heap. He was angry because he had been deceived, and now he wanted to say to that grey goose that the gander was his property. He was going to take Nils up to Lapland, and there would be no talk of his staying here on her account. But now, when he saw the young grey goose close to, he understood, not only why the gander had been carrying food to her for two days, but also why he had not wished to mention that he had helped her. She had the prettiest little head; her feather dress was like soft satin, and her eyes were mild and pleading.

When she saw the boy she wanted to run away, but the left wing was out of joint and dragged on the ground so that it interfered with her movements.

'You mustn't be afraid of me,' said the boy, and didn't look nearly so angry as he had intended to appear. 'I 'm Tummetott, Morten gander's comrade,' he continued. Then he stood there and didn't know what he wanted to say.

Occasionally one finds something in animals which makes one wonder what sort of creatures they really are. One is almost afraid that they may be transformed human beings. It was something like this with the grey goose. As soon as Tummetott said who he was, she lowered her neck and head very charmingly before him, and said in a voice that was so pretty that he couldn't believe it was a goose who spoke: 'I am very glad that you have come here to help me.   The white gander has told me that no one is as wise and as good as you.'

She said this with such dignity that the boy grew really embarrassed.

'This surely can't be a bird,' thought he.   'It is certainly some bewitched princess.'

He was filled with a desire to help her, and ran his hand under the feathers and felt along the wing-bone. The bone was not broken, but there was something wrong with the joint.   He got his finger down into the empty cavity.   'Be careful, now!' he said, and got a firm grip on the wing-bone and fitted it into the place where it ought to be.   He did it very quickly and well, considering it was the first time that he had attempted anything of the sort.   But it must have hurt very much, for the poor young goose uttered a single shrill cry, and then sank down among the stones without showing a sign of life.

The boy was terribly frightened.   He had only wished to help her, and now she was dead.   He made a big jump from the stone pile and ran away.   He thought it was as though he had murdered a human being.

The next morning it was clear and free from mist, and Akka said that now they should continue their travels. All the others were willing to go, but the white gander made excuses.   The boy understood well enough that he didn't want to leave the grey goose.   Akka did not listen to him but started off.

The boy jumped up on the gander's back, and the white one followed the flock—albeit slowly and un-willingly.   The boy was quite glad that they could fly away from the island.   He was conscience-stricken on account of the grey goose, and had not wanted to tell the gander how it had turned out when he had tried to cure her. 'It would probably be best if Morten gander never found out about this,' he thought, though he wondered, at the same time, how the white one had the heart to leave the grey goose.

But suddenly the gander turned. The thought of the young grey goose had overpowered him. It could go as it would with the Lapland trip: he couldn't go with the others when he knew that she lay alone and ill, and would starve to death.

With a few wing-strokes he was over by the stone pile; but then, there lay no young grey goose between the stones. 'Dunfin! Dunfin! Where art thou?' called the gander.

'The fox has probably been here and taken her,' thought the boy. But at that moment he heard a pretty voice answer the gander.

'Here am I, gander; here am I! I have only been taking a morning bath.' And up from the water came the little grey goose—fresh and in good trim—and told how Tummetott had pulled her wing into place, and that she was entirely well and ready to follow them on the journey.

The drops of water lay like pearl-dew on her shimmery satin-like feathers, and Tummetott thought once again that she was a real little princess.

PART TWELVE

THE BIG BUTTERFLY

THE geese travelled alongside the coast of the long island, which lay distinctly visible under them. Nils felt happy and light of heart during the trip. He was just as pleased and well satisfied as he had been glum and depressed the day before, when he roamed around down on the island and hunted for the gander.

He saw now that the interior of the island consisted of a barren high plain, with a wreath of fertile land along the coast; and he began to comprehend the meaning of something which he had heard the other evening.

He had just seated himself to rest a bit by one of the many windmills on the highland, when a couple of shepherds came along with the dogs beside them, and a large flock of sheep in their train. The boy had not been afraid because he was well concealed under the windmill stairs. But as it turned out, the shepherds came and seated themselves on the same stairway, and then there was nothing for him to do but to keep perfectly still.

One of the shepherds was young, and looked about as folks do mostly; the other was an old queer one. His body was large and knotty, but his head was small and his face had sensitive and delicate features. It appeared as though body and head didn't fit together at all.

One moment he sat silent and gazed into the mist, with an unutterably weary expression. Then he began to talk to his companion. Then the other one took out some bread and cheese from his knapsack to eat his evening meal. He answered scarcely anything, but listened very patiently, just as if he were thinking: 'I might as well give you the pleasure of letting you chatter a while.'

'Now I shall tell you something, Eric,' said the old shepherd. 'I have figured out that in former days, when human beings and animals were much larger than they are now, the butterflies, too, must have been uncommonly large. And once there was a butterfly that was many miles long and had wings as wide as seas. Those wings were blue, and shone like silver, and so gorgeous that, when the butterfly was out flying, all the other animals stood still and stared at it. It had this drawback, however, that it was too large. The wings had hard work to carry it. But probably all would have gone very well if the butterfly had been wise enough to remain on land. But it wasn't; it ventured out over the Baltic Sea. And it hadn't got very far before the storm came along and began to tear at its wings. Well, it's easy to understand, Eric, how things would go when the Baltic Sea storm commenced to wrestle with frail butterfly wings. It wasn't long before they were torn away and scattered; and then, of course, the poor butterfly fell into the sea. At first it was tossed backward and forward on the billows, and then it was stranded upon a few rocks outside Småland. And there it lay—as large and long as it was.

'Now I think, Eric, that if the butterfly had dropped on land, it would soon have rotted and fallen apart. But since it fell into the sea, it was soaked through and through with lime and became as hard as a stone. You know, of course, that we have found stones on the shore which were nothing but petrified worms. Now I believe that it went the same way with the big butterfly body. I believe that it turned into a long, narrow mountain where it lay out in the Baltic Sea. Don't you?'

He paused for a reply and the other one nodded to him. 'Go on, so I may hear what you are driving at,' said he.

'And mark you, Eric, that this very Öland, upon which you and I live, is nothing else but the old butterfly body. If you only think about it, you will notice that the island is a butterfly. Toward the north you can see the slender fore-body and the round head, and toward the south the back-body—which first broadens out and then narrows to a sharp point.'

Here he paused once more and looked at his companion rather anxiously to see how he would take this assertion.

But the young man kept on eating with the utmost calm, and nodded to him to continue.

'As soon as the butterfly had been changed into a limestone rock, many different kinds of seeds of herbs and trees came travelling with the winds and wanted to take root on it. But it was difficult for them to remain on the barren and slippery rock. It was a long time before anything but sedge could grow there. Then came sheep-sorrel and rock-rose and thorn-bush. But even to-day there is not so much growth on Alvaret that the mountain is well covered, but it shines through here and there. And no one can think of ploughing and sowing up here where the earth crust is so thin. But if you admit that Alvaret and the cliff wall around it are made of the butterfly body, then you may also want to question where that land which lies beneath the cliff wall came from.'

'Yes, it is just that,' said he who was eating. 'That I should indeed like to know.'

'Well, you must remember that Öland has lain in the sea for a good many years, and in the course of time all the things which tumble around with the waves—seaweed and sand and clams—have gathered around it, and remained lying there. And then, stone and gravel have fallen down from both the eastern and western cliff walls. In this way the island has acquired broad shores, where grain and flowers and trees can grow.

'Up here, on the hard butterfly back only sheep and cows and little horses go about. Only lapwings and plover live here, and there are no buildings except wind-mills and a few stone huts, where we shepherds crawl in. But down on the coast lie big villages and churches and parishes and fishing hamlets and a whole city.'

He looked questioningly at the other one. This one had finished his meal, and was fastening up the knapsack.

'I wonder what you want to get at?' said he.

'It is only one thing I want to know,' said the shepherd, as he lowered his voice so that he almost whispered the words, and looked into the mist with his small eyes which appeared to be worn out from spying after all that which does not exist. 'Only this I want to know: if the peasants who live on the farms beneath the cliff walls, or the fishermen who take the small herring from the sea, or the merchants in Borgholm, or the bathing guests who come here every summer, or the tourists who wander around in Borgholm's old castle ruin, or the sportsmen who come here in the autumn to hunt partridges, or the painters who sit here on Alvaret and paint the sheep and windmills—I should like to know if any of them understand that this island has been a butterfly which flew about with great shimmery wings.'

'Ah!' said the young shepherd suddenly. 'It should have occurred to some of them, as they sat on the edge of the cliff wall of an evening, and heard the nightingales trill in the groves below them, and looked over Kalmar Sound, that this island could not have come into existence in the same way as the others.'

'I want to ask,' said the old one, 'if no one has had the desire to give wings to the windmills—so large that they could reach to heaven, so large that they could lift the whole island out of the sea and let it fly like a butterfly among butterflies.'

'It may be possible that there is something in what you say,' said the young one; 'for on summer nights, when the heavens widen and open over the island, I have sometimes thought that it was as if it wanted to raise itself from the sea and fly away.'

But when the old man had finally got the young one to talk he didn't listen to him very much.

'I would like to know,' the old one said in a low tone, 'if any one can explain why one feels such a longing up here on Alvaret.   I have felt it every day of my life; and I think it preys upon each and every one who must go about here.   I want to know if no one else has understood that all this wistfulness is caused by the fact that the whole island is a butterfly that longs for its wings.'

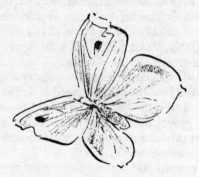

PART THIRTEEN

LITTLE KARL'S ISLAND

☆

Chapter One

THE STORM

THE wild geese had spent the night on Öland's northern point and were now on their way to the continent. A strong south wind blew over Kalmar Sound and they had been thrown northward. Still they worked their way toward land with good speed. But when they were nearing the first skerries a powerful rumbling was heard, as if a lot of strong-winged birds had come flying; and the water under them, all at once, became perfectly black. Akka drew in her wings so suddenly that she almost stood still in the air. Thereupon she lowered herself to light on the edge of the sea. But before the geese had reached the water the west storm caught up with them. Already it drove before it clouds of dust, salt scum, and small birds; it also snatched with it the wild geese, threw them on end, and cast them toward the sea.

It was a rough storm. The wild geese tried to turn back, time and again, but they couldn't do it and were driven out toward the Baltic Sea. The storm had already blown them past Öland, and the sea lay before them—empty and desolate. There was nothing for them to do but to fly before the wind.

When Akka observed that they were unable to turn

back she thought that it was needless to let the storm
drive them over the entire Baltic Sea. Therefore she
sank down to the water. Now the sea was raging and
increased in violence with every second. The sea-green
billows rolled forward with seething foam on their
crests. Each one surged higher than the other. It was
as though they raced with each other, to see which could
foam the wildest. But the wild geese were not afraid of
the swells. On the contrary, this seemed to afford them
much pleasure. They did not strain themselves with
swimming, but lay and let themselves be washed up with
the wave-crests, and down in the water-dales, and had
just as much fun as children in a swing. Their only
anxiety was that the flock should be separated. The
few land birds who drove by, up in the storm, cried with
envy: 'There is no danger for you who can swim.'

But the wild geese were certainly not out of all danger.
In the first place the rocking made them helplessly
sleepy. They wished continually to turn their heads
backward, poke their bills under their wings, and go to
sleep. Nothing can be more dangerous than to fall
asleep in this way, and Akka called out all the while:

'Don't go to sleep, wild geese! He that falls asleep
will get away from the flock. He that gets away from the
flock is lost.'

Despite all attempts at resistance one after another fell
asleep; and Akka herself came pretty near dozing off,
when she suddenly saw something round and dark rise
on the top of a wave.

'Seals! Seals! Seals!' cried Akka in a high, shrill
voice, and raised herself up in the air with resounding
wing-strokes. It was just at the crucial moment.
Before the last wild goose had time to come up from the

water, the seals were so close to her that they made a
grab for her feet.

Then the wild geese were once more up in the storm
which drove them before it out to sea. No rest did it
allow either itself or the wild geese; and no land did
they see—only desolate sea.

They lit on the water again, as soon as they dared
venture. But when they had rocked upon the waves for
a while, they became sleepy again. And when they fell
asleep the seals came swimming. If old Akka had not
been so wakeful not one of them would have escaped.

All day the storm raged; and it caused fearful havoc
among the crowds of little birds, which at this time of
year were migrating. Some were driven from their
course to foreign lands, where they died of starvation;
others became so exhausted that they sank down in the
sea and were drowned. Many were crushed against the
cliff walls, and many became a prey for the seals.

At last Akka began to wonder if she and her flock
would perish. They were now dead tired, and nowhere
did they see any place where they might rest. Toward
evening she no longer dared to lie down on the sea,
because now it filled up all of a sudden with large
ice-floes which struck against each other, and she feared
they should be crushed between these. A couple of
times the wild geese tried to stand on the ice-floes;
but one time the wild storm swept them into the water;
another time the merciless seals came creeping up on
the ice.

At sundown the wild geese were once more up in the
air. They flew on—fearful for the night. The darkness
seemed to come upon them much too quickly this night
—which was so full of dangers.

It was terrible that they, as yet, saw no land. How would it go with them if they were forced to stay out on the sea all night? They would either be crushed between the ice-floes or devoured by seals or separated by the storm.

The heavens were cloud-bedecked, the moon hid itself, and the darkness came quickly. At the same time all nature was filled with a horror which caused the most courageous hearts to quail. Distressed bird travellers' cries had sounded over the sea all day long, without any one having paid the slightest attention to them; but now, when one no longer saw who it was that uttered them, they seemed mournful and terrifying. Down on the sea the ice-floes crashed against each other with a loud rumbling noise. The seals tuned up their wild hunting songs. It was as though heaven and earth were about to clash.

Chapter Two

THE SHEEP

FOR a while Nils had sat looking down into the sea. Suddenly he thought that it began to roar louder than ever. He looked up. Right in front of him—only a couple of yards away—stood a rugged and bare mountain wall. At its base the waves dashed into a foaming spray. The wild geese flew straight toward the cliff, and the boy did not see how they could avoid being dashed to pieces against it. Hardly had he wondered that Akka hadn't seen the danger in time when they were over by the mountain. Then he also noticed that in front of them was the half-round entrance to a cave. Into this the geese steered, and the next moment they were safe.

The first thing the wild geese thought of—before they gave themselves time to rejoice over their safety—was to see if all their comrades were also harboured. Yes, there were Akka, Yksi, Kolmi, Neljä, Viisi, Kuusi, all the six goslings, the gander, Dunfin, and Tummetott; but Kaksi from Nuolja, the first left-hand goose, was missing —and no one knew anything about her fate.

When the wild geese discovered that no one but Kaksi had been separated from the flock they took the matter lightly. Kaksi was old and wise. She knew all their byways and their habits, and she, of course, would know how to find her way back to them.

Then the wild geese began to look around in the cave. Enough daylight came in through the opening so that they could see it was both deep and wide. They were delighted to think they had found such a fine night shelter when one of them caught sight of some shining, green dots, which glittered in a dark corner.

'These are eyes!' cried Akka. 'There are big animals in here.'

They rushed toward the opening, but Tummetott called to them: 'There is nothing to run away from! It's only a few sheep who are lying alongside the cave wall.'

When the wild geese had accustomed themselves to the dim daylight in the cave they saw the sheep very distinctly. The grown-up ones might be about as many as there were geese; but beside these there were a few little lambs. An old ram with long, twisted horns appeared to be the most lordly one of the flock. The wild geese went up to him with much bowing and scraping.

'Well met in the wilderness!' they greeted, but the big ram lay still and did not speak a word of welcome.

Then the wild geese thought that the sheep were displeased because they had taken shelter in their cave.

'Perhaps it does not please you that we have come in here?' said Akka. 'But we cannot help it, for we are wind-driven. We have flown about in the storm all day, and it would be very good to be allowed to stop here to-night.'

After that a long time passed before any of the sheep answered with words; but, on the other hand, it could be heard distinctly that a pair of them heaved deep sighs. Akka knew, to be sure, that sheep are always shy and peculiar; but these seemed to have no idea of how to behave. Finally an old ewe, who had a long and pathetic face and a doleful voice, said: 'There isn't one among us that refuses to let you stay; but this is a house of mourning, and we cannot receive guests as we did in former days.'

'You needn't worry about anything of that sort,' said Akka. 'If you knew what we have endured this day, you would surely understand that we are satisfied if we only get a safe spot to sleep on.'

When Akka said this, the old ewe raised herself. 'I believe that it would be better for you to fly about in the worst storm than to stop here. But, at least, you shall not go from here before we have had the privilege of offering you the best hospitality which the house affords.'

She conducted them to a hollow in the ground which was filled with water. Beside it lay a pile of grain and husks and chaff, and she bade them make the most of these.

'We have had a severe snow winter this year on the island,' she said. 'The peasants who own us came out to us with hay and oaten straw, so we shouldn't starve to death. And this trash is all there is left of the good cheer.'

The geese rushed to the food instantly. They thought that they had fared well and were in their best mood. They must have observed, of course, that the sheep were anxious; but they knew how easily scared sheep generally are, and didn't believe there was any actual danger on foot. As soon as they had eaten they intended to stand up to sleep as usual. But then the big ram got up and walked over to them. The geese thought that they had never seen a sheep with such big and coarse horns. In other respects, also, he was remarkable. He had a high, bulging forehead, intelligent eyes, and a good bearing—as though he were a proud and courageous animal.

'I cannot assume the responsibility of letting you geese

remain, without telling you that it is unsafe here,' said he.
'We cannot receive night guests just now.'

At last Akka began to comprehend that this was serious.

'We shall go away, since you really wish it,' said she.
'But won't you tell us first what it is that troubles you?
We know nothing about it. We do not even know where
we are.'

'This is the island of Lilla Karlsön!' said the ram.
'It lies outside Gottland, and only sheep and sea birds
live here.'

'Perhaps you are wild sheep?' said Akka.

'We're not far from it,' replied the ram. 'We have
nothing to do with human beings. It's an old agree-
ment between us and some peasants on a farm in Gottland, that they shall supply us with fodder in case we
have a snow winter, and as a recompense they are
permitted to take away those of us who become super-
fluous. The island is small, so it cannot feed very many
of us. But otherwise we take care of ourselves all the
year round, and we do not live in houses with doors and
locks but we reside in caves like these.'

'Do you stay out here in the winter as well?' asked
Akka, surprised.

'We do,' answered the ram. 'We have good fodder
up here on the mountain all the year round.'

'I think it sounds as if you might have it better than
other sheep,' said Akka. 'But what is the misfortune
that has befallen you?'

'It was bitter cold last winter. The sea froze, and
then three foxes came over here on the ice, and here they
have been ever since. Otherwise, there are no dangerous
animals here on the island.'

'Oh, ho! Do foxes dare to attack such as you?'

'Oh, no, not during the day; then I can protect myself and mine,' said the ram, shaking his horns. 'But they sneak upon us at night when we sleep in the caves. We try to keep awake, but one must sleep some of the time, and then they come upon us. They have already killed every sheep in the other caves, and there were herds that were just as large as mine.'

'It isn't pleasant to tell that we are so helpless,' said the old ewe. 'We cannot help ourselves any better than if we were tame sheep.'

'Do you think that they will come here to-night?' asked Akka.

'There is nothing else in store for us,' answered the old ewe. 'They were here last night and stole a lamb from us. They'll be sure to come again as long as there are any of us alive. This is what they have done in the other places.'

'But if they are allowed to keep this up you'll become entirely exterminated,' said Akka.

'Oh, it won't be long before there is no one left of the sheep on the island of Lilla Karlsön,' said the ewe.

Akka stood there hesitatingly. It was not pleasant, by any means, to venture out in the storm again, and it wasn't good to remain in a house where such guests were expected. When she had pondered a while she turned to Tummetott.

'I wonder if you will help us, as you have done so many times before,' said she.

Yes, that he would like to do, he replied.

'It is a pity for you not to get any sleep,' said the wild goose, 'but I wonder if you are able to keep awake until the foxes come, and then to awaken us, so we may fly away.'

The boy was not very pleased with this, but anything

was better than to go out in the storm again—so he
promised to keep awake.

Nils went down to the cave opening, crawled in
behind a stone that he might be shielded from the storm,
and sat down to watch.

When the boy had been sitting there a while, the storm
seemed to abate. The sky grew clear and the moonlight
began to play on the waves. The boy stepped to the
opening to look out. The cave was rather high up on
the mountain. A narrow path led to it. It was probably
here that he could expect the foxes.

As yet he saw no foxes; but, on the other hand, there
was something which, for the moment, terrified him
much more. On the land strip below the mountain
stood some giants, or other stone trolls—or perhaps they
were actual human beings. At first he thought that he
was dreaming, but now he was positive that he had not
fallen asleep. He saw the big men so distinctly that it
couldn't be an illusion. Some of them stood on the
land strip and others right on the mountain just as if
they intended to climb it. Some had big, thick heads;
others had no heads at all. Some were one-armed, and
some had humps both before and behind. He had never
seen anything so extraordinary.

Nils stood and worked himself into a state of panic
because of those trolls so that he almost forgot to keep
his eye peeled for the foxes. But now he heard a claw
scrape against a stone. He saw three foxes coming up
the steep; and as soon as he knew that he had something
real to deal with, he was calm again and not the least
bit scared. It struck him that it was a pity to awaken
only the geese and to leave the sheep to their fate. He
thought he would like to arrange things some other way.

He ran quickly to the other end of the cave, shook the big ram's horns until he awoke, and, at the same time, swung himself up on his back.

'Get up, sheep, and we 'll try to frighten the foxes a bit!' said the boy.

He had tried to be as quiet as possible, but the foxes must have heard some noise; for when they came up to the mouth of the cave they stopped and deliberated.

'It was certainly someone in there that moved,' said one. 'I wonder if they are awake.'

'Oh, go ahead, you!' said another. 'At all events, they can't do anything to us.'

When they came farther in, in the cave, they stopped and sniffed.

'Who shall we take to-night?' whispered the one who went first.

'To-night we will take the big ram,' said the last. 'After that, we 'll have easy work with the rest.'

The boy sat on the old ram's back and saw how they sneaked along.

'Now butt straight forward!' whispered the boy.

The ram butted, and the first fox was thrust, top over tail, back to the opening.

'Now butt to the left!' said the boy, and turned the big ram's head in that direction. The ram measured a terrific assault that caught the second fox in the side. He rolled around several times before he got to his feet again and made his escape. The boy had wished that the third one, too, might have got a bump, but this one had already gone.

'Now I think that they 've had enough for to-night,' said the boy.

'I think so too,' said the big ram. 'Now lie down on my back and creep into the wool! You deserve to have it warm and comfortable after all the wind and storm that you have been out in.'

Chapter Three

HELL'S HOLE

THE next day the big ram went around with the boy on his back and showed him the island. It consisted of a single massive mountain. It was like a large house with perpendicular walls and a flat roof. First the ram walked up on the mountain roof and showed the boy the good grazing lands there, and he had to admit that the island seemed to be especially created for sheep. There wasn't much else than sheep-sorrel and such little spicy growths as sheep are fond of that grew on the mountain.

But indeed there was something beside sheep fodder to look at for one who had got up to the heights. To begin with, the largest part of the sea—which now lay blue and sunlit, and rolled forward in glittering swells—was visible. Only upon two or three points did the foam spray up. To the east lay Gottland, with even and long-stretched coast; and to the south-west lay the island of Stora Karlsön, which was built on the same plan as the little island. When the ram walked to the very edge of the mountain roof, so the boy could look down the mountain walls, he noticed that they were simply filled with birds' nests; and in the blue sea beneath him lay surf-scoters and eider-ducks and kittiwakes and guillemots and razor-bills—so pretty and peaceful— busying themselves with fishing for small herring.

'This is really a favoured land,' said the boy. 'You live in a pretty place, you sheep.'

'Oh, yes! it 's pretty enough here,' said the big ram. It was as if he wished to add something; but he did not, only sighed. 'If you go about here alone you must look out for the crevices which run all around the mountain,' he continued after a little. And this was a good warning, for there were deep and broad crevices in several places. The largest of them was called Hell's Hole. That crevice was many fathoms deep and nearly one fathom wide. 'If any one fell down there, it would certainly be the last of him,' said the big ram. The boy thought it sounded as if he had a special meaning in what he said.

Then he conducted the boy down to the narrow strip of shore. Now he could see those giants which had frightened him the night before at close range. They were nothing but tall rock pillars. The big ram called them 'shore boulders.' The boy couldn't see enough of them. He thought that if there had ever been any trolls who had turned into stone they ought to look just like that.

Although it was pretty down on the shore the boy liked it still better on the mountain height. It was ghastly down here, for everywhere they came across dead sheep. It was here that the foxes had held their orgies. He saw skeletons whose flesh had been eaten, and bodies that were half eaten, and others which they had scarcely tasted but had allowed to lie untouched. It was heart-rending to see how the wild beasts had thrown themselves upon the sheep just for sport—just to hunt them and tear them to death.

The big ram did not pause in front of the dead but walked by them in silence. But the boy, meanwhile, could not help seeing all the horror.

Then the big ram went up on the mountain height again; but when he was there he stopped and said: 'I someone who is capable and wise could see all the misery which prevails here he surely would not be able to rest until these foxes had been punished.'

'The foxes must live, too,' said the boy.

'Yes,' said the big ram, 'those who do not tear in pieces more animals than they need for their sustenance, they may as well live. But these are wicked.'

'The peasants who own the island ought to come here and help you,' said the boy.

'They have rowed over a number of times,' replied the ram, 'but the foxes always hid themselves in the caves and crevices, so they could not get near them to shoot them.'

'You surely cannot mean, father, that a poor little creature like me should be able to get at them, when neither you nor the peasants have succeeded in getting the better of them.'

'He that is little and spry can put many things to rights,' said the big ram.

They talked no more about this and the boy went over and seated himself among the wild geese who fed on the highland. Although he had not cared to show his feelings before the ram he was very sad on the sheep's account, and he would have been glad to help them. 'I can at least talk with Akka and Morten gander about the matter,' he thought. 'Perhaps they can help me with a good suggestion.'

A little later the white gander took the boy on his back and went over the mountain plain in the direction of Hell's Hole.

He wandered, care-free, on the open mountain top— apparently unconscious of how large and white he was. He didn't seek protection behind bushes, or any other shelter, but went straight ahead. It was strange that he was not more careful, for it was apparent that he had fared badly in yesterday's storm. He limped on his right leg, and the left wing hung and dragged as if it might be broken.

He acted as if there were no danger, pecked at a grass blade here and another there, and did not look about him in any direction. Nils lay stretched out full length on his back, and looked up toward the blue sky. He was so accustomed to riding now that he could both stand and lie down on goose-back.

While the gander and the boy were so care-free, they did not observe, of course, that the three foxes had come up on the mountain plain.

And the foxes, who knew that it was wellnigh impossible to take the life of a goose on an open plain, thought at first that they wouldn't chase after the gander. But as they had nothing else to do they finally sneaked down on one of the long passes and tried to steal up to him. They went about it so cautiously that the gander couldn't see a shadow of them.

They were not far off when the gander made an attempt to raise himself into the air. He spread his wings but he did not succeed in lifting himself. When the foxes seemed to grasp the fact that he couldn't fly, they hurried forward with greater eagerness than before. They no longer concealed themselves in the cleft but came up on the high land. They covered themselves as well as they could behind tufts and hollows, and came nearer and nearer the gander—without his seeming to notice that he was being hunted. At last the foxes were so near that they could make the final leap. Simultaneously all three threw themselves with one long jump at the gander.

But still at the last moment he must have noticed
something, for he ran out of the way, so the foxes missed
him. This, at any rate, didn't matter very much, for the
gander only had a couple of yards start, and, into the
bargain, he limped. Anyway, the poor thing ran ahead
as fast as he could.

The boy sat upon the goose-back—backwards—and
shrieked and called to the foxes:

'You have eaten yourselves too fat on mutton, foxes.
You can't catch up with a goose even.'

He teased them so that they became crazed with rage
and thought only of rushing forward.

The white one ran straight to the big cleft. When he
was there he made one stroke with his wings and got
over. Just then the foxes were almost upon him.

The gander hurried on with the same haste as before,
even after he had got across Hell's Hole. But he had
hardly been running two yards before the boy patted him
on the neck and said: 'Now you can stop, gander.'

At that instant they heard a number of wild howls
behind them, and a scraping of claws and heavy falls.
But of the foxes they saw nothing more.

The next morning the lighthouse keeper on Great
Karl's Island found a bit of bark poked under the
entrance door, and on it had been cut, in slanting,
angular letters: 'The foxes on the little island have fallen
down into Hell's Hole. Take care of them!'

And this the lighthouse keeper did, too.

PART FOURTEEN

TWO CITIES

☆

Chapter One

THE CITY AT THE BOTTOM OF THE SEA

IT was a calm and clear night. The wild geese did not trouble themselves to seek shelter in any of the caves, but stood sleeping on the mountain top, and Nils had lain down in the short, dry grass beside the geese.

It was bright moonlight that night, so bright that it was difficult for the boy to go to sleep. He lay there and thought about just how long he had been away from home; and he worked out that it was three weeks since he had started on the trip. At the same time he remembered that this was Easter eve.

'It is to-night that all the witches come home from Blakulla,' thought he, and laughed to himself. For he was just a little afraid of the sea nymph and the elf, but he didn't believe in witches the least little bit.

If there had been any witches out that night he should have seen them, to be sure. It was so light in the heavens that not the tiniest black speck could move in the air without his seeing it.

While the boy lay there with his nose in the air and thought about this, his eye rested on something lovely. The moon's disk was whole and round, and rather high, and over it a big bird came flying. He did not fly past the moon, but he moved just as though he might have flown out from it. The bird looked black against the light background, and the wings extended from one rim of the disk to the other. He flew on, evenly, in the same direction, and the boy thought that he was painted on the moon's disk. His body was small, his neck long and slender, his legs hung down, long and thin. It couldn't be anything but a stork.

A couple of seconds later Herr Ermenrich, the stork, lit beside the boy. He bent down and poked him with his bill to awaken him.

Instantly the boy sat up. 'I'm not asleep, Herr Ermenrich,' he said. 'How does it happen that you are out in the middle of the night, and how is everything at Glimminge castle? Do you want to speak with mother Akka?'

'It's too light to sleep to-night,' answered Herr Ermenrich. 'Therefore I decided to go over to Karl's Island and hunt you up, friend Tummetott. I learned from a sea-gull that you were spending the night here. I have not as yet moved over to Glimminge castle, but am still living at Pommern.'

Nils was simply overjoyed to think that Herr Ermenrich had sought him out. They chatted about all sorts of things, like old friends. At last the stork asked the boy if he wouldn't like to go out riding for a while on this beautiful night.

Oh, yes! that the boy wanted to do, if the stork would manage it so that he got back to the wild geese before sunrise. This he promised, so off they went.

Again Herr Ermenrich flew straight toward the moon. They rose and rose; the sea sank deep down, but the flight went so light and easy that it seemed almost as if the boy lay still in the air.

When Herr Ermenrich began to descend the boy thought that the flight had lasted an unreasonably short time.

They landed on a desolate bit of seashore, which was covered with fine, even sand. All along the coast ran a row of flying-sand drifts, with lyme-grass on their tops. They were not very high but they prevented the boy from seeing anything inland.

Herr Ermenrich stood on a sand-hill, drew up one leg, and bent his head backwards so he could stick his bill under the wing.

'You can roam around on the shore for a while,' he said to Tummetott, 'while I rest myself. But don't go so far away you cannot find your way back to me again!'

To start with the boy intended to climb a sand-hill and see how the land behind it looked. But when he had walked a couple of paces he stubbed the toe of his wooden shoe against something hard. He stooped down and saw that a small copper coin lay on the sand. It was so worn with verdigris that it was almost transparent. It was so poor that he didn't even bother to pick it up, but only kicked it out of the way.

But when he straightened himself up once more he was perfectly astounded, for two paces away from him stood a high, dark wall with a big, turreted gate.

The moment before, when the boy bent down, the sea lay there, shimmering and smooth, while now it was hidden by a long wall with towers and battlements. Directly in front of him, where before there had been only a few seaweed banks, the big gate of the wall opened.

The boy understood well enough that it was a ghostly

play of some sort; but this was nothing to be afraid of, he thought. It wasn't any dangerous troll, or any other evil—such as he always dreaded to encounter at night. Both the wall and the gate were so beautifully constructed that he only desired to see what there might be at the back of them. 'I must find out what this can be,' thought he, and went in through the gate.

In the deep archway there were guards, dressed in brocaded and puffed suits, with long-handled spears beside them, who sat and threw dice. They thought only of the game and took no notice of the boy who hurried past them.

Just within the gate he found an open space paved with large, even flagstones. All around this were high and magnificent buildings; and between these opened long, narrow streets. On the square—facing the gate— it fairly swarmed with people. The men wore long, fur-trimmed capes over satin suits; plume-bedecked hats sat obliquely on their heads; on their chests hung superb chains. They were all so regally dressed that the whole lot of them might have been kings.

The women went about in high head-dresses and long robes with tight-fitting sleeves. They, too, were beautifully dressed, but their splendour was not to be compared with that of the men.

This was exactly like the old story-book which mother occasionally took from the chest and showed to him. Nils simply couldn't believe his eyes.

But that which was even more wonderful to look upon than either the men or the women was the city itself. Every house was built in such a way that a gable faced the street. And the gables were so highly ornamented that one could believe they wished to compete with each other as to which one could show the most beautiful decorations.

When you suddenly see so much that is new, you cannot manage to treasure it all in your memory. But at least the boy could recall that he had seen stepped gables which on the various landings bore statues of Christ and His Apostles: gables where there were images in niche after niche all along the wall, gables that were inlaid with multicoloured bits of glass, and gables that were striped and checked with white and black marble. As the boy admired all this a sudden sense of haste came over him.

'Anything like this my eyes have never seen before. Anything like this they will never see again,' he said to himself. And he began to run in toward the city—up one street and down another.

The streets were straight and narrow, but not empty and gloomy, as they were in the cities with which he was familiar. There were people everywhere. Old women sat by their open doors and spun without a spinning-wheel—only with the help of a shuttle. The merchants' shops were like market-stalls—opening on to the street. All the craftsmen did their work out of doors. In one place they were boiling crude oil; in another tanning hides; in a third there was a long rope-walk.

If only Nils had had time enough he could have learned how to make all sorts of things. Here he saw how armourers hammered out thin breastplates; how turners tended their irons; how the shoemakers soled soft, red shoes; how the gold-wire drawers twisted gold thread, and how the weavers inserted silver and gold into their weaving.

But the boy did not have the time to stay. He just

rushed on, so that he could manage to see as much as possible before it would all vanish again.

The high wall ran all round the city and shut it in, as a hedge shuts in a field. He saw it at the end of every street ornamented with towers and battlements. On the top of the wall walked warriors in shining armour.

When he had run from one end of the city to the other he came to yet another gate in the wall. Outside this

lay the sea and harbour. The boy saw olden-time ships, with rowing-benches straight across and high structures fore and aft. Some were taking on cargo, others were just casting anchor. Carriers and merchants hurried about. All over it was life and bustle.

But not even here did he seem to have the time to linger. He rushed into the city again, and now he came up to the market-place. There stood the cathedral with its three high towers and deep vaulted arches filled with statues. The walls had been so highly decorated by sculptors that there was not a stone without its own special ornamentation. And what a magnificent display of gilded crosses and gold-trimmed altars and priests in golden vestments, shimmered through the open gate! Directly opposite the church there was a house with a notched roof and a single, slender, sky-high tower. That

was probably the courthouse. And between the courthouse and the cathedral, all around the square, stood
the beautiful gabled houses with their multiplicity of
adornments.

Nils had run himself both warm and tired. He
thought that now he had seen the most remarkable
things, and therefore he began to walk more leisurely.
The street which he had turned into now was surely the
one where the inhabitants purchased their fine clothing.
He saw crowds of people standing before the little stalls
where the merchants spread brocades, stiff satins, heavy
gold cloth, shimmery velvet, delicate veiling, and laces
as sheer as a spider's web.

Before, when the boy ran so fast, no one had paid any
attention to him. The people must have thought that
it was only a little grey rat that darted by them. But
now, when he walked down the street, very slowly, one
of the salesmen caught sight of him and began to beckon
to him.

At first Nils was uneasy and wanted to hurry out
of the way, but the salesman only beckoned and smiled,
and spread out on the counter a lovely piece of satin
damask as if he wanted to tempt him.

The boy shook his head. 'I will never be so rich that
I can buy even a yard of that cloth,' thought he.

But now they had caught sight of him in every stall,
all along the street. Wherever he looked salesmen
stood and beckoned to him. They left their rich
customers and thought only of him. He saw how they
hurried into the most hidden corner of the stall to fetch
the best that they had to sell, and how their hands
trembled with eagerness and haste as they laid it upon
the counter.

When the boy continued to go on one of the merchants jumped over the counter, caught hold of him, and spread before him silver cloth and woven tapestries which shone with brilliant colours.

Nils couldn't do anything but laugh at him. The salesman certainly must understand that a poor little

creature like him couldn't buy such things. He stood still and held out his two empty hands, so they would understand that he had nothing and let him go in peace.

But the merchant raised a finger and nodded and pushed the whole pile of beautiful things over to him.

'Can he mean that he will sell all this for a gold piece?' wondered the boy.

The merchant brought out a tiny worn and poor coin —the smallest that one could see—and showed it to him. And he was so eager to sell that he increased his pile with a pair of large, heavy, silver goblets.

Then the boy began to dig down in his pockets. He knew, of course, that he didn't possess a single coin, but he couldn't help feeling for it.

All the other merchants stood still and tried to see how the sale would come off, and when they observed that the boy began to search in his pockets, they flung themselves over the counters, filled their hands full of gold and silver ornaments, and offered them to him. And they all showed him that what they asked in payment was just one little penny.

But the boy turned both vest and breeches pockets inside out, so they should see that he owned nothing. Then tears filled the eyes of all these regal merchants, who were so much richer than he. At last he was moved because they looked so distressed, and he pondered if he could not in some way help them. And then he happened to think of the rusty coin which he had but lately seen on the strand.

He started to run down the street, and luck was with him so that he came to the self-same gate which he had happened upon first. He dashed through it, and commenced to search for the little green copper penny which lay on the strand a while ago.

He found it too, very promptly; but when he had picked it up, and wanted to run back to the city with it, he saw only the sea before him. No city wall, no gate, no sentinels, no streets, no houses could now be seen—only the sea.

The boy couldn't help that the tears came to his eyes. He had believed in the beginning that that which he saw was nothing but an hallucination, but this he had already forgotten. He only thought about how pretty everything was. He felt a genuine, deep sorrow because the city had vanished.

That moment Herr Ermenrich awoke and came up to him. But he didn't hear him, and the stork had to poke the boy with his bill to attract attention to himself.

'I believe that you stand here and sleep just as I do,' said Herr Ermenrich.

'Oh, Herr Ermenrich!' said the boy. 'What was that city which stood here just now?'

'Have you seen a city?' said the stork. 'You have slept and dreamt, as I say.'

'No! I have not dreamt,' said Tummetott, and he told the stork all that he had experienced.

Then Herr Ermenrich said : 'For my part, Tummetott, I believe that you fell asleep here on the strand and dreamed all this. But I will not conceal from you that Bataki, the raven, who is the most learned of all birds, once told me that in former times there was a city on this shore called Vineta. It was so rich and so fortunate that no city has ever been more glorious; but its inhabitants, unluckily, gave themselves up to arrogance and love of display. As a punishment for this, says Bataki, the city of Vineta was overtaken by a flood and sank into the sea. But its inhabitants cannot die, neither is their city destroyed. And one night in every hundred years it rises in all its splendour up from the sea and remains on the surface just one hour.'

'Yes, it must be so,' said Tummetott, 'for this I have seen.'

'But when the hour is up, it sinks again into the sea, if, during that time, no merchant in Vineta has sold anything to a single living creature. If you, Tummetott, only had had an ever so tiny coin to pay the merchants, Vineta might have remained up here on the shore; and its people could have lived and died like other human beings.'

'Herr Ermenrich,' said the boy, 'now I understand why you came and fetched me in the middle of the night. It was because you believed that I should be able to save the old city. I am so sorry it didn't turn out as you wished, Herr Ermenrich.'

He covered his face with his hands and wept. It wasn't easy to say which one looked the more disconsolate —the boy or Herr Ermenrich.

Chapter Two

THE LIVING CITY

On the afternoon of Easter Monday the wild geese and Tummetott were on the wing. They travelled over Gottland.

The large island lay smooth and even beneath them. The ground was checked just as it was in Skåne and there were many churches and farms. But there was this difference, however, that there were more leafy meadows between the fields here, and the farms were not built round a courtyard. And there were no large manors with ancient tower-ornamented castles and large parks.

The wild geese had taken the route over Gottland on account of Tummetott. He had been altogether unlike himself for two days and hadn't spoken a cheerful word. This was because he had thought of nothing but that city which had appeared to him in such a strange way. He had never seen anything so magnificent and royal, and he could not be reconciled with himself for having failed to save it. Usually he was not chicken-hearted, but now he actually grieved for the beautiful buildings and the stately people.

Both Akka and the gander tried to convince Tummetott that he had been the victim of a dream or an hallucination, but the boy wouldn't listen to anything of that sort. He was so positive that he had really seen what he had seen that no one could move him from this conviction. He went about so disconsolate that his travelling companions became worried about him.

Just when the boy was most depressed old Kaksi came
back to the flock.   She had been blown toward Gottland,
and had been compelled to travel over the whole island
before she had learned through some crows that her
comrades were on Little Karl's Island.   When Kaksi
found out what was wrong with Tummetott she said
impulsively:

'If Tummetott is grieving over an old city, we'll soon
be able to comfort him.   Just come along and I'll take
you to a place that I saw yesterday!   You will not need
to be distressed very long.'

Thereupon the geese had taken farewell of the sheep,
and were on their way to the place which Kaksi wished
to show Tummetott.   Depressed as he was, he couldn't
keep from looking at the land over which he travelled,
as usual.

He thought it looked as though the whole island had
in the beginning been just such a high, steep cliff as
Little Karl's Island—though much bigger of course.
But afterwards it had in some way been flattened out.
Someone had taken a big rolling-pin and rolled over it,
as if it had been a lump of dough.   Not that the island
had become altogether flat and even, like a bread-cake,
for it wasn't like that.   While they had travelled along
the coast he had seen white lime walls with caves and
crags in several directions; but in most of the places they
were levelled and sank inconspicuously down toward the
sea.

In Gottland they had a pleasant and peaceful holiday
afternoon.   It turned out to be mild spring weather;
the trees had large buds; spring blossoms patterned the
ground in the leafy meadows; the poplars' long, thin
pendants swayed; and in the little gardens, which one

finds around every cottage, the gooseberry bushes were green.

The warmth and the spring-budding had tempted the people out into the gardens and roads, and wherever a number of them were gathered together they were playing. It was not the children alone who played but the grown-ups also. They were throwing stones at a given point, and they threw balls in the air so high that they almost touched the wild geese. It looked cheerful and pleasant to see big folks at play; and Nils certainly would have enjoyed it if he had been able to forget his grief because he had failed to save the city.

Anyway, he had to admit that this was a lovely trip. There was so much singing and sound in the air. Little children played round dances and sang as they played. The Salvation Army was out. He saw a lot of people dressed in black and red—sitting upon a wooded hill, playing on guitars and brass instruments. On one road came a great crowd of people. They were Good Templars who had been on a pleasure trip. He recognised them by the big banners with the gold inscriptions which waved above them. They sang song after song as long as he could hear them.

After that the boy could never think of Gottland without thinking of the games and songs at the same time.

He had been sitting and looking down for a long while; but now he happened to raise his eyes. No one can describe his amazement. Before he was aware of it the wild geese had left the interior of the island and gone westward—toward the sea coast. Now the wide, blue sea lay before him. However, it was not the sea that was remarkable but a city which appeared on the seashore.

Nils came from the east, and the sun had just begun
to go down in the west. When he came nearer the city
its walls and towers and high, gabled houses and churches
stood there, perfectly black, against the light evening sky.
He couldn't see therefore what it really looked like, and
for a couple of moments he believed that this city was
just as beautiful as the one he had seen on Easter night.

When he got right up to it he saw that it was both like
and unlike that city from the bottom of the sea. There
was the same contrast between them, as there is between
a man whom one sees arrayed in purple and jewels one
day, and on another day dressed in rags.

Yes, this city had probably, once upon a time, been
like the one which he sat and thought about. This one,
also, was enclosed by a wall with towers and gates. But
the towers in this city, which had been allowed to remain
on land, were roofless, hollow, and empty. The gates
were without doors; sentinels and warriors had disappeared. All the glittering splendour was gone.
There was nothing left but the naked, grey stone skeleton.

When Nils came farther into the city he saw that
the larger part of it was made up of small, low houses;
but here and there were still a few high, gabled houses
and a few churches, which were from the olden time.
The walls of the gabled houses were whitewashed and
entirely without ornamentation; but because the boy had
so lately seen the buried city he seemed to understand
how they had been decorated: some with statues, and
others with black and white marble. And it was the
same with the old churches; the majority of them were
roofless with bare interiors. The window openings were
empty, the floors were grass-grown, and ivy clambered
along the walls. But now he knew how they had looked

at one time : that they had been covered with statues and paintings, that the chancel had had decorated altars and gilded crosses, and that priests had moved about arrayed in gold vestments.

The boy saw also the narrow streets, which were

almost deserted on holiday afternoons. He knew, however, what a stream of stately people had once upon a time sauntered about on them. He knew that they had been like large workshops filled with all sorts of workmen.

But that which Nils Holgersson did not see was that the city, even to-day, was beautiful and remarkable. He saw neither the cheery cottages in the side streets, with their black walls and white corners and red pelargoniums behind the shining window-panes, nor the many pretty gardens and avenues, nor the beauty in the weed-clad ruins. His eyes were so filled with glory of the past that he could not see anything good in the present.

The wild geese flew back and forth over the city a couple of times so that Tummetott might see everything. Finally they sank down on the grass-grown floor of a church ruin to spend the night.

While they were arranging themselves for sleep, Tummetott was still awake and looked up through the open arches to the pale pink evening sky. When he had been sitting there a while, he found he didn't want to grieve any more because he couldn't save the buried city.

No, that he didn't want to do, now that he had seen this one. If that city, which he had seen, had not sunk into the sea again, then it would perhaps become as dilapidated as this one in a little while. Perhaps it could not have withstood time and decay, but would have stood there with roofless churches and bare houses and desolate, empty streets—just like this one. It was better that it should remain in all its glory down in the deep.

'It was best that it happened as it happened,' thought he. 'If I had the power to save the city, I don't believe that I should care to do it.' Then he no longer grieved over that matter.

And there are probably many among the young who think in the same way. But when people are old, and have become accustomed to being satisfied with little, then they are more happy over the Visby that exists, than over a magnificent Vineta at the bottom of the sea.

PART FIFTEEN

THE LEGEND OF SMÅLAND

THE wild geese had made a good trip over the sea and had alighted in Tjust Township, in northern Småland. That township didn't seem able to make up its mind whether it wanted to be land or sea. Fiords ran in everywhere, and cut the land up into islands and peninsulas and points and capes. The sea was so intensive that the only things which could hold themselves above it were hills and mountains. All the lowlands were hidden away under the water.

It was evening when the wild geese came in from the sea; and the land with the little hills lay prettily between the shimmering fiords. Here and there, on the islands, the boy saw cabins and cottages; and the farther inland he came the bigger and better became the dwelling-houses. Finally, they grew into large, white manors. Along the shores there was generally a border of trees; and within this lay field-plots, and on the tops of the little hills there were trees again. He could not help thinking of Blekinge. Here again was a place where land and sea met, in such a pretty and peaceful sort of way, just as if they tried to show each other the best and loveliest which they possessed.

The wild geese alighted upon a bare island a good way in on Goose-fiord. With the first glance at the shore they observed that spring had made rapid strides while they had been away on the islands. The big, fine trees were not as yet leaf-clad, but the ground under them

203

was carpeted with white anemones, yellow star of Beth-
lehem, and blue anemones.

When the wild geese saw the flower carpet they feared
that they had lingered too long in the southern part of
the country. Akka said instantly that there was no time
to hunt up any of the stopping places in Småland. By
the next morning they must travel northward, over
Östergötland.

Nils would then see nothing of Småland and this
grieved him. He had heard more about Småland than
he had about any other province and he had longed to
see it with his own eyes.

The summer before, when he had served as goose-boy
with a farmer in the neighbourhood of Jordberga, he had
met a pair of Småland children almost every day, who
also tended geese. These children had irritated him
terribly with their Småland.

It wasn't fair to say that Osa, the goose-girl, had
annoyed him. She was much too wise for that. But the
one who could be really tiresome was her brother, little
Mats.

'Have you heard, Nils Goose-boy, how it went when
Småland and Skåne were created?' he would ask, and
if Nils Holgersson said no, he began immediately to relate
the old folk legend.

'Well, it was at that time when God was creating the
world. While He was in the midst of His work Saint
Peter came walking by. He stopped and looked on, and
then he asked if it was hard to do. "Well, it isn't
exactly easy," said God. Saint Peter stood there a little
longer, and when he noticed how easy it was to lay out
one landscape after another, he too wanted to try his
hand at it. "Perhaps you need to rest yourself a little,"

said Saint Peter. "I could attend to the work in the meantime for you." But this God did not wish. "I do not know if you are so much at home in this art that I can trust you to take hold where I leave off," He answered. Then Saint Peter was angry and said that he believed he could create just as fine countries as God himself.

'It happened that God was just then creating Småland. It wasn't even half ready, but it looked as though it would be an indescribably pretty and fertile land. It was difficult for God to say no to Saint Peter, and, apart from this, He thought very likely that a thing so well begun no one could spoil. Therefore He said : "If you like, we will prove which one of us two understands this sort of work the better. You, who are only a novice, shall go on with this which I have begun, and I will create a new land." To this Saint Peter agreed at once; and so they went to work—each one in his place.

'God moved southward a bit, and there He undertook to create Skåne. It wasn't long before He finished it, and soon He asked if Saint Peter had finished, and would come and look at His work. "I had mine ready long ago," said Saint Peter; and from the sound of his voice it could be heard how pleased he was with what he had accomplished.

'When Saint Peter saw Skåne he had to acknowledge that there was nothing but good to be said of that land. It was a fertile land and easy to cultivate, with wide plains wherever one looked, and hardly a sign of hills. It was evident that God had really tried to make it such that people should feel at home there. "Yes, this is a good country," said Saint Peter, "but I think that mine is better." "Then we 'll take a look at it," said God.

'The land was already finished in the north and east when Saint Peter began the work, but the southern and western parts, and the whole interior, he had created all by himself. Now when God came up there, where Saint

Peter had been at work, He was so horrified that He stopped short and exclaimed: "What on earth have you been doing with this land, Saint Peter?"

'Saint Peter, too, stood and looked around perfectly astonished. He had had the idea that nothing could be so good for a land as a great deal of warmth. Therefore he had gathered together an enormous mass of stones and mountains, and erected a highland, and this he had done so that it should be near the sun, and receive much help from the sun's heat. Over the stone heaps he had spread a thin layer of soil, and then he had thought that everything was well arranged.

'But while he was down in Skåne a couple of heavy showers had come up, and more was not needed to show what his work amounted to. When God came to inspect the land, all the soil had been washed away, and the bare mountain foundation showed through. Where it was about the best lay clay and heavy gravel over the rocks, but it looked so poor that it was easy to understand that hardly anything except spruce and juniper and moss and heather could grow there. But one thing was plentiful, and that was water. It had filled up all the clefts in the mountain; and lakes and rivers and brooks, these one saw everywhere, to say nothing of swamps and morasses which spread over large tracts. And the most exasperating thing of all was that while some districts had too much water, it was so scarce in others that whole fields lay like dry moors, where sand and earth whirled up in clouds with the least little breeze.

'"What can have been your meaning in creating such a land as this?" said God. Saint Peter made excuses and declared he had wanted to build up a land so high that it should have plenty of warmth from the sun. "But then you will also get much of the night chill," said God, "for that too comes from heaven. I am very much afraid the little that can grow here will freeze."

'This, to be sure, Saint Peter hadn't thought about.

'"Yes, this will be a poor and frostbound land," said God. "It can't be helped."'

When little Mats had got this far in his story, Osa, the goose-girl, protested:

'I cannot bear, little Mats, to hear you say that it is so miserable in Småland,' said she. 'You forget entirely how much good soil there is. Only think of Möre district, by Kalmar Sound! I wonder where you'll find richer corn crops. There are fields upon fields, just like here in Skåne. The soil is so good that I cannot imagine anything that couldn't grow there.'

'I can't help that,' said little Mats. 'I'm only relating what others have said before.'

'And I have heard many say that there is not a more beautiful coast land than Tjust. Think of the bays and islets, and the manors and the groves!' said Osa.

'Yes, that's true enough,' little Mats admitted.

'And don't you remember,' continued Osa, 'the school teacher said that such a lovely and picturesque district as that bit of Småland which lies south of Lake Vettern is not to be found in all Sweden? Think of the beautiful lake and the yellow mountains, and of Gränna and Jönköping, with its match factory, and think of Husk-varna, and all the big factories there!'

'Yes, that's true enough,' said little Mats once again.

'And think of Visingsö, little Mats, with the ruins and the oak forests and the legends! Think of the valley through which Emån flows, with all the villages and flour-mills and saw-mills, and the carpenter shops!'

'Yes, that is true enough,' said little Mats, and looked troubled.

All of a sudden he had looked up. 'Now we are pretty stupid,' said he. 'All this, of course, lies in God's Småland, in that part of the land which was already finished when Saint Peter undertook the job. It's only natural that it should be pretty and fine there. But in Saint Peter's Småland it looks as it says in the legend. And it wasn't surprising that God was distressed when He saw it,' continued little Mats, as he took up the thread of his story again. 'Saint Peter didn't lose his courage, at all events, but tried to comfort God. "Don't be so grieved over this!" said he. "Only wait until I have created people who can till the swamps and break up fields from the stone hills."

'That was the end of God's patience and He said: "No! you can go down to Skåne, which I have made into a good and easily cultivated country, and make the Skåninge, but the Smålander I will create myself." And so God created the Smålander, and made him quick-witted and contented and happy and thrifty and

enterprising and capable, that he might be able to
get his livelihood in his poor country.'

Then little Mats was silent; and if Nils Holgersson had
also kept still, all would have gone well; but he couldn't
possibly refrain from asking how Saint Peter had
succeeded in creating the Skåninge.

'Well, what do you think yourself?' said little Mats,
and looked so scornful that Nils Holgersson threw himself upon him, to hit him. But Mats was only a little
thing, and Osa, the goose-girl, who was a year older than
he, ran forward instantly to help him. Good-natured
though she was, she sprang like a lion as soon as any one
touched her brother. And Nils Holgersson did not care
to fight a girl, but turned his back and didn't look at
those Småland children for the rest of the day.

PART SIXTEEN

THE CROWS

☆

Chapter One

THE EARTHEN CROCK

In the south-west corner of Småland lies a township called Sunnerbo. It is a rather smooth and even country. And one who sees it in winter, when it is covered with snow, cannot imagine that there is anything under the snow but fallow land, rye-fields, and clover meadows as is generally the case in flat countries. But in the beginning of April, when the snow finally melts away in Sunnerbo, it is apparent that that which lies hidden under it is only dry, sandy heaths, bare rocks, and big, marshy swamps. There are fields here and there, to be sure, but they are so small that they are scarcely worth mentioning; and one also finds a few little red or grey farmhouses hidden away in some birch wood—almost as if they were afraid to show themselves.

Where Sunnerbo township touches the boundaries of Halland, there is a sandy heath which is so far-reaching that he who stands upon one edge of it cannot look across to the other. Nothing except heather grows on the heath, and it wouldn't be easy either to make other plants thrive there. To start with, one would have to uproot the heather; for it is thus with heather: although it has only a little shrunken root, small shrunken branches, and dry, shrunken leaves, it fancies that it is

a tree. Therefore it acts just like real trees—spreads
itself out in forest fashion over wide areas, holds together
faithfully, and causes all foreign growths that wish to
crowd in upon its territory to die out.

The only place on the heath where the heather is not
all powerful is a low, stony ridge which passes over it.
There you'll find juniper bushes, mountain ash, and a
few large, fine birches. At the time when Nils Holgersson travelled round with the wild geese a little cabin
stood there, with a bit of cleared ground around it. But
the people who had lived there at one time had, for some
reason or other, moved away. The little cabin was
empty and the ground lay unused.

When the tenants left the cabin they closed the oven,
fastened the window-hooks, and locked the door. But
no one had thought of the broken window-pane which
was only stuffed with a rag. After the showers of a
couple of summers the rag had mouldered and shrunk,
and finally a crow had succeeded in poking it out.

The ridge of the heather heath was really not as
desolate as one might think, for it was inhabited by
many crow-folk. Naturally the crows did not live there
all the year round. They moved to foreign lands in the
winter; in the autumn they travelled from one grain-field
to another all over Götaland and picked grain; during the
summer they spread themselves over the farms in
Sunnerbo township, and lived upon eggs and berries and
birdlings; but every spring, when nesting time came,
they came back to the heather.

The one who had poked the rag from the window was
a crow-cock named Garm Whitefeather; but he was
never called anything but Fumle or Drumle, or out and
out Fumle-Drumle, because he always acted awkwardly

and stupidly, and wasn't good for anything except to make fun of. Fumle-Drumle was bigger and stronger than any of the other crows, but that didn't help him in the least; he was—and remained—a common laughing stock. And it didn't profit him, either, that he came from very good family. If everything had gone smoothly he should have been leader for the whole flock, because this honour had, from time immemorial, belonged to the oldest Whitefeather. But long before Fumle-Drumle was born the power had gone from his family, and was now wielded by a cruel wild crow named Wind-Rush.

This transference of power was due to the fact that the crows on Crow Ridge desired to change their manner of living. Possibly there are many who think that everything in the shape of crow lives in the same way; but this is not so. There are entire crow-folk who lead honourable lives—that is to say, they only eat grain, worms, caterpillars, and dead animals; and there are others who lead a regular bandit's life, who throw themselves upon baby hares and small birds, and plunder every single bird's nest they set eyes on.

The ancient Whitefeathers had been strict and temperate; and as long as they had led the flock the crows had been compelled to conduct themselves in such a way that other birds could speak no ill of them. But the crows were numerous, and poverty was great among them. In the end they could not stand that strictly moral life, so they rebelled against the Whitefeathers and gave the power to Wind-Rush, who was the worst nest-plunderer and robber that could be imagined—if his wife, Wind-Air, wasn't worse still. Under their government the crows had begun to lead such a life that now they were more feared than pigeon-hawks and eagle-owls.

Naturally Fumle-Drumle had nothing to say in the flock. The crows were all of the opinion that he did not in the least take after his forefathers, and that he would be no good as a leader. No one would have mentioned him if he hadn't constantly committed fresh blunders.

A few, who were quite sensible, sometimes said that perhaps it was lucky for Fumle-Drumle that he was such a gawky fellow, otherwise Wind-Rush and Wind-Air would hardly have allowed him—who was of the old chieftain stock—to remain with the flock.

Now, on the other hand, they were rather friendly toward him, and willingly took him along with them on their hunting expeditions. There all could observe how much more skilful and daring they were than he.

None of the crows knew that it was Fumle-Drumle who had pecked the rag out of the window, and had they known of this they would have been very much astonished. A thing as daring as to approach a human being's dwelling they had never believed of him. He kept the thing to himself very carefully, and he had his own good reasons for it. Wind-Rush and Wind-Air always treated him well in the daytime, and when the others were around; but one very dark night, when the comrades sat on the night branch, he was attacked by a couple of crows and nearly murdered. After that he moved every night after dark from his usual sleeping quarters into the empty cabin.

Now one afternoon when the crows had put their nests in order on Crow Ridge they happened upon a remarkable find. Wind-Rush, Fumle-Drumle, and a couple of others had flown down into a big hollow in one corner of the heath. The hollow was nothing but a gravel-pit, but the crows could not be satisfied with such a simple explanation; they flew down in it continually, and turned every single sand grain to try and discover why human beings had dug it. While the crows were pottering around down there, a mass of gravel fell from one side. They rushed up to it, and had the good fortune to find amongst the fallen stones and stubble a large earthen crock, which was locked with a wooden clasp! Naturally they wanted to know if there was anything in it, and they tried both to peck holes in the crock and to bend up the clasp, but they had no success.

They stood there helpless and examined the crock, then they heard someone say:

'Shall I come down and assist you crows?'

They glanced up quickly. On the edge of the hollow sat a fox looking down on them. He was one of the prettiest foxes, both in colour and form, that they had ever seen. The only fault with him was that he had lost an ear.

'If you desire to do us a service,' said Wind-Rush, 'we shall not say nay.'

At the same time both he and the others flew up from the hollow. Then the fox jumped down in their place, bit at the jar, and pulled at the lock—but he couldn't open it either.

'Can you make out what there is in it?' said Wind-Rush.

The fox rolled the jar back and forth and listened attentively.

'It must be silver money,' said he.

This was more than the crows had expected.

'Do you think it can be silver?' they said, and their eyes were ready to pop out of their heads with greed; for remarkable as it may sound there is nothing in the world which crows love as much as silver money.

'Hear how it rattles!' said the fox and rolled the crock around once more. 'Only I can't understand how we shall get at it.'

'That will surely be impossible,' said the crows.

The fox stood and rubbed his head against his left leg, and pondered. Now perhaps he might succeed, with the help of the crows, in becoming master of that little imp who always eluded him.

'Oh! I know someone who could open the crock for you,' said the fox.

'Then tell us! Tell us!' cried the crows; and they were so excited that they tumbled down into the pit.

'That I will do, if you'll first promise me that you will agree to my terms,' said he.

Then the fox told the crows about Tummetott, and said that if they could bring him to the heath he would open the crock for them.. But in payment for this

counsel he demanded that they should deliver Tummetott to him, as soon as he had got the silver money for
them. The crows had no reason to spare Tummetott, so
agreed to the bargain at once. It was easy enough to
agree to this, but it was harder to find out where
Tummetott and the wild geese were stopping.

Wind-Rush himself travelled away with fifty crows,
and said that he should soon return. But one day after
another passed without the crows on Crow Ridge seeing
a shadow of him.

Chapter Two

KIDNAPPED BY CROWS

THE wild geese were up at daybreak, so that they should have time to get themselves a bite of food before starting out on the journey toward Östergötland. The island in Goose-fiord, where they had slept, was small and barren, but in the water all around it were plants of which they could eat their fill. It was worse for the boy, however. He couldn't manage to find anything eatable.

As he stood there hungry and drowsy, and looked around in all directions, his glance fell upon a pair of squirrels, who played upon a wooded point, directly opposite the rock island. He wondered if the squirrels still had any of their winter supplies left, and asked the white gander to take him over to the point that he might ask them for a couple of hazel-nuts.

Instantly the white one swam across the sound with him; but as bad luck would have it the squirrels had so much fun chasing each other from tree to tree that they didn't bother about listening to the boy. They drew farther into the grove. He hurried after them and was soon out of the gander's sight, who stayed behind and waited on the shore.

Nils waded forward between some white anemone stems—which were so high they reached to his chin—when he felt that someone caught hold of him from behind and tried to lift him up. He turned round and saw that a crow had grabbed him by the shirt-band. He tried to break loose, but before this was possible another crow ran up, gripped him by the stocking, and knocked him over.

If Nils Holgersson had immediately cried for help the white gander certainly would have been able to save him; but the boy probably thought that he could protect himself, unaided, against a couple of crows. He kicked and struck out but the crows didn't let go their hold, and they soon succeeded in raising themselves into the air with him. To make matters worse they flew so recklessly that his head struck against a branch. He received a hard knock over the head, it grew black before his eyes, and he lost consciousness.

When he opened his eyes once more he found himself high above the ground. He regained his senses slowly; at first he knew neither where he was, nor what he saw. When he glanced down he saw that under him was spread a tremendously big woolly carpet, which was woven in greens and reds, and in large irregular patterns. The carpet was very thick and fine, but he thought it was a pity that it had been so badly used. It was actually ragged; long tears ran through it; in some places large pieces were torn away. And the strangest of all was that it appeared to be spread over a mirror floor; for under the holes and tears in the carpet shone bright and glittering glass.

The next thing the boy observed was that the sun came rolling up in the heavens. Instantly the mirror-glass under the holes and tears in the carpet began to shimmer in red and gold. It looked very gorgeous, and the boy was delighted with the pretty colour scheme, although he didn't exactly understand what it was that he saw. But now the crows descended and he saw at once that the big carpet under him was the earth, which

was dressed in green cone-trees and naked brown leaf-
trees, and that the holes and tears were shining fiords
and little lakes.

He remembered that the first time he had travelled
up in the air, he had thought that the earth in Skåne
looked like a piece of checked cloth. But this country
which resembled a torn carpet—what might this be?

He began to ask himself a lot of questions. Why
wasn't he sitting on the gander's back? Why did a
great swarm of crows fly around him? And why was he
being pulled and knocked hither and thither so that he
was about to break in pieces?

Then, all at once, the whole thing dawned on him.
He had been kidnapped by a couple of crows. The
white gander was still on the shore, waiting, and to-day
the wild geese were going to travel to Östergötland. He
was being carried south-west; this he understood because
the sun's disk was behind him. The big forest carpet
which lay beneath him was surely Småland.

'What will become of the gander now, when I cannot
look after him?' thought the boy, and began to call to the
crows to take him back to the wild geese instantly. He
wasn't at all uneasy on his own account. He believed
that they were carrying him off simply in a spirit of
mischief.

The crows didn't pay the slightest attention to his
exhortations, but flew on as fast as they could. After a
bit one of them flapped his wings in a manner which
meant: 'Look out! Danger!' Soon thereafter they
came down in a spruce forest, pushed their way between
prickly branches to the ground, and put the boy down
under a thick spruce, where he was so well concealed
that not even a falcon could have sighted him.

Fifty crows surrounded him, with bills pointed toward him to guard him.

'Now perhaps I may hear, crows, what your purpose is in carrying me off,' said he.

But he was hardly permitted to finish the sentence before a big crow hissed at him:

'Keep still! or I 'll bore your eyes out.'

It was evident that the crow meant what he said, and there was nothing for the boy to do but obey. So he sat there and stared at the crows, and the crows stared at him.

The longer he looked at them the less he liked them. It was dreadful how dusty and unkempt their feather dresses were—as though they knew neither baths nor oiling. Their toes and claws were grimy with dried-in mud, and the corners of their beaks were covered with food drippings. These were very different birds from the wild geese—that he observed. He thought they had a cruel, sneaky, watchful, and bold appearance, just like cut-throats and vagabonds.

'It is certainly a real robber band that I 've fallen in with,' thought he.

Just then he heard the wild geese's call above him.

'Where are you? Here am I. Where are you? Here am I.'

He understood that Akka and the others had gone out to search for him; but before he could answer them the big crow, who appeared to be the leader of the band, hissed in his ear: 'Think of your eyes!' And there was nothing else for him to do but to keep still.

The wild geese may not have known that he was so near them, but had just happened, incidentally, to travel over this forest. He heard their call a couple of times more, then it died away.

'Well, now you 'll have to get along by yourself, Nils Holgersson,' he said to himself. 'Now you must prove whether you have learned anything during these weeks in the open.'

A moment later the crows gave the signal to break up; and since it was still their intention, apparently, to carry him along in such a way that one held on to his shirt-band and one to a stocking, the boy said:

'Is there not one among you so strong that he can carry me on his back? You have already travelled so badly with me that I feel as if I were in pieces. Only let me ride! I 'll not jump from the crow's back, that I promise you.'

'Oh, you needn't think that we care how you have it,' said the leader.

But now the largest of the crows—a dishevelled and uncouth one, who had a white feather in his wing—came forward and said:

'It would certainly be best for all of us, Wind-Rush, if Tummetott got there whole, rather than half, and there-fore I shall carry him on my back.'

'If you can do it, Fumle-Drumle, I have no objection,' said Wind-Rush. 'But don't lose him!'

With this much was already gained, and the boy actually felt pleased again.

'There is no point in losing my spirits because I have been kidnapped by the crows,' thought he. 'I 'll surely be able to manage those poor little things.'

The crows continued to fly south-west, over Småland. It was a glorious morning, sunny and calm, and the birds down on the earth were singing their best love-songs. In a high, dark forest sat the thrush himself with drooping wings and swelling throat, and struck up tune after tune.

'How pretty you are! How pretty you are! How pretty you are!' sang he. 'No one is so pretty. No one

is so pretty. No one is so pretty.' As soon as he had finished this song he began it all over again.

But just then Nils rode over the forest, and when he had heard the song a couple of times, and noticed that the thrush knew no other, he put both hands up to his mouth as a speaking-trumpet, and called down:

'We've heard all this before! We've heard all this before!'

'Who is it? Who is it? Who is it? Who makes fun of me?' asked the thrush, and tried to catch a glimpse of the one who called.

'It is Kidnapped-by-Crows who makes fun of your song!' answered the boy. At that the crow chief turned his head and said:

'Be careful of your eyes, Tummetott!'

But the boy thought: 'Oh, I don't care about that. I want to show you that I'm not afraid of you!'

Farther and farther inland they travelled, and there were woods and lakes everywhere. In a birch grove sat the wood-dove on a bare branch and before her stood the cock dove. He blew up his feathers, cocked his head, raised and lowered his body until the breast feathers rattled against the branch. All the while he cooed:

'Thou, thou, thou art the loveliest in all the forest. No one in the forest is so lovely as thou, thou, thou!'

But up in the air the boy rode past, and when he heard Mr. Dove he couldn't keep still.

'Don't you believe him! Don't you believe him!' cried he.

'Who, who, who is it lies about me?' cooed Mr. Dove, and tried to get a sight of the one who shrieked at him.

'It is Caught-by-Crows that lies about you!' replied the boy.

Again Wind-Rush turned his head toward the boy and commanded him to shut up, but Fumle-Drumle, who was carrying him, said:

Let him chatter, then all the little birds will think that we crows have become quick-witted and funny birds.'

'Oh, they 're not such fools, either,' said Wind-Rush; but he liked the idea just the same, for after that he let the boy call out as much as he liked.

They flew mostly over forests and woodlands, but there were churches and parishes and little cabins in the outskirts of the forest. In one place they saw a pretty old manor. It lay with the forest behind it and the sea in front of it, had red walls and a turreted roof, great maples  about the grounds, and big, thick gooseberry bushes in the orchard. On the top of the weathercock sat the starling, and sang so loud that every note was heard by the wife, who sat on eggs in the nesting-box in a pear-tree.

'We have four pretty little eggs,' sang the starling.

'We have four pretty little round eggs. We have the whole nest filled with fine eggs.'

When the starling sang the song for the thousandth time the boy rode over the place. He put his hands up to his mouth, as a pipe, and called:

'The magpie will get them! The magpie will get them!'

'Who is it that wants to frighten me?' asked the starling, and flapped his wings uneasily.

'It is Captured-by-Crows that frightens you!' said the boy.

This time the crow chief didn't attempt to hush him up. Instead, both he and his flock were having so much fun that they cawed with satisfaction.

The farther inland they came, the larger were the lakes, and the more plentiful were the islands and points. And on a lake shore stood a drake who kowtowed before the duck.

'I 'll be true to you all the days of my life. I 'll be true to you all the days of my life,' said the drake.

'It won't last until the summer's end!' cried the boy.

'Who are you?' called the drake.

'My name's Stolen-by-Crows!' cried the boy.

At dinner time the crows alighted in a pasture. They

walked about and procured food for themselves, but none of them thought about giving the boy anything. Then Fumle-Drumle came riding up to the chief with a dog-rose branch, with a few dried hips on it.

'Here's something for you, Wind-Rush,' said he. 'This is pretty food, and suitable for you.'

Wind-Rush sniffed contemptuously.

'Do you think that I want to eat old, dry hips?' said he.

'And I who thought that you would be pleased with them!' said Fumle-Drumle, and threw away the dog-rose branch as if in despair. But it fell right in front of the boy, and he wasn't slow about grabbing it and eating until he was satisfied.

When the crows had eaten they began to chatter.

'What are you thinking about, Wind-Rush? You are so quiet to-day,' said one of them to the leader.

'I'm thinking that in this district there lived, once upon a time, a hen who was very fond of her mistress; and in order really to please her, she went and laid a nest full of eggs, which she hid under the storehouse floor. The mistress of the house wondered, of course, where the hen was keeping herself such a long time. She searched for her but did not find her. Can you guess, Longbill, who it was that found her and the eggs?'

'I think I can guess it, Wind-Rush, but when you have told about this I will tell you something like it. Do you remember the big, black cat in Hinneryd's parish house? She was dissatisfied because they always took the new-born kittens from her and drowned them. Just once did she succeed in keeping them concealed, and that was when she had hid them in a haystack, outdoors. She was pretty well pleased with those young kittens, but I believe that I got more pleasure out of them than she did.'

Now they became so excited that they all talked at once.

'What kind of an accomplishment is that—to steal little kittens?' said one. 'I once chased a young hare who was almost full grown. That meant following him from covert to covert.'

He got no further before another took the words from him.

'It may be fun, perhaps, to annoy hens and cats, but I find it still more remarkable that a crow can worry a human being. I once stole a silver spoon——'

But now the boy thought he was too good to sit and listen to such gabble.

'Now listen to me, you crows!' said he. 'I think you ought to be ashamed of yourselves to talk about all your wickedness. I have lived amongst wild geese for three weeks, and of them I have never heard or seen anything but good. You must have a bad chief, since he permits you to rob and murder in this way. You ought to begin to lead new lives, for I can tell you that human beings have grown so tired of your wickedness they are trying with all their might to root you out. And then there will soon be an end of you.'

When Wind-Rush and the crows heard this they were so furious that they intended to throw themselves upon him and tear him in pieces. But Fumle-Drumle laughed and cawed and stood in front of him.

'Oh, no, no!' said he, and seemed absolutely terrified. 'What think you that Wind-Air will say if you tear Tummetott in pieces before he has got that silver money for us?'

'It has to be you, Fumle-Drumle, that's afraid of womenfolk,' said Wind-Rush.

But, at any rate, both he and the others left Tummetott in peace.

Shortly after that the crows went on. Until now the boy thought that Småland wasn't such a poor country as he had heard. Of course it was woody and full of mountain ridges, but alongside the islands and lakes lay cultivated grounds, and any real desolation he hadn't come upon. But the farther inland they came the fewer were the villages and cottages. Towards the last he thought that he was riding over a veritable wilderness where he saw nothing but swamps and heaths and juniper hills.

The sun had gone down, but it was still perfect daylight when the crows reached the large heather heath. Wind-Rush sent a crow on ahead to say that he had met with success; and when it was known, Wind-Air, with several hundred crows from Crow Ridge, flew to meet the arrivals. In the midst of the deafening cawing which the crows emitted, Fumle-Drumle said to the boy:

'You have been so comical and so jolly during the trip that I am really fond of you. Therefore I want to give you some good 'advice. As soon as we alight you'll be requested to do a bit of work which may seem very easy to you, but beware of doing it!'

Soon thereafter Fumle-Drumle put Nils Holgersson down in the bottom of the sand-pit. The boy flung himself down, rolled over, and lay there as though he was simply done up with fatigue. Such a lot of crows fluttered about him that the air rustled like a wind-storm, but he didn't look up.

'Tummetott,' said Wind-Rush, 'get up now! You shall help us with a matter which will be very easy for you.'

The boy didn't move, but pretended to be asleep. Then Wind-Rush took him by the arm and dragged him over the sand to an earthen crock of old-time make that was standing in the pit.

'Get up, Tummetott,' said he, 'and open this crock!'

'Why can't you let me sleep?' said the boy. 'I'm too tired to do anything to-night. Wait until to-morrow!'

'Open the crock!' said Wind-Rush, shaking him.

'How shall a poor little child be able to open such a crock? Why, it's quite as large as I am myself.'

'Open it,' commanded Wind-Rush once more, 'or it will be a sorry thing for you!'

The boy got up, tottered over to the crock, fumbled the clasp, and let his arms fall.

'I'm not usually so weak,' said he. 'If you will only let me sleep until morning I think that I'll be able to manage that clasp.'

But Wind-Rush was impatient, and he rushed forward and pinched the boy in the leg. That sort of treatment the boy didn't care to suffer from a crow. He jerked himself loose quickly, ran a couple of paces backward, drew his knife from its sheath, and held it extended in front of him.

'You'd better be careful!' he cried to Wind-Rush.

This one too was so enraged that he didn't dodge the danger. He rushed at the boy, just as though he'd been blind, and ran so straight against the knife, that it entered through his eye into the head. The boy drew the knife back quickly, but Wind-Rush only struck out with his wings, then he fell down—dead.

'Wind-Rush is dead! The stranger has killed our chieftain, Wind-Rush!' cried the nearest crows, and then there was a terrible uproar. Some wailed, others cried for vengeance. They all ran or fluttered up to the boy, with Fumle-Drumle in the lead. But he acted badly as usual. He only fluttered and spread his wings over the boy, and prevented the others from coming forward and running their bills into him.

The boy thought that things looked very bad for him now. He couldn't run away from the crows, and there was no place where he could hide. Then he happened to think of the earthen crock. He took a firm hold on the clasp and pulled it off. Then he hopped into the crock to hide in it. But the crock was a poor hiding place, for it was nearly filled to the brim with little, thin, silver coins. The boy couldn't get far enough down, so he stooped and began to throw out the coins.

Until now the crows had fluttered round him in a thick swarm and pecked at him, but when he threw out the coins they immediately forgot their thirst for vengeance and hurried to gather the money. The boy threw out handfuls of it, and all the crows—yes, even Wind-Air herself—picked them up. And every one who succeeded in picking up a coin ran off to the nest with the utmost speed to conceal it.

When the boy had thrown out all the silver pennies from the crock he glanced up. Not more than a single crow was left in the sand-pit. That was Fumle-Drumle, with the white feather in his wing, he who had carried Tummetott.

'You have rendered me a greater service than you

yourself understand,' said the crow, with a very different voice, and a different intonation than the one he had used heretofore, 'and I want to save your life. Sit down on my back, and I 'll take you to a hiding place where you can be secure for to-night. To-morrow I 'll arrange it so that you will get back to the wild geese.'

Chapter Three

THE CABIN

THE following morning when the boy awoke he lay in a bed. When he saw that he was in a house with four walls around him, and a roof over him, he thought that he was at home.

'I wonder if mother will come soon with some coffee,' he muttered to himself where he lay half awake. Then he remembered that he was in a deserted cabin on Crow Ridge, and that Fumle-Drumle with the white feather had borne him there the night before.

The boy was sore all over after the journey he had made the day before, and he thought it was lovely to lie still while he waited for Fumle-Drumle who had promised to come and fetch him.

Curtains of checked cotton hung before the bed, and he drew them aside to look out into the cabin. It dawned upon him instantly that he had never seen a cabin like this. The walls consisted of nothing but a couple of rows of logs; then the roof began. There was no interior ceiling, so he could look clear up to the roof-tree. The cabin was so small that it appeared to have been built rather for such as he than for real people. However, the fireplace and chimney were so large he thought that he had never seen larger. The entrance door was in a gable wall at the side of the fireplace, and was so narrow that it was more like a wicket than a door. In the other gable wall he saw a low and broad window with many panes. There was scarcely any movable furniture in the cabin. The bench on one side and the table under the window were also fixed to the wall—also the big bed where he lay and the many-coloured cupboard.

The boy could not help wondering who owned the cabin and why it was deserted. It certainly looked as though the people who had lived there expected to return. The coffee-pot and the gruel-pot stood on the hearth, and there was some wood in the fireplace; the oven rake and baker's peel stood in a corner; the spinning-wheel was put near a bench; on the shelf over the window lay oakum and flax, a couple of skeins of yarn, a candle, and a box of matches.

Yes, it surely looked as if those who had lived there had intended to come back. There were bed-clothes on the bed; and on the walls there still hung long strips of cloth, upon which three riders named Kasper, Melchior, and Baltasar were painted. The same horses and riders were pictured many times. They rode around the whole cabin and continued their ride even up toward the joists.

But in the roof the boy saw something which brought him to his senses in a jiffy. It was a couple of loaves of big bread-cakes that hung there upon a spit. They looked old and mouldy but it was bread all the same. He gave them a knock with the oven rake and one piece fell to the floor. He ate, and stuffed his bag full. It was incredible how good bread was, anyway.

He looked around the cabin once more to try and discover if there was anything else which he might find useful to take along.

'I may as well take what I need, since no one else cares about it,' he thought. But most of the things were too

Inside the cabin

big and heavy. The only things that he could carry might be a few matches.

He clambered up on the table and swung, with the help of the curtains, up to the window-shelf. While he stood there and stuffed the matches into his bag the crow with the white feather came in through the window.

'Well, here I am at last,' said Fumle-Drumle as he alighted on the table. 'I couldn't get here any sooner because we crows have elected a new chieftain in Wind-Rush's place.'

'Whom have you chosen?' said the boy.

'Well, we have chosen one who will not permit robbery and injustice. We have elected Garm Whitefeather, lately called Fumle-Drumle,' answered he, drawing himself up until he looked absolutely regal.

'That was a good choice,' said Nils, and congratulated him.

'You may well wish me luck,' said Garm; then he told the boy about the time they had had with Wind-Rush and Wind-Air.

During this recital the boy heard a voice outside the window which he thought sounded familiar.

'Is he here?' inquired the fox.

'Yes, he's hidden in there,' answered a crow voice.

'Be careful, Tummetott!' cried Garm. 'Wind-Air stands without with that fox who wants to eat you.'

More he didn't have time to say, for Smirre dashed against the window. The old, rotten window-frame gave way, and the next second Smirre stood upon the table by the window. Garm Whitefeather, who didn't have time to fly away, he killed instantly. Thereupon he jumped down to the floor and looked around for the boy.

He tried to hide behind a big oakum spiral, but Smirre had already spied him, and was crouched for the final spring. The cabin was so small, and so low, the boy realized that the fox could reach him without the least difficulty. But just at that moment Nils was not without weapons of defence. He struck a match quickly, touched the curtains, and when they were in flames he threw them down upon Smirre Fox. When the fire enveloped the fox he was seized with a mad terror. He thought no more about the boy but rushed wildly out of the cabin.

But it looked as if the boy had escaped one danger to throw himself into a greater one. From the tuft of oakum which he had flung at Smirre the fire had spread to the bed-hangings. He jumped down and tried to smother it, but it blazed too quickly now. The cabin was soon filled with smoke, and Smirre Fox, who had remained just outside the window, began to grasp the state of affairs within.

'Well, Tummetott,' he called out, 'which do you choose now: to be broiled alive in there or to come out here to me? Of course, I should prefer to have the pleasure of eating you; but in whichever way death meets you it will be dear to me.'

The boy could not help thinking that the fox was right, for the fire was making rapid headway. The whole bed was now in a blaze and smoke rose from the floor; and along the painted wall-strips the fire crept from rider to rider. The boy jumped up in the fireplace and tried to open the oven door, when he heard a key which turned slowly in the lock. It must be human beings coming. And in the dire extremity in which he found himself he was not afraid, but only glad. He was already on the threshold when the door opened. He saw a couple of children facing him; but how they looked when they saw the cabin in flames he took no time to find out, but rushed past them into the open.

He didn't dare run far. He knew, of course, that Smirre Fox lay in wait for him, and he understood that he must remain near the children. He turned round to see what sort of folk they were, but he hadn't looked at them a second before he ran up to them and cried:

'Oh, good day, Osa goose-girl! Oh, good day, little Mats!'

For when the boy saw those children he forgot entirely where he was. Crows and burning cabin and talking animals had vanished from his memory. He was walking on a stubble-field, in West Vemmenhög, tending a goose flock; and beside him, in the field, walked those same Småland children with their geese. As soon as he saw them he ran upon the stony ridge and shouted:

'Oh, good day, Osa goose-girl! Oh, good day, little Mats!'

But when the children saw such a little creature coming up to them with outstretched hands they grabbed hold of each other, took a couple of steps backward, and looked scared to death.

When the boy noticed their terror he woke up and remembered who he was. And then it seemed to him that nothing worse could happen to him than that those children should see how he had been bewitched. Shame and grief, because he was no longer a human being, over-powered him. He turned and fled. He knew not whither.

But a glad meeting awaited the boy when he came

down to the heath. For there, in the heather, he spied something white, and toward him came the white gander, accompanied by Dunfin. When the white one saw the boy running with such speed he thought that dreadful fiends were pursuing him. He flung him in all haste upon his back and flew off with him.

PART SEVENTEEN

THE OLD PEASANT WOMAN

THREE tired travellers were out in the late evening in
search of a night shelter. They travelled over a poor
and desolate portion of northern Småland. But the sort
of resting place which they wanted they should have
been able to find; for they were no weaklings who asked
for soft beds or comfortable rooms.

'If one of these long mountain ridges had a peak so
high and steep that a fox couldn't in any way climb up
to it, then we should have a good sleeping place,' said
one of them.

'If a single one of the big swamps was thawed out, and
was so marshy and wet that a fox wouldn't dare venture
out on it, this, too, would be a right good night shelter,'
said the second.

'If the ice on one of the large lakes we travel past were loose so that a fox could not come out on it, then we should have found just what we are seeking,' said the third.

The worst of it was that when the sun had gone down two of the travellers became so sleepy that every second they were ready to fall to the ground. The third one, who could keep himself awake, grew more and more uneasy as night approached.

'Then it was a misfortune that we came to a land where lakes and swamps are frozen, so that a fox can get around everywhere. In other places the ice has melted away; but now we're well up in the very coldest Småland, where spring has not as yet arrived. I don't know how I shall ever manage to find a good sleeping place! Unless I find some spot that is well protected, Smirre Fox will be upon us before morning.'

He gazed in all directions, but he saw no shelter where he could lodge. It was a dark and chilly night, with wind and drizzle. It grew more terrible and disagreeable around him every second.

This may sound strange, perhaps, but the travellers didn't seem to have the least desire to ask for shelter on any farm. They had already passed many parishes without knocking at a single door. Little hillside cabins on the outskirts of the forest, which all poor wanderers are glad to run across, they took no notice of either. One might almost be tempted to say they deserved to have a hard time of it, since they did not seek help where it was to be had for the asking.

But finally, when it was so dark that there was scarcely a glimmer of light left under the skies and the two who needed sleep journeyed on in a kind of half-sleep, they

happened to come to a farmyard which was a long way off
from all neighbours.   And not only did it lie there desolate, but it appeared to be uninhabited as well.   No
smoke rose from the chimney; no light shone through the
windows; no human being moved on the place.   When
the one among the three who could keep awake saw the
place he thought: 'Now come what may we must try to
get in here.   Anything better we are not likely to find.'

Soon after that all three stood in the farmyard.   Two
of them fell asleep the instant they stood still, but the
third looked about him eagerly to find where they could
get under cover.   It was not a small farm.   Beside the
dwelling-house and stable and boiler-house, there were
long buildings with barns and storehouses and tool sheds.
But it all looked awfully poor and dilapidated.   The
houses had grey, moss-grown, leaning walls, which
seemed ready to topple over.   In the roofs were yawning
holes, and the doors hung aslant on broken hinges.   It
was apparent that no one had taken the trouble to drive
a nail into a wall on the place for a long time.

Meanwhile he who was awake had discovered which
building was the cowshed.   He roused his travelling companions from their sleep and conducted them to the
cowshed door.   Luckily this was not fastened with anything but a hook, which he could easily push up with a
rod.   He heaved a sigh of relief at the thought that they
should soon be in safety.   But when the cowshed door
swung open with a sharp creaking he heard a cow begin
to bellow:

'Are you coming at last, mistress?' said she.   'I
thought that you were not going to give me any supper
to-night.'

The one who was awake stopped in the doorway,

absolutely terrified when he discovered that the cowshed was not empty. But he soon saw that there was not more than one cow and three or four chickens, and then he took courage again.

'We are three poor travellers who want to come in somewhere, where no fox can assail us and no human being capture us,' said he. 'We wonder if this can be a good place for us.'

'I cannot believe but what it is,' answered the cow. 'To be sure the walls are poor, but the fox does not walk through them as yet; and no one lives here except an old peasant woman, who isn't at all likely to make a captive of any one. But who are you?' she continued, as she twisted in her stall to get a sight of the newcomers.

'I am Nils Holgersson from Vemmenhög, who has been transformed into an elf,' replied the first of the travellers, 'and I have with me a tame goose, whom I generally ride, and a grey goose.'

'Such rare guests have never before been within my four walls,' said the cow, 'and you shall be welcome, although I would have preferred that it had been my mistress come to give me my supper.'

The boy led the geese into the cowshed, which was rather large, and placed them in an empty manger, where they fell asleep instantly. For himself, he made a little bed of straw and expected that he, too, should go to sleep at once.

But this was impossible, for the poor cow, who hadn't had her supper, wasn't still an instant. She shook her flanks, moved round in the stall, and complained of how hungry she was. The boy couldn't get a wink of sleep, but lay there and lived over all the things that had happened to him during these last days.

He thought of Osa, the goose-girl, and little Mats, whom he had encountered so unexpectedly; and he fancied that the little cabin which he had set on fire must have been their old home in Småland. Now he recalled that he had heard them speak of just such a cabin, and of the big heather heath which lay below it. Now they had wandered back there to see their old home again, and then, when they had reached it, it was in flames.

It was indeed a great sorrow which he had brought upon them and it hurt him very much. If he ever again became a human being he would try to compensate them for the damage and disappointment.

Then his thoughts wandered to the crows. And when he thought of Fumle-Drumle who had saved his life, and had met his own death so soon after he had been elected chieftain, he was so distressed that tears filled his eyes.

He had had a pretty rough time of it these last few days. But, anyway, it was a rare stroke of luck that the gander and Dunfin had found him.

The gander had said that as soon as the wild geese discovered that Tummetott had disappeared, they had asked all the small animals in the forest about him. They soon learned that a flock of Småland crows had carried him off. But the crows were already out of sight, and whither they had directed their course no one had been able to say. That they might find the boy as soon as possible, Akka had commanded the wild geese to start out—two and two—in different directions, to search for him. But after a two days' hunt, whether or not they had found him, they were to meet in north-western Småland on a high mountain top, which resembled an abrupt, chopped-off tower, and was called Taberg. After Akka had given them the best directions, and

All the while the cow fussed and fumed in the stall

described carefully how they should find Taberg, they had separated.

The white gander had chosen Dunfin as travelling companion, and they had flown about hither and thither with the greatest anxiety for Tummetott. During this flight they had heard a thrush, who sat in a tree top, cry and wail that someone, who called himself Kidnapped-by-Crows, had made fun of him. They had talked with the thrush, and he had shown them in which direction that Kidnapped-by-Crows had travelled. Afterwards they had met a cock dove, a starling, and a drake; they had all wailed about a little culprit who had disturbed their song, and who was named Caught-by-Crows, Captured-by-Crows, and Stolen-by-Crows. In this way they were enabled to trace Tummetott all the way to the heather heath in Sunnerbo parish.

As soon as the gander and Dunfin had found Tummetott, they had started toward the north, in order to reach Taberg. But it had been a long road to travel, and the darkness was upon them before they had sighted the mountain top.

'If we only get there by to-morrow, surely all our troubles will be over,' thought the boy, and dug down into the straw to make it warmer. All the while the cow fussed and fumed in the stall. Then, all of a sudden, she began to talk to the boy.

'Everything is wrong with me,' said the cow. 'I am neither milked nor tended. I have no night fodder in my manger, and no bed has been made under me. My mistress came here at dusk to put things in order for me, but she felt so ill that she had to go in soon again, and she has not returned.'

'It's distressing that I should be little and powerless,'

said the boy. 'I don't believe that I am able to help you.'

'You can't make me believe that you are powerless because you are little,' said the cow. 'All the elves that I 've ever heard of were so strong that they could pull a whole load of hay and strike a cow dead with one fist.'

The boy couldn't help laughing at the cow.

'They were a very different kind of elf from me,' said he. 'But I 'll loosen your halter and open the door for you, so that you can go out and drink in one of the pools on the place, and then I 'll try to climb up to the hayloft and throw down some hay in your manger.'

'Yes, that would be some help,' said the cow.

The boy did as he had said, and when the cow stood with a full manger in front of her he thought that at last he should get some sleep. But he had hardly crept down in the bed before she began, anew, to talk to him.

'You 'll be clean put out with me if I ask you for one thing more,' said the cow.

'Oh, no I won't, if it 's only something that I 'm able to do,' said the boy.

'Then I will ask you to go into the cabin, directly opposite, and find out how my mistress is getting along. I fear some misfortune has come to her.'

'No! I can't do that,' said the boy. 'I dare not show myself before human beings.'

'Surely you 're not afraid of an old and sick woman,' said the cow. 'But you do not need to go into the cabin. Just stand outside the door and peep in through the crack!'

'Oh, if that is all you ask of me, I 'll do it, of course,' said the boy.

With that he opened the cowshed door and went out

in the yard.   It was a fearful night.   Neither moon nor stars shone, the wind blew a gale, and the rain came down in torrents.   And the worst of all was that seven great owls sat in a row on the eaves of the cabin.   It was awful just to hear them, where they sat and grumbled at the weather, but it was even worse to think what would

happen to him if one of them should set eyes on him. That would be the last of him.

'Pity him who is little!' said the boy as he ventured out in the yard.   And he had a right to say this, for he was blown down twice before he got to the house; once the wind swept him into a pool, which was so deep that he came near drowning.   But he got there nevertheless.

He clambered up a pair of steps, scrambled over a threshold, and came into the entrance.   The cabin door was closed, but down in one corner a large piece had been cut away, that the cat might go in and out.   It was no difficulty whatever for the boy to see how things were in the cabin.

He had hardly cast a glance in there before he staggered back and turned his head away.   An old, grey-haired woman lay stretched out on the floor within. She neither moved nor moaned, and her face shone strangely white. It was as if an invisible moon had thrown a feeble light over it.

The boy remembered that when his grandfather had died his face had also become so strangely white. And he understood that the old woman who lay on the cabin floor must be dead. Death had probably come to her so suddenly that she didn't even have time to lie down on her bed.

As he thought of being alone with the dead in the middle of the dark night, he was terribly afraid. He threw himself headlong down the steps, and rushed back to the cowshed.

When he told the cow what he had seen in the cabin she stopped eating.

'So my mistress is dead,' said she. 'Then it will soon be over for me as well.'

'There will always be someone to look after you,' said the boy comfortingly.

'Ah, you don't know,' said the cow, 'that I am already twice as old as a cow usually is before she is laid upon the slaughter-bench. But then I do not care to live any longer, since she, in there, can come no more to care for me.'

She said nothing more for a while, but the boy observed, no doubt, that she neither slept nor ate. It was not long before she began to speak again.

'Is she lying on the bare floor?' she asked.

'She is,' said the boy.

'She had a habit of coming out to the cowshed,' she continued, 'and talking about everything that troubled her. I understood what she said, although I could not answer her. These last few days she talked of how afraid she was lest there would be no one with her when she died. She was anxious for fear no one should close her eyes and fold her hands across her breast after she was dead. Perhaps you 'll go in and do this?'

The boy hesitated. He remembered that when his grandfather had died, mother had been very careful about putting everything to rights. He knew this was something which had to be done. But, on the other hand, he felt that he didn't dare go to the dead in the ghostly night. He didn't say no, neither did he take a step toward the cowshed door. For a couple of seconds the old cow was silent, just as if she had expected an answer. But when the boy said nothing she did not repeat her request. Instead, she began to talk with him of her mistress.

There was much to tell, first and foremost, about all the children whom she had brought up. They had been in the cowshed every day, and in the summer they had taken the cattle to pasture on the swamp and in the groves, so the old cow knew all about them. They had been splendid, all of them, and happy and industrious. A cow knew well enough what her caretakers were good for.

There was also much to be said about the farm. It had not always been as poor as it was now. It was very large—although the greater part of it consisted of swamps and stony groves. There was not much room for fields, but there was plenty of good fodder everywhere. At one time there had been a cow for every stall in the cowshed; and the oxshed, which was now empty, had at one time been filled with oxen. And then there was life and gaiety, both in cabin and cowshed. When the mistress opened the cowshed door she would hum and sing, and all the cows lowed with gladness when they heard her coming.

But the master had died when the children were so small that they could not be of any assistance, and the mistress had to take charge of the farm, and all the work and responsibility. She had been as strong as a man, and had both ploughed and reaped. In the evenings, when she came into the cowshed to milk, sometimes she was so tired that she wept. Then she dashed away her tears and was cheerful again.

'It doesn't matter. Good times are coming again for me too, if only my children grow up. Yes, if they only grow up.'

But as soon as the children were grown a strange longing came over them. They didn't want to stay at home, but went away to a strange country. Their mother never got any help from them. A couple of her children were married before they went away, and they had left their children behind, in the old home. And now these children followed the mistress in the cowshed, just as her own had done. They tended the cows, and were fine, good folk. And, in the evenings, when the mistress was so tired out that she could fall asleep in the middle of the milking, she would rouse herself again to renewed courage by thinking of them.

'Good times are coming for me, too,' said she, and shook off sleep, 'when once they are grown.'

But when these children grew up they went away to their parents in the strange land. No one came back, no one stayed at home—the old mistress was left alone on the farm.

Probably she had never asked them to remain with her.

'Think you, Rödlinna, that I would ask them to stay here with me, when they can go out in the world and have things comfortable?' she would say as she stood in the stall with the old cow. 'Here in Småland they have only poverty to look forward to.'

But when the last grandchild was gone, it was all up with the mistress. All at once she became bent and grey and tottered as she walked, as if she no longer had the strength to move about. She stopped working. She did not care to look after the farm but let everything go to rack and ruin. She didn't repair the houses, and she sold both the cows and the oxen. The only one that she kept was the old cow who now talked with Tummetott. Her she let live because all the children had tended her.

She could have taken maids and farm-hands into her service, who would have helped her with the work, but she couldn't bear to see strangers around her, since her own had deserted her. Perhaps she was better satisfied to let the farm go to ruin, since none of her children were coming back to take it after she was gone. She did not mind that she herself became poor, because she didn't value that which was only hers. But she was troubled lest the children should find out how hard was her life.

'If only the children do not hear of this! If only the children do not hear of this!' she sighed as she tottered through the cowhouse.

The children wrote constantly and begged her to come out to them, but this she did not wish. She didn't want to see the land that had taken them away from her. She was angry with it.

'It's foolish of me, perhaps, that I do not like that land which has been so good for them,' said she. 'But I don't want to see it.'

She never thought of anything but the children, and of this—that they must needs have gone. When summer came she led the cow out to graze in the big swamp. All day she would sit on the edge of the swamp, her hands in her lap, and on the way home she would say: 'You see, Rödlinna, if there had been large, rich fields here, in place of these barren swamps, then there would have been no need for them to leave.'

She could become furious with the swamp which spread out so big and did no good.   She could sit and talk about how it was the swamp's fault that the children had left her.

This last evening she had been more trembly and feeble than ever before. She could not even do the milking. She had leaned against the manger and talked about two strangers who had been to see her, and had asked if they might buy the swamp. They wanted to drain it, and sow and raise grain on it. This had made her both anxious and glad.

'Do you hear, Rödlinna,' she had said, 'do you hear? They said that grain can grow on the swamp. Now I shall write to the children to come home. Now they 'll not have to stay away any longer, for now they can get their bread here at home.'

It was this that she had gone into the cabin to do. . . .

The boy heard no more of what the old cow said. He had opened the cowshed door and gone across the yard, and to the dead of whom he had but lately been so afraid.

It was not so poor in the cabin as he had expected. It was well supplied with the sort of things one generally finds among those who have relatives in America.   In a corner there was an American rocking chair; on the

table before the window lay a brocaded plush cover;
there was a pretty bedspread on the bed; on the walls, in
carved-wood frames, hung the photographs of the
children and grandchildren who had gone away; on the
bureau stood high vases and a couple of candlesticks,
with thick, spiral candles in them.

The boy searched for a match-box and lighted these
candles, not because he needed more light than he
already had, but because he thought that this was one
way to honour the dead.

Then he went up to her, closed her eyes, folded her
hands across her breast, and stroked back the thin grey
hair from her face.

He thought no more about being afraid of her. He
was so deeply grieved because she had been forced to live
out her old age in loneliness and longing. He, at least,
would watch over her dead body this night.

He hunted up the psalm book, and seated himself to
read a couple of psalms in an undertone. But in the
middle of the reading he paused—because he had begun
to think about his mother and father.

Think, that parents can long so for their children!
This he had never known. Think, that life can be as
though it were over for them when the children are away!
Think, if those at home longed for him in the same way
that this old peasant woman had longed!

This thought made him happy, but he dared not
believe in it. He had not been such a one that anybody
could long for him.

But what he had not been, perhaps he could become.
Round about him he saw the portraits of those who
were away. They were big, strong men and women
with earnest faces. There were brides in long veils and

gentlemen in fine clothes, and there were children with waved hair and pretty white dresses. And he thought that they all stared blindly into vacancy—and did not want to see.

'Poor you!' said the boy to the portraits. 'Your mother is dead. You cannot make reparation now, because you went away from her. But my mother is living!'

Here he paused, and nodded and smiled to himself. 'My mother is living,' said he. 'Both father and mother are living.'

PART EIGHTEEN

FROM TABERG TO HUSKVARNA

Nils sat awake nearly all night, but toward morning he fell asleep and then he dreamed of his father and mother. He could hardly recognize them. They had both grown grey and had old and wrinkled faces. He asked how this had come about, and they answered that they had aged so because they had longed for him. He was touched and astonished, for he had always believed that they were glad to be rid of him.

When the boy awoke the morning was come, with fine, clear weather. First, he himself ate a bit of bread which he found in the cabin; then he gave morning feed to geese and cow, and opened the cowshed door so that the cow could go over to the nearest farm. When the cow came along all by herself the neighbours would no doubt understand that something was wrong with her mistress. They would hurry over to the desolate farm to see how the old woman was getting along, and then they would find her dead body and bury it.

The boy and the geese had barely raised themselves into the air, when they caught a glimpse of a high mountain, with almost perpendicular walls and an abrupt, broken-off top, and they understood that this must be Taberg. On the summit stood Akka, with Yksi and Kaksi, Kolmi and Neljä, Viisi and Kuusi, and all six goslings and waited for them. There was a rejoicing and a cackling and a fluttering and a calling which no one can describe, when they saw that the gander and Dunfin had succeeded in finding Tummetott.

⁓The woods grew pretty high up on Taberg's sides, but her highest peak was barren; and from there one could look far out in all directions. If one gazed toward the east, or south, or west, then there was hardly anything to be seen but a poor highland with dark spruce-trees, brown morasses, ice-clad lakes, and bluish mountain ridges. The boy couldn't help thinking that it was true that the one who had created this hadn't taken very great pains with his work, but had thrown it together in a hurry. But if one glanced to the north it was altogether different. Here it looked as if it had been worked out with the utmost care and affection. In this direction one saw only beautiful mountains, soft valleys, and winding rivers, all the way to the big Lake Vätter, which lay ice-free and transparently clear, and shone as if it wasn't filled with water but with blue light.

It was Vätter that made it so pretty to look toward the north, because it looked as though a blue light had risen up from the lake, and spread itself over land also. Groves and hills and roofs, and the spires of Jönköping City—which shimmered along Vätter's shores—lay enveloped in pale blue which caressed the eye. If there were countries in heaven, they, too, must be blue like this, thought the boy, and imagined that he had got a faint idea of how it must look in Paradise.

Later in the day, when the geese continued their journey, they flew up toward the blue valley. They were in holiday mood; they called and made such a racket that no one who had ears could help hearing them.

This happened to be the first really fine spring day they had had in this district. Until now the spring had done its work under rain and bluster; and now, when it had all of a sudden become fine weather, the people were filled with such a longing after summer warmth and green woods that they could hardly perform their tasks. And when the wild geese rode by, high above the ground, cheerful and free, there wasn't one who did not drop what he had in hand and glance at them.

The first ones who saw the wild geese that day were miners on Taberg, who were digging ore at the mouth of the mine. When they heard them cackle, they paused in their drilling for ore, and one of them called to the birds: 'Where are you going? Where are you going?'

The geese didn't understand what he said, but the boy leaned forward over the goose-back and answered for them: 'Where there is neither pick nor hammer!'

When the miners heard the words, they thought it was their own longing that made the goose cackle sound like human speech.

'Take us along with you! Take us along with you!' they cried.

'Not this year!' shrieked the boy. 'Not this year!'

The wild geese followed the river Tabergsån down toward Monk Lake, and all the while they made the same racket. Here, on the narrow land strip between Munke-jön and Vätter Lakes, lay Jönköping with its great factories. The wild geese rode first over Munksjö paper-mills. The lunch hour was just over and the big workmen were streaming down to the mill gate. When they heard the wild geese, they stopped a moment to listen to them.

'Where are you going? Where are you going?' called the workmen.

The wild geese understood nothing of what they said, but the boy answered for them:

'There, where there are neither engines nor machines.'

When the workmen heard the answer, they believed it was their own longing that made the goose cackle sound like human speech.

'Take us along with you!'

'Not this year!' answered the boy. 'Not this year!'

Next the geese rode over the well-known match factory which lies on the shores of Vettern, large as a fortress, and lifts its high chimneys toward the sky. Not a soul moved out in the yards, but in a large hall young working women sat and filled match-boxes. They had opened a window on account of the beautiful weather, and through it came the wild geese's call. The one who sat nearest the window leaned out, with a match-box in her hand, and cried:

'Where are you going? Where are you going?'

'To that land where there is no need of either light or matches!' said the boy.

The girl thought that what she had heard was only goose cackle; but since she thought she had distinguished a couple of words, she called out in answer:

'Take me along with you!'

'Not this year!' replied the boy. 'Not this year!'

East of the factories rises Jönköping, on the most glorious spot that any city can occupy. The narrow Vettern has high, steep sand shores, both on the eastern and western sides; but straight south the sand walls are broken down, just as if to make room for a large gate through which one reaches the lake. And in the middle of the gate, with mountains to the left and mountains to the right, with Monk Lake behind it and Vettern in front of it, lies Jönköping.

The wild geese travelled forward over the long, narrow city, and behaved here just as they had done in the country. But in the city there was no one who answered them. It was not to be expected that city people should pause out in the streets and call to the wild geese.

The trip extended farther along Vettern's shores, and after a little they came to Sanna sanatorium. Some of the patients had gone out on the veranda to enjoy the spring air, and in this way they heard the goose cackle.

'Where are you going?' asked one of them with such a feeble voice that he was scarcely heard.

'To that land where there is neither sorrow nor sickness!' answered the boy.

'Take us along with you!' said the sick one.

'Not this year!' answered the boy. 'Not this year!'

When they had travelled still farther on they came to Huskvarna. It lay in a valley. The mountains around it were steep and beautifully formed. A river rushed along the heights in long and narrow falls. Big workshops and factories lay below the mountain walls; and scattered over the valley bottom were the working men's homes, encircled by little gardens; and in the centre of the valley lay the schoolhouse. Just as the wild geese came along a bell rang and a crowd of school children marched out in line. They were so numerous that the whole schoolyard was filled with them.

'Where are you going? Where are you going?' the children shouted when they heard the wild geese.

'Where there are neither books nor lessons to be found!' answered the boy.

'Take us along!' shrieked the children.

'Not this year, but next!' cried the boy. 'Not this year, but next!'

PART NINETEEN

THE BIG BIRD LAKE

☆

Chapter One

JARRO, THE WILD DUCK

On the eastern shore of Vettern lies Mount Omberg; east of Omberg lies Dagmosse; east of Dagmosse lies Lake Tåkern. Around the whole of Tåkern spreads the big, even Östergötland plain.

Tåkern is a pretty large lake and in olden times it must have been still larger. But then the people thought it covered entirely too much of the fertile plain, so they attempted to drain the water from it, that they might sow and reap on the lake bottom. But they did not succeed in laying waste the entire lake, which had evidently been their intention; therefore it still hides a lot of land. Since the draining the lake has become so shallow that hardly at any point is it more than six feet deep. The shores have become marshy and muddy; and out in the lake little mud islets stick up above the water's surface.

Now there is one which loves to stand with its feet in the water, if it can just keep its body and head in the air, and that is the reed. And it cannot find a better place to grow upon than the long, shallow Tåkern shores, and around the little mud islets. It thrives so well that it grows taller than a man's height, and so thick that it is almost impossible to push a boat through it. It forms a broad green enclosure around the whole lake, so that it is only accessible in a few places where the people have taken away the reeds.

But if the reeds shut the people out, they give, in return, shelter and protection to many other things. In the reeds there are a lot of little dams and canals with green, still water, where duckweed and pondweed run to seed, and where gnat eggs and blackfish and worms are hatched out in uncountable masses. And all along the shores of these little dams and canals there are many well-concealed places, where sea birds hatch their eggs and bring up their young without being disturbed, either by enemies or food worries.

An incredible number of birds live in the Tåkern reeds; and more and more gather there every year as it becomes known what a splendid sanctuary it is. The first who settled there were the wild ducks and they still live there by thousands. But they no longer own the entire lake, for they have been obliged to share it with swans, grebes, coots, loons, fen-ducks, and a lot of others.

Tåkern is certainly the largest and choicest bird lake in the whole country; and the birds may count themselves lucky as long as they own such a retreat. But it is uncertain just how long they will be in control of reeds and mud-banks, for human beings cannot forget that the lake extends over a considerable portion of good and fertile soil; and every now and then the proposition to drain it comes up among them. And if these propositions were carried out the many thousands of water birds would be forced to move from this quarter.

At the time when Nils Holgersson travelled around with the wild geese there lived at Tåkern a wild duck named Jarro. He was a young bird who had only lived one summer, one autumn, and a winter; now, it was his first spring. He had just returned from South Africa and had reached Tåkern in such good season that the ice was still on the lake.

One evening, when he and the other young wild ducks played at racing backward and forward over the lake, a hunter fired a couple of shots at them and Jarro was wounded in the breast. He thought he should die; but in order that the one who shot him shouldn't get him into his power he continued to fly as long as he possibly could. He didn't know whither he was directing his course, but only struggled to get far away. When his strength failed him, so that he could not fly any farther, he was no longer on the lake. He had flown a bit inland, and now he sank down before the entrance to one of the big farms which lie along the shores of Tåkern.

A moment later a young farm-hand happened along. He saw Jarro and came and lifted him up. But Jarro, who asked for nothing but to be allowed to die in peace, gathered his last powers and nipped the farm-hand in the finger so he should let go of him.

Jarro didn't succeed in freeing himself. The encounter had this good in it at any rate: the farm-hand noticed that the bird was alive. He carried him very gently into the cottage and showed him to the mistress of the house, a young woman with a kindly face. At once she took Jarro from the farm-hand, stroked him on the back, and wiped away the blood which trickled down through the neck feathers. She looked him over very carefully, and when she saw how pretty he was, with his dark-green, shining head, his white neck-band, his brownish-red back, and his blue speculum, she must have thought that it was a pity for him to die. She promptly put a basket in order and tucked the bird into it.

All the while Jarro fluttered and struggled to get loose; but when he understood that the people didn't intend to

kill him he settled down in the basket with a sense of pleasure. Now it was evident how exhausted he was from pain and loss of blood. The mistress carried the basket across the floor to place it in the corner by the fireplace, and before she put it down Jarro was already fast asleep.

In a little while Jarro was awakened by someone who nudged him gently. When he opened his eyes he experienced such an awful shock that he almost lost his senses. Now he was lost! for there stood *the* one who was more dangerous than either human beings or birds of prey. It was no less a thing than Caesar himself, the long-haired dog, who nosed around him inquisitively.

How pitifully scared had he not been last summer,

when he was still a little yellow-down duckling, every time it had sounded over the reed stems:

'Caesar is coming! Caesar is coming!'

When he had seen the brown-and-white spotted dog with the cruel teeth come wading through the reeds, he had believed that he beheld death itself. He had always hoped that he would never have to live through that moment when he should meet Caesar face to face.

But, to his sorrow, he must have fallen down in the very yard where Caesar lived, for there he stood right over him.

'Who are you?' he growled. 'How did you get into

the house? Don't you belong down among the reed banks?'

It was with great difficulty that he gained the courage to answer.

'Don't be angry with me, Caesar, because I came into the house!' said he. 'It isn't my fault. I have been wounded by gunshot. It was the people themselves who laid me in this basket.'

'Oho! So it's the people themselves that have placed you here,' said Caesar. 'Then it is surely their intention to cure you, although, for my part, I think it would be wiser for them to eat you up since you are in their power. But, at any rate, you are tabooed in the house. You needn't look so scared. We're not down on Tåkern now.'

With that Caesar laid himself to sleep in front of the blazing log fire. As soon as Jarro understood that this terrible danger was past, extreme lassitude came over him and he fell asleep anew.

The next time Jarro awoke he saw that a dish of grain and water stood before him. He was still quite ill, but he felt hungry nevertheless, and began to eat. When the mistress saw that he ate she came up and petted him, and looked pleased. After that Jarro fell asleep again. For several days he did nothing but eat and sleep.

One morning Jarro felt much better and stepped from the basket and wandered along the floor. But he hadn't gone very far before he fell over and lay there. Then came Caesar, who opened his big jaws and grabbed him. Jarro believed, of course, that the dog was going to bite him to death; but Caesar carried him back to the basket without harming him. Because of this, Jarro acquired such a confidence in the dog Caesar, that on his next walk in the cottage, he went over to the dog and lay down beside him. Thereafter Caesar and he became good friends, and every day, for several hours, Jarro lay and slept between Caesar's paws.

But an even greater affection than he felt for Caesar did Jarro feel toward his mistress. Of her he had not the least fear, but rubbed his head against her hand when she came and fed him. Whenever she went out of the cottage he sighed with regret, and when she came back he cried welcome to her in his own language.

Jarro forgot entirely how afraid he had been of both dogs and humans in other days. He thought now that they were gentle and kind, and he loved them. He wished that he were well, so he could fly down to Tåkern and tell the wild ducks  that their enemies were not dangerous, and that they need not fear them.

He had observed that the human beings, as well as Caesar, had calm eyes, which it did one good to look into. The only one in the cottage whose glance he did not care to meet, was Clawina, the house cat. She did him no harm, either, but he couldn't feel any confidence in her. Then, too, she quarrelled with him constantly, because he loved human beings.

'You think they protect you because they are fond of

you,' said Clawina. 'You just wait until you are fat enough! Then they 'll wring the neck off you. I know them, I do.'

Jarro, like all birds, had a tender and affectionate heart, and he was unutterably distressed when he heard this. He couldn't imagine that his mistress would wish to wring the neck off him, nor could he believe any such thing of her son, the little boy who sat for hours beside his basket, and babbled and chattered. He seemed to think that both of them had the same love for him that he had for them.

One day, when Jarro and Caesar lay on the usual spot before the fire, Clawina sat on the hearth and began to tease the wild duck.

'I wonder, Jarro, what you wild ducks will do next year, when Tåkern is drained and turned into grain-fields?' said Clawina.

'What 's that you say, Clawina?' cried Jarro, and jumped up, scared through and through.

'I always forget, Jarro, that you do not understand human speech, like Caesar and myself,' answered the cat. 'Or else you surely would have heard how the men, who were here in the cottage yesterday, said that all the water was going to be drained from Tåkern, and that next year the lake bottom would be as dry as a house floor. And now I wonder where you wild ducks will go.'

When Jarro heard this talk he was so furious that he hissed like a snake.

'You are just as mean as a common coot!' he screamed at Clawina. 'You only want to incite me against human beings. I don't believe they want to do anything of the sort. They must know that Tåkern is the wild ducks' property. Why should they make so many birds homeless and unhappy? You have certainly told me all this to scare me. I hope that you may be torn in pieces by Gorgo, the eagle! I hope that my mistress will cut off your whiskers!'

But Jarro couldn't shut Clawina up with this outburst. 'So you think I 'm lying,' said she. 'Ask Caesar, then. He was also in the house last night. Caesar never lies.'

'Caesar,' said Jarro, 'you understand human speech much better than Clawina. Say that she hasn't heard aright! Think how it would be if the people drained Tåkern and changed the lake bottom into fields! Then there would be no more pondweed or duck food for the grown wild ducks, and no blackfish or worms or gnat eggs for the ducklings. Then the reed banks would disappear, where now the ducklings conceal themselves until they are able to fly. All ducks would be compelled to move away from here and seek another home. But where shall they find a retreat like Tåkern? Caesar, say that Clawina has not heard aright!'

It was extraordinary to watch Caesar's behaviour during this conversation. He had been wide awake the whole time before, but now, when Jarro turned to him, he panted, laid his long nose on his forepaws, and was sound asleep within the wink of an eyelid.

The cat looked down at Caesar with a knowing smile. 'I believe that Caesar doesn't care to answer you,' she said to Jarro. 'It is with him as with all dogs; they will never acknowledge that humans can do any wrong. But you can rely upon my word, at any rate. I shall tell you why they wish to drain the lake just now. As long as you wild ducks still had the power on Tåkern, they did not wish to drain it, for, at least, they got some good out of you; but now, grebes and coots and other birds, who are no good as food, have infested nearly all the reed banks, and the people don't think they need let the lake remain on their account.'

Jarro didn't trouble himself to answer Clawina, but raised his head and shouted in Caesar's ear:

'Caesar! You know that on Tåkern there are still so many ducks left that they fill the air like clouds. Say it isn't true that human beings intend to make all of these homeless!'

Then Caesar sprang up with such a sudden outburst at Clawina that she had to save herself by jumping up on a shelf.

'I 'll teach you to keep quiet when I want to sleep,' bawled Caesar. 'Of course I know that there is some talk about draining the lake this year. But there 's been talk of this many times before without anything coming of it. And that draining business is a matter in which I take no stock whatever. For how would it go with the game if Tåkern were laid waste. You 're a donkey to gloat over a thing like that. What will you and I have to amuse ourselves with, when there are no more birds on Tåkern?'

Chapter Two

THE DECOY-DUCK

A COUPLE of days later Jarro was so well that he could fly all about the house. Then he was petted a good deal by the mistress, and the little boy ran out in the yard and plucked the first grass-blades for him which had sprung up. When the mistress caressed him, Jarro thought that although he was now so strong that he could fly down to Tåkern at any time, he shouldn't care to be separated from the human beings. He had no objection to remaining with them all his life.

But early one morning the mistress placed a halter, or noose, over Jarro, which prevented him from using his wings, and then she turned him over to the farm-hand who had found him in the yard. The farm-hand poked him under his arm, and went down to Tåkern with him.

The ice had melted away while Jarro had been ill. The old, dry autumn leaves still stood along the shores and islets, but all the water-growths had begun to take root down in the deep, and the green stems had already reached the surface. And now nearly all the migratory birds were at home. The curlews' hooked bills peeped out from the reeds. The grebes glided about with new feather collars around the neck, and the jack-snipes were gathering straw for their nests.

The farm-hand got into a scow, laid Jarro in the bottom of the boat, and began to pole himself out on the lake. Jarro, who had now accustomed himself to expect only good of human beings, said to Caesar, who was also in the party, that he was very grateful toward the farm-hand for taking him out on the lake. But there was no need to keep him so closely guarded, for he did not intend to fly away. To this Caesar made no reply. He was very silent that morning.

The only thing which struck Jarro as being a bit peculiar was that the farm-hand had taken his gun along. He couldn't believe that any of the good folk in the cottage would want to shoot birds. And, besides, Caesar had told him that the people didn't hunt at this time of the year.

'It is a prohibited time,' he had said, 'although this doesn't concern me, of course.'

The farm-hand went over to one of the little reed-enclosed mud islets. There he stepped from the boat, gathered some old reeds into a pile, and lay down behind it. Jarro was permitted to wander around on the ground, with the halter over his wings, and tethered to the boat, with a long string.

Suddenly Jarro caught sight of some young ducks and drakes, in whose company he had formerly raced backwards and forwards over the lake. They were a long way off, but Jarro called them to him with a couple of loud shouts. They responded, and a large and beautiful flock approached. Before they got there Jarro began to tell them about his marvellous rescue and of the kindness of human beings. Just then two shots sounded behind him. Three ducks sank down in the reeds, lifeless, and Caesar bounced out and captured them.

Then Jarro understood. The human beings had only saved him that they might use him as a decoy-duck. And they had also succeeded. Three ducks had died on his account. He thought he should die of shame. He thought that even his friend Caesar looked contemptuously at him; and when they came home to the cottage he didn't dare lie down and sleep beside the dog.

The next morning Jarro was again taken out on the shallows. This time, too, he saw some ducks. But when he observed that they flew toward him he called to them:

'Away! Away! Be careful! Fly in another direction! There's a hunter hidden behind the reed-pile. I'm only a decoy-bird!'

And he actually succeeded in preventing them from coming within shooting distance.

Jarro had scarcely had time to taste of a grass-blade, so busy was he in keeping watch. He called out his warning as soon as a bird drew nigh. He even warned the grebes, although he detested them because they crowded the ducks out of their best hiding places. But he did not wish that any bird should meet with misfortune on his account. And, thanks to Jarro's vigilance, the farm-hand had to go home without firing off a single shot.

Despite this fact Caesar looked less displeased than on the previous day; and when evening came he took Jarro in his mouth, carried him over to the fireplace, and let him sleep between his forepaws.

Nevertheless Jarro was no longer contented in the cottage but was grievously unhappy. His heart suffered at the thought that humans never had loved him. When the mistress or the little boy came forward to caress him, he stuck his bill under his wing and pretended that he slept.

For several days Jarro continued his distressful watch service, and already he was known all over Tåkern.

Then it happened one morning while he called as usual:
'Have a care, birds! Don't come near me! I'm only
a decoy-duck,' that a grebe-nest came floating toward
the shallows where he was tied. This was nothing
especially remarkable. It was a nest from the year
before; and since grebe-nests are built in such a way that

they can move on water like boats, it often happens that
they drift out toward the lake. Still Jarro stood there
and stared at the nest, because it came so straight toward
the islet that it looked as though someone had steered its
course over the water.

As the nest came nearer Jarro saw that a little human
being—the tiniest he had ever seen—sat in the nest and
rowed it forward with a pair of sticks. And this little
human called to him:

'Go as near the water as you can, Jarro, and be ready
to fly. You shall soon be freed.'

A few seconds later the grebe-nest lay near land, but
the little oarsman did not leave it, but sat huddled up
between branches and straw. Jarro too held himself

almost immovable. He was actually paralysed with fear
lest the rescuer should be discovered.

The next thing which occurred was that a flock of wild
geese came along. Then Jarro woke up to business and
warned them with loud shrieks; but in spite of this they
flew backwards and forwards over the shallows several
times. They held themselves so high that they were
beyond shooting distance; still the farm-hand let himself
be tempted to fire a couple of shots at them. These shots
were hardly fired before the little creature ran up on land,
drew a tiny knife from its sheath, and with a couple of
quick strokes cut loose Jarro's halter.

'Now fly away, Jarro, before the man has time to load
again!' he cried, while he himself ran down to the grebe-
nest and poled away from the shore.

The hunter had had his gaze fixed upon the geese, and
hadn't observed that Jarro had been freed; but Caesar
had followed more carefully that which happened; and
just as Jarro raised his wings he dashed forward and
grabbed him by the neck.

Jarro cried pitifully, and the boy who had freed him
said quietly to Caesar:

'If you are just as honourable as you look, surely you
cannot wish to force a good bird to sit here and entice
others into trouble.'

When Caesar heard these words, he grinned viciously
with his upper lip, but the next second he dropped Jarro.

'Fly, Jarro!' said he. 'You are certainly too good to
be a decoy-duck. It wasn't for this that I wanted to
keep you here, but because it will be lonely in the cottage
without you.'

Chapter Three

THE LOWERING OF THE LAKE

It was indeed very lonely in the cottage without Jarro. The dog and the cat found the time long when they didn't have him to wrangle over; and the housewife missed the glad quacking which he had indulged in every time she entered the house. But the one who longed most for Jarro was the little boy, Per Ola. He was but three years old and the only child; and in all his life he had never had a playmate like Jarro. When he heard that Jarro had gone back to Tåkern and the wild ducks he couldn't be satisfied with this, but thought constantly of how he should get him back again.

Per Ola had talked a good deal with Jarro while he lay still in his basket, and he was certain that the duck understood him. He begged his mother to take him down to the lake that he might find Jarro and persuade him to come back to them. Mother wouldn't listen to this; but the little one didn't give up his plan on that account.

The day after Jarro had disappeared Per Ola was running about in the yard. He played by himself as usual, but Caesar lay on the veranda; and when mother let the boy out, she said:

'Take care of Per Ola, Caesar!'

Now if all had been as usual Caesar would have obeyed the command, and the child would have been so well guarded that he couldn't have run the least risk. But Caesar was not himself these days. He knew that the farmers who lived along Tåkern had held frequent conferences about the lowering of the lake, and that they had almost settled the matter. The ducks must leave, and Caesar should never more behold a glorious chase. He was so preoccupied with thoughts of this misfortune that he did not remember to watch over Per Ola.

And the little one had scarcely been alone in the yard a minute before he realized that now the right moment was come to go down to Tåkern and talk with Jarro. He opened a gate and wandered down toward the lake on the narrow path which ran along the banks. As long as he could be seen from the house he walked slowly, but afterwards he increased his pace. He was very much afraid that mother, or someone else, should call to him that he couldn't go. He didn't wish to do anything naughty, only to persuade Jarro to come home; but he felt that those at home would not have approved of the undertaking.

When Per Ola came down to the lake shore he called Jarro several times. Thereupon he stood for a long time and waited, but no Jarro appeared. He saw several birds that resembled the wild duck, but they flew by without noticing him, and he could understand that none among them was the right one.

When Jarro didn't come to him the child thought that it would be easier to find him if he went out on the lake. There were several good craft lying along the shore, but they were tied. The one that lay loose, and at liberty, was an old leaky scow which was so unfit that no one thought of using it. But Per Ola scrambled up in it without caring that the whole bottom was filled with water. He had not strength enough to use the oars, but,

instead, he seated himself to swing and rock in the scow.
Certainly no grown person would have succeeded in
moving a scow out on Tåkern in that manner; but when
the level of the water is high—and ill luck to the fore—
little children have a marvellous faculty for getting out
to sea. Per Ola was soon riding around on Tåkern and
calling for Jarro.

When the old scow was rocked like this—out to sea—
its cracks opened wider and wider, and the water actually
streamed into it. Per Ola didn't pay the slightest attention to this. He sat upon the little bench in front and
called to every bird he saw, and wondered why Jarro
didn't appear.

At last Jarro caught sight of Per Ola. He heard that
someone called him by the name which he had borne
among human beings, and he understood that the little
boy had gone out on Tåkern to search for him. Jarro was
unspeakably happy to find that one of the humans really
loved him. He shot down toward Per Ola like an
arrow, seated himself beside him, and let him caress him.
They were both very happy to see each other again, but
suddenly Jarro noticed the condition of the scow. It
was half filled with water and was almost ready to sink.
Jarro tried to tell Per Ola that he, who could neither fly
nor swim, must try to get upon land; but Per Ola didn't
understand him. Then Jarro did not wait an instant
but hurried away to get help.

Jarro came back in a little while, and carried on his
back a tiny thing, who was much smaller than Per Ola
himself. If he hadn't been able to talk and move the little
boy would have believed that it was a doll. Instantly
the tiny elf ordered Per Ola to pick up a long, slender
pole that lay in the bottom of the scow and try to pole

it toward one of the reed islands. Per Ola obeyed him, and he and the tiny creature together steered the scow. With a couple of strokes they were on a little reed-encircled island, and now Per Ola was told that he must step on land. And just the very moment that Per Ola set foot on land the scow was filled with water and sank to the bottom.

When Per Ola saw this he was sure that father and mother would be very angry with him. He would have started to cry if he hadn't found something else to think about soon; namely, a flock of big, grey birds, who alighted on the island. The little midget took him up to them, and told him their names, and what they said. And this was so funny that Per Ola forgot everything else.

Meanwhile the people on the farm had discovered that Per Ola had disappeared and had started to search for him. They searched the outhouses, looked in the well, and hunted through the cellar. Then they went out into the highways and by-paths, wandered to the neighbouring farm to find out if he had strayed over there, and searched for him also down by Tåkern. But no matter how much they sought they did not find him.

Caesar, the dog, understood very well that the farmer-folk were looking for Per Ola, but he did nothing to lead them on the right track; instead, he lay still as though the matter didn't concern him.

Later in the day Per Ola's footprints were discovered down by the boat-landing. And then came the discovery that the old, leaky scow was no longer on the strand. Then they began to understand how the whole affair had come about.

The farmer and his helpers immediately took out the

boats and went in search of the child. They rowed
around on Tåkern until late in the evening without
seeing the least shadow of him. They couldn't help
believing that the old scow had gone down, and that the
little one lay dead on the lake bottom.

In the evening Per Ola's mother hunted around on
the strand. Every one else was convinced that Per Ola
was drowned, but she could not bring herself to believe
this. She searched all the time. She searched between
reeds and bulrushes; tramped and tramped on the muddy
shore, never thinking of how deep her foot sank and
how wet she had become. She was utterly desperate.
Her heart ached in her breast. She did not weep, but
wrung her hands and called for her child in loud, piercing
tones.

Round about her she heard swans' and ducks' and
curlews' calls. She thought that they followed her,
and moaned and wailed too. 'Surely they too must
be in trouble, since they moan so,' thought she. Then
she remembered: these were only birds that she heard
complain. They surely had no worries.

It was strange that they did not quieten down after
sunset. But she heard all these uncountable bird
throngs, which lived along Tåkern, send forth cry upon
cry. Several of them followed her wherever she went;
others came rustling past on light wings. All the air
was filled with moans and lamentations.

But the anguish which she herself was suffering opened
her heart. She thought that she was not so far removed
from all other living creatures as people usually think.
She understood much better than ever before how birds
fared. They had their constant worries for home and
children: they, as she. There was surely not such a great

difference between them and her as she had heretofore believed.

Then she began to think that it was as good as settled that these thousands of swans and ducks and loons would lose their homes here by Tåkern. 'It will be very hard for them,' she thought. 'Where will they bring up their children now?'

She stood still and mused on this. It appeared to be an excellent and agreeable accomplishment to change a lake into fields and meadows, but let it be some other lake than Tåkern; some other lake which was not the home of so many thousand creatures.

She remembered how on the following day the proposition to lower the lake was to be decided, and she wondered if this was why her little son had been lost— just to-day.

Was it God's meaning that sorrow should come and open her heart, just to-day, before it was too late to avert the cruel act?

She walked rapidly up to the house and began to talk with her husband about this. She spoke of the lake, and of the birds, and said that she believed it was God's judgment on them both. And she soon found that he was of the same opinion.

They already owned a large place, but if the lake-draining was carried into effect, such a goodly portion of the lake bottom would fall to their share that their property would be nearly doubled. For this reason they had been more eager for the undertaking than any of the other shore owners. The others had been worried about expenses, and anxious lest the draining should not prove any more successful this time than it was the last. Per Ola's father knew in his heart that it was he who had influenced them to undertake the work. He had exercised all his eloquence, so that he might leave to his son a farm twice as large as his father had left to him.

He stood and pondered if God's hand was behind the fact that Tåkern had taken his son from him on the day before he was to draw up the contract to lay it waste. The wife didn't have to say many words to him before he answered:

'It may be that God does not want us to interfere with His order. I'll talk with the others about this to-morrow and I think we'll conclude that all may remain as it is.'

While the farmer-folk were talking this over, Caesar lay before the fire. He raised his head and listened very attentively. When he thought that he was sure of the outcome he walked up to the mistress, took her by the skirt, and led her to the door.

'But, Caesar!' said she, and wanted to break loose. 'Do you know where Per Ola is?' she exclaimed.

Caesar barked joyfully, and threw himself against the door. She opened it, and Caesar dashed down toward Tåkern. The mistress was so positive he knew where Per Ola was that she rushed after him. And no sooner had they reached the shore than they heard a child's cry out on the lake.

Per Ola had had the best day of his life, in company with Tummetott and the birds; but now he had begun to cry because he was hungry and afraid of the darkness. And he was glad when father and mother and Caesar came for him.

PART TWENTY

ULVÅSA-LADY

☆

THE PROPHECY

ONE night when Nils lay and slept on an island in Tåkern he was awakened by oar-strokes. He had hardly got his eyes open before there fell such a dazzling light on them that he began to blink.

At first he couldn't make out what it was that shone so brightly out here on the lake; but he soon saw that a scow with a big burning torch stuck up on a spike, aft, lay near the edge of the reeds. The red flame from the torch was clearly reflected in the night-dark lake; and the brilliant light must have lured the fish, for round about the flame in the deep a mass of dark specks were seen, that moved continually and changed places.

There were two old men in the scow. One sat at the oars, and the other stood on a bench in the stern and held in his hand a short spear which was coarsely barbed. The one who rowed was apparently a poor fisherman. He was small, dried up and weather-beaten, and wore a thin, threadbare coat. One could see that he was so used to being out in all sorts of weather that he didn't mind the cold. The other was well fed and well dressed, and looked like a prosperous and self-complacent farmer.

'Now, stop!' said the farmer, when they were opposite the island where the boy lay. At the same time he plunged the spear into the water. When he drew it out again a long, fine eel came with it.

'Look at that!' said he, as he released the eel from the spear. 'That was one who was worth while. Now I think we have so many that we can turn back.'

His comrade did not lift the oars but sat and looked round.

'It is lovely out here on the lake to-night,' said he.

And so it was. It was absolutely still, so that the entire water surface lay in undisturbed rest with the exception of the streak where the boat had gone forward. This lay like a path of gold and shimmered in the torchlight. The sky was clear and dark blue and thickly studded with stars. The shores were hidden by the reed islands except toward the west. There Mount Omberg loomed up high and dark, much more impressive than usual, and cut away a big, three-cornered piece of the vaulted heavens.

The other one turned his head to get the light out of his eyes, and looked about him.

'Yes, it is lovely here in Östergylln,' said he. 'Still, the best thing about the province is not its beauty.'

'Then what is it that's best?' asked the oarsman.

'That it has always been a respected and honoured province.'

'That may be true enough.'

'And then this, that one knows it will always continue to be so.'

'But how in the world can one know this?' said the one who sat at the oars.

The farmer straightened up where he stood and braced himself with the spear.

'There is an old story which has been handed down from father to son in my family, and in it one learns what will happen to Östergötland.'

'Then you may as well tell it to me,' said the oarsman.

'We do not tell it to any one and every one, but I do not wish to keep it a secret from an old comrade.

'At Ulvåsa, here in Östergötland,' he continued, and one could tell by the tone of his voice that he talked of something which he had heard from others, and knew by heart, 'many, many years ago, there lived a lady who had the gift of looking into the future, and telling people what was going to happen to them—just as certainly and accurately as though it had already occurred. For this she became widely noted; and it is easy to understand that people would come to her, both from far and near, to find out what they were going to pass through of good or evil.

'One day, when Ulvåsa-lady sat in her hall and spun, as was customary in former days, a poor peasant came into the room and seated himself on the bench near the door.

'"I wonder what you are sitting and thinking about, dear lady," said the peasant after a little.

'"I am sitting and thinking about high and holy things," answered she.

'"Then it is not fitting, perhaps, that I ask you about something which weighs on my heart," said the peasant.

'"It is probably nothing else that weighs on your heart than that you may reap much grain on your field. But I am accustomed to receive communications from the emperor about how it will go with his crown, and from the pope about how it will go with his keys."

'"Such things cannot be easy to answer," said the peasant. "I have also heard that no one seems to go from here without being dissatisfied with what he has heard."

'When the peasant said this, he saw that Ulvåsa-lady bit her lip, and moved higher up on the bench.

'"So this is what you have heard about me," said she. "Then you may as well tempt fortune by asking me about the thing you wish to know, and you shall see if I answer so that you will be satisfied."

'After this the peasant did not hesitate to state his errand. He said that he had come to ask how it would go with Östergötland in the future. There was nothing which was so dear to him as his native province, and he felt that he should be happy until his dying day if he could get a satisfactory reply to his query.

'"Oh, is that all you wish to know," said the wise lady. "Then I think that you will be content. For here where I now sit, I can tell you that it will be like this with Östergötland: it will always have something to boast of ahead of other provinces."

'"Yes, that was a good answer, dear lady," said the peasant. "And now I would be entirely at peace if I could only comprehend how such a thing should be possible."

'"Why should it not be possible?" said Ulvåsa-lady. "Don't you know that Östergötland is already renowned? Or think you there is any place in Sweden that can boast of owning, at the same time, two such cloisters as the ones in Alvastra and Vreta, and such a beautiful cathedral as the one in Linköping?"

'"That may be so," said the peasant. "But I 'm an old man, and I know that people's minds are changeable. I fear that there will come a time when they won't want to give us any glory, either for Alvastra or Vreta or for the cathedral."

'"Herein you may be right," said Ulvåsa-lady, "but

you need not doubt prophecy on that account. I shall now build up a new cloister on Vadstena, and that will become the most celebrated in the north. Thither both the high and the lowly shall make pilgrimages, and all shall sing the praises of the province because it has such a holy place within its confines."

'The peasant replied that he was right glad to know this. But he also knew, of course, that everything was perishable; and he wondered much what would give distinction to the province if Vadstena Cloister should once fall into disrepute.

'"You are not easy to satisfy," said Ulvåsa-lady, "but surely I can see so far ahead that I can tell you, before Vadstena Cloister shall have lost its splendour, there will be a castle erected close by which will be the most magnificent of its period. Kings and dukes will be guests there, and it shall be accounted an honour to the whole province that it owns such an ornament."

'"This I am also glad to hear," said the peasant. "But I 'm an old man, and I know how it generally turns out with this world's glories. And if the castle goes to ruin, I wonder much what there will be that can attract the people's attention to this province."

'"It 's not a little that you want to know," said Ulvåsa-lady, "but, certainly, I can look far enough into the future to see that there will be life and movement in the forests around Finspång. I see how cabins and smithies arise there, and I believe that the whole province shall be renowned because iron will be moulded within its confines."

'The peasant didn't deny that he was delighted to hear this. "But if it should go so badly that even Finspång's foundry went down in importance, then it would

hardly be possible that any new thing could arise of which
Östergötland might boast."

"'You are not easy to please," said Ulvåsa-lady, "but
I can see so far into the future that I mark how, along
the lake shores, great manors—large as castles—are
built by gentlemen who have carried on wars in
foreign lands. I believe that the manors will bring the
province just as much honour as anything else that I
have mentioned."

"'But if there comes a time when no one lauds the
great manors?" insisted the peasant.

"'You need not be uneasy at all events," said Ulvåsa-
lady. "I see how health springs bubble on Medevi
meadows, by Vätter's shores. I believe that the wells
at Medevi will bring the land as much praise as you can
desire."

"'That is a mighty good thing to know," said the
peasant. "But if there comes a time when people will
seek their health at other springs?"

"'You must not give yourself any anxiety on that
account," answered Ulvåsa-lady. "I see how people
dig and labour from Motala to Mem. They dig a canal
right through the country, and then Östergötland's
praise is again on every one's lips."

'But, nevertheless, the peasant looked distraught.

"'I see that the rapids in Motala stream begin to draw
wheels," said Ulvåsa-lady, and now two bright red spots
came to her cheeks, for she began to be impatient, "I
hear hammers resound in Motala, and looms clatter in
Norrköping."

"'Yes, that's good to know," said the peasant, "but
everything is perishable, and I'm afraid that even this
can be forgotten and go into oblivion."

'When the peasant was not satisfied even now, there was an end to the lady's patience.

'"You say that everything is perishable," said she, "but now I shall still name something which will always be like itself; and that is that such arrogant and pigheaded peasants as you will always be found in this province—until the end of time."

'Hardly had Ulvåsa-lady said this before the peasant rose—happy and satisfied—and thanked her for a good answer. Now, at last, he was satisfied, he said.

'"Verily, I understand now how you look at it," then said Ulvåsa-lady.

'"Well, I look at it in this way, dear lady," said the peasant, "that everything which kings and priests and noblemen and merchants build and accomplish, can only endure for a few years. But when you tell me that in Östergötland there will always be peasants who are honour-loving and persevering, then I know also that it will be able to keep its ancient glory. For it is only those who go bent under the eternal labour with the soil, who can hold this land in good repute and honour—from one time to another."'

PART TWENTY-ONE

THE HOMESPUN CLOTH

NILS rode forward—way up in the air. He had the great Östergötland plain under him, and sat and counted the many white churches which towered above the small leafy groves around them. It wasn't long before he had counted fifty. After that he became confused and couldn't keep track of the counting.

Nearly all the farms were built up with large, white-washed two-storey houses, which looked so imposing that the boy couldn't help admiring them. 'There can't be any peasants in this land,' he said to himself, 'since I do not see any peasant farms.'

Immediately all the wild geese shrieked:

'Here the peasants live like gentlemen. Here the peasants live like gentlemen.'

On the plains the ice and snow had disappeared and the spring work had begun.

'What kind of long crabs are those that creep over the fields?' asked the boy after a bit.

'Ploughs and oxen. Ploughs and oxen,' answered the wild geese.

The oxen moved so slowly down on the fields, that one could scarcely perceive they were in motion, and the geese shouted to them:

'You won't get there before next year! You won't get there before next year!'

But the oxen were equal to the occasion. They raised their muzzles in the air and bellowed:

'We do more good in an hour than such as you do in a whole lifetime!'

In a few places the ploughs were drawn by horses. They went along with much more eagerness and haste than the oxen, but the geese couldn't keep from teasing these either.

'Aren't you ashamed to be doing ox-duty?' cried the wild geese.

'Aren't you ashamed yourselves to be doing lazy man's duty?' the horses neighed back at them.

But while horses and oxen were at work in the fields, the stable ram walked about in the barnyard. He was newly clipped and touchy, knocked over the small boys, chased the shepherd dog into his kennel, and then strutted about as though he alone were lord of the whole place.

'Rammie, rammie, what have you done with your wool?' asked the wild geese, who rode by up in the air.

'That I have sent to Drag's woollen mills in Norrköping!' replied the ram with a long, drawn-out bleat.

'Rammie, rammie, what have you done with your horns?' asked the geese.

But horns the ram had never possessed, to his sorrow, and one couldn't offer him a greater insult than to ask after them. He ran around a long time, and butted at the air, so furious was he.

On the country road came a man who drove a herd of Skåne pigs that were not more than a few weeks old, and were going to be sold up country. They trotted along bravely, as little as they were, and kept close together, as if they sought protection.

'Nuff, nuff, nuff, we came away too soon from father

and mother. Nuff, nuff, nuff, how will it go with us poor children?' said the little pigs.

The wild geese didn't have the heart to tease such poor little creatures.

'It will be better for you than you can ever believe,' they cried as they flew past them.

The wild geese were never so merry as when they flew over a flat country. Then they did not hurry themselves, but flew from farm to farm, and joked with the tame animals.

As Nils rode over the plain, he happened to think of a legend which he had heard a long time ago. He didn't remember it exactly, but it was something about a petticoat, half of which was made of gold-woven velvet and half of grey homespun cloth. But the one who owned the petticoat adorned the homespun cloth with such a lot of pearls and precious stones that it looked richer and more gorgeous than the gold cloth.

He remembered this about the homespun cloth, as he looked down on Östergötland, because it was made up of a large plain, which lay wedged in between two mountainous forest tracts, one to the north the other to the south. The two forest heights lay there, a lovely blue, and shimmered in the morning light, as if they were decked with golden veils; and the plain, which simply spread out one winter-naked field after another, was not, in and of itself, prettier to look upon than grey homespun.

But the people must have been contented on the plain, because it was generous and kind, and they had tried to decorate it in the best way possible. High up, where Nils rode by, he thought that cities and farms, churches and factories, castles and railway stations, were scattered over it, like large and small trinkets. It shone on the roofs, and the window-panes glittered like jewels. Yellow country roads, shining railway tracks, and blue canals ran along between the districts like embroidered loops. Linköping lay around its cathedral like a pearl-setting around a precious stone, and the gardens in the country were like little brooches and buttons. There was not much regulation in the pattern, but it was a display of grandeur which one could never tire of looking at.

The geese had left Omberg district, and travelled toward the east along Göta Canal. This was also getting itself ready for the summer. Workmen repaired the canal banks and tarred the huge lock gates. They were working everywhere to receive spring fittingly, even in the cities. There masons and painters stood on scaffoldings and made fine the exteriors of the houses while maids were cleaning the windows. Down at the harbour sailing-boats and steamers were being washed and dressed up.

At Norrköping the wild geese left the plain and flew up toward Kolmården. For a time they had followed an old, hilly, country road, which wound around cliffs, and ran forward under wild mountain walls—when the boy suddenly let out a shout. He had been sitting and swinging his foot back and forth, and one of his wooden shoes had slipped off.

'Gander, gander, I have dropped my shoe!' cried the boy.

The gander turned about and sank toward the ground; then the boy saw that two children, who were walking along the road, had picked up his shoe.

'Gander, gander,' screamed the boy excitedly, 'fly

upward again! It is too late. I cannot get my shoe
back again.'

Down on the road stood Osa, the goose-girl, and her
brother, little Mats, looking at a tiny wooden shoe that
had fallen from the skies.

Osa, the goose-girl, stood silent a long while, and
pondered over the find. At last she said, slowly and
thoughtfully:

'Do you remember, little Mats, that when we went
past Öved Cloister, we heard that the people in a farmyard had seen an elf who was dressed in leather breeches,
and had wooden shoes on his feet, like any other working
man? And do you recollect when we came to Vittskövle, a girl told us that she had seen a Goa-Nisse with
wooden shoes, who flew away on the back of a goose?
And when we ourselves came home to our cabin, little
Mats, we saw a goblin who was dressed in the same way,
and who also straddled the back of a goose and flew
away. Maybe it was the same one who rode along on
his goose up here in the air and dropped his wooden
shoe.'

'Yes, it must have been,' said little Mats.

They turned the wooden shoe about and examined it
carefully, for it isn't every day that one happens across
a Goa-Nisse's wooden shoe on the highway.

'Wait, wait, little Mats!' said Osa, the goose-girl.
'There is something written on one side of it.'

'Why, so there is—but they are such tiny letters.'

'Let me see! It says—it says: "Nils Holgersson from
West Vemmenhög." That's the most wonderful thing
I've ever heard!' said little Mats.

HANS ANDERSEN'S FAIRY TALES

translated by Naomi Lewis

A marvellous collection of fairy tales from Hans Andersen, chosen and newly translated by the eminent writer and critic Naomi Lewis. All the best-known and most-loved stories, Thumbelina, The Snow Queen, The Emperor's New Clothes, are included as well as the less familiar, The Goblin at the Grocer's and Dance, Dolly, Dance. Hans Andersen's timeless tales have been delighting generations of readers for over 150 years – no child should be without them.

KING ARTHUR AND HIS KNIGHTS OF THE ROUND TABLE

Roger Lancelyn Green

The immortal tales from the Court of King Arthur are tales about good overcoming evil, full of mystery, enchantment and chivalry. These stories about Merlin, King Arthur, Queen Guinevere and the Knights of the Round Table have been told for hundreds of years but are retold here with freshness, vitality and dignity. From the sword in the stone and the coming of King Arthur, the forging of Excalibur and the making of the Round Table, to the quest for the Holy Grail and Arthur's last battle, these age-old stories are as exciting as they were when they were first told.

FRANKENSTEIN

Mary Shelley

The fable of the scientist who creates a man-monster, and of the terrible events which follow, is one of the best-known horror stories ever. From the moment that Frankenstein's creation comes alive, the gripping story that unfolds with its murders and terrors is one that fills the reader with horror and trepidation – and a determination and compulsion to read on.

Some Puffin Classics

PINOCCHIO
Carlo Collodi

When the old wood-carver Gepetto decides to make a wonderful puppet who can dance and turn somersaults, he has no idea of the trouble in store. For as the puppet takes shape, it gradually comes to life, learning to talk and play pranks, providing a constant source of exasperation and delight. This translation is by E. Harden.

ENGLISH FAIRY TALES
Joseph Jacobs

This anthology of traditional stories is a delightful combination of old favourites and little-known stories, collected by the scholar and story-teller Joseph Jacobs at the end of the nineteenth century. There are classics such as Jack and the Beanstalk, Tom Thumb and The Story of the Three Bears, as well as the less familiar The Laidly Worm of Spindleston Heugh and Mr Miacca. A classic collection to be enjoyed over and over again.

WELSH LEGENDS AND FOLK TALES
Gwyn Jones

Heroic deeds and high adventure abound in this rich collection of legends and folk tales from Wales. There's the story of Lleu and the bride made of flowers because of a mother's curse, the tale of the giant Rhitta and his strange obsession with collecting beards, and the classic love story of Trystan and Esyllt, among many others, all beautifully retold.